KASHMIR ON FIRE

Onaly A. Kapasi, MD

Rev. date: 11/25/2015

To order additional copies of this book, contact:
Xlibris
1-888-795-4274
www.Xlibris.com
Orders@Xlibris.com
717682

CONTENTS

Author's *First* Book Published in 2014

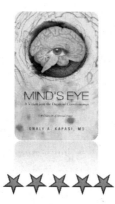

Mind's Eye – A Vision in the Depth of Consciousness

Poetry anthology opens portal to inner consciousness, & reflective understanding

Book of personal poems reflecting Life, Passion and Love.

This anthology of personal poems is prompted by personal experiences of the author

The book has received favorable reviews and compared to the works of Rumi by some

All the proceeds of his books are distributed to benefit medical charities

To my parents, Dayumbai and Abdulkarim Kapasi
for
instilling values of secular, nonsectarian existence
and
much, much more.

To Sameera, Sameer, Rohan, Aarav, Milan, and Maya

for their love.

PREFACE

This is a story of two very close friends, Krishna and Mustafa, who are friends from preschool days and who now share a room in a medical school students' hostel in Srinagar, the capital of the war-torn state of Kashmir. The friendship between Krishna, a Kashmiri pandit, and Mustafa, a Shia Muslim, survived recent sectarian violence introduced by an insurgence of fanatical fighters from a neighboring country that had vested interest in Indian Kashmir. Mustafa hoped to return to Kashmir after completion of a specialty training in Delhi or Bombay, and Krishna hoped to go abroad to explore far frontiers of medicine; his planned destination was the United States of America.

This is a story of a proud, God-fearing community, the Kashmiri people, and the transformation of their motherland, Kashmir, within a short time—from a major, most sought after tourist destination in India to a violent state, froth with sectarian violence. Pasted at every corner were signs of plebiscite, which reappeared after the local police brought them down.

Mustafa Sheikh is the son of Muzzaffer Sheikh, a lead reporter at the *Kashmir Gazette*, a local newspaper that brought real-life stories of the strife in Kashmir to its people. The gazette is a popular newspaper in Srinagar, the capital, and also in other parts of Kashmir, mainly because of its no-gloss, candid reporting of the violence in Kashmir and the mind-set of its perpetrators.

Muzzaffer Sheikh, a Shia Muslim, grew up listening to bedtime stories of Khan Abdul Gaffar Khan, the famous Pashtun freedom fighter, who stood shoulder to shoulder with Mahatma Gandhi; of Subash Chandra Bose, yet another freedom fighter who revolted against the British Raj; and of the journey of Prince Srivastava (Gautama Buddha) in search of divine truth. He listened to stories of the prophets Ibrahim (Abraham); Nuh (Noah); Musa (Moses); Mohamed; Isa (Jesus); Krishna, the child god; and Rama and Sita. These stories told over his childhood espoused an understanding of the societal importance of a secular, nonsectarian coexistence. The study of Islam taught Muzzaffer that men and women were equal, and his readings of philosophers like Marcus Aurelius inculcated the discipline of listening to his inner voice, a voice of his inner consciousness. These early childhood stories molded Muzzaffer Sheikh's thinking, which made him a very formidable reporter at the gazette, one who did not shy away from truthful reporting of the prevailing events unfolding in Kashmir and of the non-Islamic ideology of the mujahideen. Nonetheless, Muzzaffer Sheik's razor-sharp reporting infuriated fanatical groups in his community who were propagating their own brand of Islam, a brand of intolerance, violence, and hatred. These fanatics criticized him, castigated him, and even labeled him as an Indian agent and anti-Islam, a *kafir* (an Arabic word meaning "a disbeliever, one that does not believe in God").

Muzzaffer was aware of the power of the press mostly from reading foreign articles, in which Islam was branded as a terrorist religion, and in America, Islam was synonymous with terrorism, mostly judging from the frequent sound bites on the airwaves and the written words in the newspapers. In reality, Islam, the most modern of all monotheistic religions, taught tolerance and equality. He was aware that in a masjid, a white worshiper is not differentiated from a black worshiper or a pauper from the prince, as they all pray as equals in the house of God. He was also aware that the Islamic gospel was misinterpreted by a minority in Kashmir and also elsewhere for a personal agenda. The group that terrorized Kashmir was driving modern Kashmir to the dark ages.

Mustafa, Muzzaffer Sheik's son, was born on *Milad*, the same day as the prophet Mohamed-ul-Mustafa (570 CE), and as is customary with Muslims, he was named after the prophet. In many ways, he was an extension of his father, a "fruit that fell near the tree." He had a puritanical desire of serving the Kashmiri people. He was aware that even the most basic medical care was not available to the masses in Kashmir, mostly resulting from unrest, lack of security, lack of basic medical equipment, and a lack of disease prevention. He was determined to bring about a change someday during his lifetime. His younger sister, Fizza, was, however, different; she was a romantic who loved to write poetries and read with great passion the works of Rumi, written in its original Farsi language. She loved the Sufi philosophy of worshiping God in rhyme and rhythm, even though the philosophy was ill understood and castigated by mainstream Islam. Fizza was known to frequently sneak out of the house without wearing the mandatory hijab (covering of the face and body), a custom enforced by radical individuals practicing a fanatical brand of Islam, enforcing it by threats to life and of excommunication.

Miriam, Mustafa and Fizza's mother, was pragmatic and not idealistic as her husband; she understood quite well the mind-set of 'Kashmiri fanatics,' who chanted calls for plebiscite, inciting people with their brand of Islam. Miriam harbored a fear of harm to her brood, arising from her husband's candid and truthful reporting of the strife in Kashmir. She frequently cautioned her husband of the potential for harm resulting from his reporting. Nevertheless, she ignored an occasional retort and insult when she shopped at the *Subzi Mandi*, the vegetable market. Miriam was educated in a conventional school system (madrassa)[1] up to sixth grade, much like most other girls of her time, but she had gathered a wealth of knowledge from reading and listening to her parents and visitors, who came to her father's household. She was gifted with an uncanny sixth sense very similar to a jungle animal that knows of an impending danger. She prompted caution to her husband and children, and over time, her children came to accept and recognize her ability to sense danger. In matters concerning her her family, she was a tigress. Both her children inherited her uncanny sense of awareness. For instance, returning from school one day, Mustafa and Fizza chose a different route home for no apparent reason other than a gut instinct only to find out later of a roadside bomb blast, which maimed many.

Krishna, Mustafa's best friend, was a Kashmiri pandit, a Brahman—the highest caste amongst Hindus. Krishna's father, Bishma, was a merchant, who had inherited a business that had spanned over three generations. His great-grandfather imported water from the sacred river Ganges (Ganga) for the Kashmiri Hindus and also imported sandalwood used for cremation and other religious ceremonies. He exported locally grown saffron and sacred pinecone[2] necklaces to New Delhi and other parts of India. Bishma expanded the business to supply local grocery stores with grain and other sundry items for daily use, such as toothpaste, hair oil, and soap.

---

1   Madrassa is an Arabic word for an educational institution either religious or secular.

2   Pinecone is the third eye symbolizing the pineal gland and is of mystical importance in many ancient cultures and found in architectural ruins in Indonesia, Babylon, Egypt, Greece, and Rome and held as a priceless possession to an Indian ascetic.

Krishna was born on *Janmashtami*, Lord Krishna's birthday, therefore named after the child god Krishna. Krishna was the only child, and even though his father wanted him to take over the family business, he had decided to pursue higher education, and he is now in a medical school. Nonetheless, he could chant most religious scriptures in its original language, Sanskrit, a tradition spanning a few centuries, originating from the ancient Vedic Indus Valley civilization of Mohenjo Daro and *Indraprastha* (the *Indra* civilization of the legendary *Pandavas* of the epic *Mahabharata*).

Mohenjo Daro, Ancient Indus Valley Civilization

Krishna wanted to become a brain surgeon, as most medical students aspired during his time, mostly from a false belief that a brain surgeon was like an astronaut, exploring unknown territories.

Unlike Hindus in other parts of India, Kashmiri pandits, an offshoot of *Saraswat Brahmans*, relished a rich Kashmiri cuisine of lamb, mutton, and poultry, and they also pickled marinated meat.

Before the British came as traders and later ruled India, Hindus and Muslims lived in harmony and worked side by side. The coexistence was centuries old, and the fabled Mogul king Akbar had married a Rajput Hindu princess, Jodha Bai, who was permitted to practice her own religion in his court by the king's decree. Raja Akbar was remembered for, amongst other things, advocating religious tolerance and equality. The bloodshed that followed the division of the Indian nation into India and Pakistan was mostly engineered by a disenchanted British Raj, which left India inciting the two major religious groups of India—the Hindus and Muslims to demand a partition of India into India, a predominantly Hindu state, and Pakistan, a predominantly Muslim state.

Kashmir was a direct victim of this unholy division of India. Families were divided, some living in Azad Kashmir in Pakistan and others in the Indian Kashmir. Similarly, Bengal was divided into East Bengal belonging to Pakistan and West Bengal belonging to India, dividing homes and families arbitrarily, thereby resulting in bloodshed and loss of lives and Hindu-Muslim mistrust. The partition of India was no different from British colonies of Kenya, Uganda, and Tanganyika, which were also arbitrarily divided. The African nation was divided without consideration of its people, language, or cultural heritage, thereby dividing families and friends. The arbitrariness of the British Raj in Africa was also seen when the British monarch Queen Victoria gifted Mount Kilimanjaro, a part of the Usambara-Pare ranges of Kenya and a sister mountain to Mount Kenya, to her cousin Kaiser Wilhelm for his birthday in 1886.

Mustafa and Krishna, childhood friends, both grew up with a keen desire to be doctors; Mustafa with aspirations of serving Kashmir and Krishna a desire to explore new frontiers beyond India. They studied together and competed for academic excellence throughout their education from early grade school to medical school. Mustafa excelled in academics in the medical school and helped his best friend, Krishna, with his medical curriculum and research.

They shared books, as Krishna's father was able to buy the latest medical books in Delhi, and Mustafa's dad received regular free consignments of nonmedical books from the MacMillan press.

Mustafa celebrated *Diwali*, the Hindu festival of lights that signified a triumph of good over evil, with Krishna. He especially loved the milk cake that Krishna's mother made from condensed milk and cottage cheese, a specialty of Kashmiri pandits. He also loved the saffron-cashew *burfi*, which was absolutely delectable. Krishna celebrated Muslim holidays with Mustafa and at times went to the masjid with him. Krishna loved vermicelli cooked in milk with raisins, dried apricots, and nuts (*sheer korma*) served at Muslim *Idd* holidays at the end of a month of fasting. He also loved apricot *halwa*, *qubani ka meetha*, chicken cooked in yogurt, and fried dough triangles stuffed with ground lamb (*samosa*). Srinagar was a close-knit town, and their teachers, friends, and neighbors were all aware of the strong bond between these two boys.

Krishna did not have a sister, so Fizza tied on him a *rakhi*, a thread tied on the wrist of a brother as a contractual obligation between a brother and sister each year, promising the sister her brother's protection against evil.

Both Krishna and Mustafa were fond of debating and sat by the Dal Lake's shore or sat on the railings of the bridge on the Jhelum River arguing about the most insignificant and mundane subjects at most times.

Dal Lake and Zabarwan Mountains

Living where they did, they were aware of the political uncertainty of Kashmir. Mustafa lived on the west side of the Nishat Bagh on the banks of the Dal Lake. It was a very peaceful location, with the Zabarwan Mountains as its backdrop. There was never a day passed when they did not see columns of army vehicles either going to the mountains bordering Pakistan or returning from the mountains. Sometimes they heard distant sounds of gunfire in the middle of the night and at times saw men with covered faces buying rations for the mujahideen, the so-called freedom fighters in Kashmir.

India was a rising nation, mainly because of its brand of democracy granting freedom of speech and equality and its secular religious policies bestowing religious freedom to all and also because of its educational policy of free or subsidized education, with exceptions of minor bumps, such as the state-sanctioned massacre of Muslims in Gujarat in 2002 and the recently publicized molestation of women in India. India was an emerging nation, rising much rapidly in comparison to its neighbors to the north and west.

Mustafa and Krishna both understood that self-rule (plebiscite) advocated by the mujahideen was not a viable option for Kashmir, as Kashmir was a land locked state between India to the south and the mountain ranges to the north. Whereas India chose the pathway of a nonaligned, democratic nation, its neighbor Pakistan did not have a lasting democracy, and it was froth with military rule and military coups, and it remained in the shackles of foreign dependence, mainly the United States, who favored it in return for allowing a strategic military presence in the area. India, in its past two hundred years, had not attacked or carried out an act of aggression on any nation, but it had been attacked by China and Pakistan several times. China attacked India because of its need to capture strategic posts in India, and its neighbor Pakistan attacked for its insatiable desire to supersede India, a kind of an ongoing sibling rivalry inherent with divided nations. Both Krishna and Mustafa believed that China would one day need to commandeer as much adjacent landmass as possible, for economic and strategic reasons and also for its exponential population growth, an absolute necessity of land for the people of China. They both believed that the paper tiger had awakened and was the new and coming threat in their part of the world.

Social and religious needs had drawn Kashmiri Hindus to live mostly around the *mandir*—their place of worship—in a locality known as *Hindu Mohalla*, and Kashmiri Muslims similarly lived in *Muslim Mohalla*. This division was mostly for convenience, not dissimilar to the Jama Masjid community in Old Delhi, where Muslims predominated. Interestingly enough, the Kashmiri carpet weavers—mostly members of the Muslim community—lived next to each other and in close proximity with traders selling wool, dye, and pigments essential for their craft. The merchants selling wool, dye, and pigments were mostly Hindus. In this case too, convenience drew the two communities together in symbiosis. The Muslim *meenakari* weavers of gold and silk threads lived in their own *mohalla*; so did the *Kasai* (butchers). These communities, or *mohallas*, were mainly drawn out of convenience or necessity. There were no walls or fortresses separating one *mohalla* from the other, but the *Kasai* (butchers) lived on the outskirts of the city by selection, just as the crematorium was on the far side of the river. Not unlike most other city-societies, the wealthy Kashmiri lived in luxury and mostly developed their community on the other side of the Nigeen Lake—no different from the rich in Mumbai, Fort Lauderdale, San Diego, or Boston—similar to the Western description of living on the other side of the track. These affluent Kashmiri people shopped in their own locality and in shops that were owned by Sikhs and Sindhis who had opened high-end stores, selling the same stuff as in the lower side of the city but packaged differently and at a higher price, like a Gucci made in Italy sold in the affluent area and an identical imitation made in China sold at roadside stands in the poor section.

There was rumor of an insurgence of foreign fighters from Pakistan and Afghanistan, who had training camps in the Himalayan mountain ranges and the Hindu Kush Mountains, also known as *Pariyatra Parvata* during the Indus Valley civilization.

Occasionally, a dead body appeared, floating in the lake or down the river, and a sense of impending violence and uncertainty grew, but within the medical campus and in the medical community, life remained calm and untouched by the insurgency. An eight-foot-tall wall surrounding the perimeter of the medical campus seemed to keep evil out of it, or maybe it was the necessity of medical care that made it a protected sanctuary. At times, a wounded shooter would be left at the doorstep of the hospital casualty room; and at most times, the story would be that of an unknown shooter or a stray bullet was the alleged cause of the gunshot wound. The calluses on the hands and feet of these wounded victims and their lean body mass told a story of a hard life. Their sinews were strong, their look gaunt, and eyes drawn from strain and lack of sleep. These were not ordinary folks, as their austere look told a story of many past death-defying encounters. The medical students labeled these patients as the 'living dead.' Even to a third-year medical student, these were not ordinary farmers of the valley but the mujahideen shot by Indian soldiers. The police who interrogated the victims left, satisfied that it was a case of a stray bullet; a policy of 'live and let live' was prevalent, and as long as the fighters did not harm the citizenry or the police, the police did not do much. The local traders sold food, nitrogen fertilizer, chemicals, lead and steel pipes, wood (mostly walnut for making gun butts), jute ropes, small roofing nails, and other paraphernalia that could be weaponized by the insurgents. Occasionally, one would hear gangs of local hooligans threatening a shopkeeper who refused to trade with the mujahideen, which raised a suspicion of a symbiosis between the hooligans and the mujahideen.

Muzzaffer Sheikh wrote unbiased investigative reports on the insurgency and incidences of unchecked hooliganism and believed that the Kashmiri police was complicit. He once interviewed a wounded mujahid for several days and brought him food and clean clothes, and after several days, the "unknown victim" shared his story. The story in the gazette was of a fourteen-year-old who was cajoled and inducted into the mujahideen with promises of fame and fortune and a rite of passage to heaven as a *shaheed* (martyr). A few days after his discharge from the hospital, a body was found in the lake, but nobody claimed it from the morgue, so Muzzaffer did an investigative reporting, only to find out that it was none other than the victim he had interviewed in the hospital. He could not get any other information or find a next of kin, so he decided to have the gazette pay for the fallen mujahid's funeral. At the funeral *namaz* (prayers), an informant shared the details of the dead person. He wrote an article in the gazette, naming the article "The Unknown Truth" but without divulging his source. His business of reporting the truth in his war-torn city was very risky, but he was a determined Kashmiri, and like some others in the community, once he had set his mind on a job, nothing would have made him waver, not even his wife's voice of caution. Miriam had an inner sense of impending danger to her family. She could see the rapid change in her friends and even the traders in the bazaar. The other day at the banks of the river, women washing their clothes found a human body in the water, but no one reported it to the authorities. This was so unlike the God-fearing nature of Kashmiris, who were proud people renowned for their fortitude and humanity. The community seemed to be losing its sense of morality, and most hoped for a change.

This is a love story of two people, a Hindu and a Muslim, a story that transcends all religious and cultural norms.

Acknowledgements

Cover page: Sarrah Hussain
Interior graphics, paintings and editing: Shamim Kapasi-Rampuri

CHAPTER 1

Raksha Bandhan

The setting sun spread a golden crimson hue over the waters of the Dal Lake; the leaves of the walnut trees were mostly auburn by now. The winter was approaching in the valley of Kashmir. Winters, as all knew, were usually cold, and the chilly mountain winds were bone-piercing cold. The shepherd had sheared his lamb and sold most of the lamb's wool at the bazaar, leaving just enough for their homes to be used by their womenfolk to stuff quilts and stitch *Bandhis* (an inner waistcoat) and *dharies* (wool carpets). The apple orchards were now bare of fruit. Most of the fruits were exported out to markets in Delhi, Bombay, Ahmadabad, and other large wholesale markets. Some fruits for home consumption were buried under the snow in the mountains for winter storage and dug out for spring consumption. The apricots were dried and stored, and the weavers had readied their looms for the cold winter months, when most weavers worked indoors in the warmth of an open fire, and men and women ventured to go out only with a *Kangri*, a small earthen pot with burning charcoal strung from the neck over the chest by a rope to keep warm. The shikaras (colorful gondolas of Kashmir) were pulled from the water for repair and winter storage until the return of spring, when tourists arrived in droves from all parts of India and abroad. But now with fear of violence, the tourists had stopped coming to Kashmir, and the local crafts, furs, and rugs had to be sold to brokers who bought the wares at rock-bottom prices, leaving a very small amount of cash for the artisans. These families could not make ends meet, and some of the men had to look for work elsewhere and away from Kashmir, and the youngsters were lured by the mujahideen, who promised easy cash and a passage to heaven. The economic downturn worked to the advantage of the mujahideen, who exploited the situation, telling the people that the Indian government was responsible for the scarcity and that there would be a bountiful feast once Kashmir was independent. They were also able to recruit men by enticing them with monetary advances to feed their families.

The Friday evening prayers had just started. Mr. Sheikh prayed at home, as he had stopped going to the masjid because he was warned several times to stop "writing mujahideen stories" in the gazette and was also harassed frequently. He preferred praying in his house, as it was peaceful and a personal preference during these troubled times.

It was the day of *Raksha Bandhan*, a Hindu custom when sisters tie a *rakhi*, a thread, on the wrist of their brothers for the brother to pledge protection of the sister. Fizza had prepared a tray of fruits and milk cake and had bought a *rakhi* from a mail-order catalogue, which she believed was perfect for Krishna, her *rakhi* brother. She had made sandalwood paste for the *tikka*, a traditional mark applied on the forehead of a brother as a part of the ceremony. Krishna had promised to pass by after his pathology laboratory session that ended at about 7:00 p.m., which was perfect, as the Sheikhs would have completed the night *Maghrib* prayers.

As Krishna walked to his locker to put away his white coat and wash his hands, he heard the *Aazan*, the prayer call for the *Maghrib* prayers. He nervously bit his lip, as he had promised Fizza to be at the Sheikhs' just after the *Maghrib namaz*, but the lab went beyond its usual time, so he was slightly late. He almost ran to his Rajdoot motorcycle and kick-started the engine. The 450cc engine roared as he started off from the students' parking towards the bridge over the Jhelum River. He instinctively killed the engine at the bridge and stopped by the riverside to give the Sheikhs a little more time and so as to not disturb the *Maghrib* prayer. About forty minutes past sunset, he got back on his bike and roared away across the bridge towards the Sheikhs' home. He heard a car backfire several times at a distance, which almost sounded like an automatic weapon similar to the sound of a Kalashnikov. As he reached the shoreline, he was surprised by the sound of powerboats jettisoning away, as usually, the lakeshore was calm and quiet at *Maghrib*, especially during winter, when most boats were stowed. *Unusual*, he said to himself. He believed those were at least two powerboats, a sound he was able to recognize well, as he was an avid water-skier.

He parked his Rajdoot motorcycle on its stand by pulling it backwards to lock the stand, but it did not lock, so he kicked the stand forward to lock. Having secured the bike, he walked to the house but remembered the *Zarda* (a Kashmiri halvah made of cottage cheese and dried fruits) and a sari he purchased for Fizza a few days ago, so he returned to his bike to pick up the package from the side holster of his bike.

Hiding the package behind his back to surprise Fizza, he walked to the door, which was partly open to his astonishment. A thought came to his mind that Fizza must have heard his motorcycle as he came down the pathway to the house. He opened the door and froze when he saw Fizza lying on the floor just beside the door in a pool of blood. The contents of her *rakhi thali*, the *rakhi*, sweets, the *dahi*, and the sandalwood paste for the *tikka* (a dot that is applied on the forehead of a brother) were all strewn a distance away. He called out for Amma and Uncle. Not hearing a response, he walked from the dining room to the kitchen, where he saw Amma stooped over where she was cooking *Zarda*, his favorite sweet dish. The smell of burning milk and smoke rising from the smoldering pot filled the kitchen air. Amma's skull was blown off by a high-caliber bullet shot from a close proximity, and there was blood all over the kitchen. He had never seen a more gruesome sight before. Instinctively, he went to the bedroom where *Unclejee* prayed, only to find him genuflected in *Sajda*, with blood still pouring out of his multiple bullet wounds. He instinctively made the appropriate emergency calls and attempted to resuscitate Unclejee, as he was the only one with a heartbeat. The police arrived before the ambulance, and when the ambulance arrived, it was not equipped with lifesaving equipment, and the EMTs lacked the appropriate lifesaving skills. The police questioned Krishna briefly, jotting down his personal and contact information, and ordered an immediate transfer of the three bodies to the hospital, as Unclejee had died by that time too.

Krishna got on his bike and rode directly to the medical school, where Mustafa was attending Dr. Kapoor's late evening marathon class on the interpretation of EKG. Krishna waved from the doorway, beckoning him to step out of the class. Mustafa was surprised with his friend's request but noted blood on his pristine white shirtsleeve, so he walked out. Krishna took him home in the Hindu enclave of Srinagar with an excuse that his dad was unwell. Once safely home, he saw Krishna's parents waiting in the *angan* (the inner courtyard), as Krishna had called them on his way to the hospital. Krishna informed Mustafa of the mass execution of his family. Krishna's dad, who had lived in Kashmir most of his life, was aware of similar past assassinations by the mujahideen, so he assumed that the cowardly, murderous act was the work of the thugs within the mujahideen organization. Mustafa was in complete disbelief, and he instinctively got up to leave, but Krishna gently sat him back in the chair. Krishna's dad cautioned Mustafa of an imminent danger to his life, as the killers would be looking for him to complete the annihilation of the Sheikh family. He told him that the killers would not want to leave a family member alive for fear of a reprisal and to avoid future vengeful killings. He told him that the killers would most likely attend the funeral with the expectation to find him there. He told him that it was imperative for him to leave Kashmir that very night and to go as far away from Srinagar as he could in the next twenty-four hours. They all sat at the dinner table to strategize Mustafa's emergency exit from Srinagar, but no one had an appetite for food, even though hot *aloo puri* (curry) was served. Mustafa was completely numbed by the news of his family's death and could not think. Time seemed to have frozen.

Krishna's dad, Bishma, had a *lorry*, a British word for a cargo truck, scheduled to leave Srinagar for Delhi at dawn with some local goods, so he sent a runner to summon his trusted workers to ready it for an immediate departure. Krishna, with the aptness of a medical student, made a list of things that needed to be done prior to his friend's hasty departure—clothes, food, cash, and toiletries; he also made sure that his passport was at the medical students' hostel. Krishna left for the hostel with their driver to pack an emergency bag for his friend's immediate departure. During that time, Bishma personally supervised the loading of the lorry. He stacked the merchandise, keeping a seven-foot crawl space in the center for hiding Mustafa during the risky passage out of Srinagar. He padded the space with carpets and a wool *kambal* (blanket) to keep its occupant warm and comfortable for the long journey on a bone-chilling-cold Kashmiri night. He was aware of the border checkpoints and their liaison with the mujahideen. He could not take the chance of Mustafa being found during a border inspection, as that would be a death sentence. As a last precaution, he summoned his most trusted employee, Ganesh Hanuman, a young man he had brought home from an *Anarth Ashram* (orphanage for destitute children), offering him a home, refuge, and education and later a job in his business. He was to accompany Mustafa to Delhi and assist and protect him during the journey and also stay in Delhi until the time Mustafa felt settled and safe. He gave him cash and names of trusted contacts in Jammu and Delhi in case there was a need for emergency assistance. As a last precaution, he gave the workers who helped load the lorry overnight chores to keep them from leaving the shop that night, only as an additional precaution.

CHAPTER 2

North–South Corridor NH 1A
(Indian National Highway 1A)

Ganesh took the National Highway One to New Delhi

The lorry was to take the much travelled highway NH 1A from Srinagar, which ran from Uri in Kashmir to Jalandhar in Punjab and onwards to Delhi. The road was hazardous, as there were frequent terrorist attacks on border patrols and civilians. Night travel was more dangerous, but Bishma made the decision fully aware of the greater risk to Mustafa's life therefore did not wait for day travel. The travel would take them across Jawahar Tunnel, also known as the Banihal Tunnel, which was completed in 1959 and at that time the longest tunnel in Asia at about 1.77 miles long and at about 7,198 feet above sea level. The road was hazardous because of frequent blizzards and avalanches in the area during the winter months. There were many checkpoints barricaded by sandbags and razor wiring on the way, an attestation of the insurgency and many years of strife in Kashmir. The distance between Srinagar and Jammu was about three hundred kilometers but took greater than ten hours in the day, but a night travel was much slower, and formalities at the checkpoints took much longer.

The lorry left Srinagar at 7:45 p.m. after a *puja* and *Ashirwad* (blessings) and Sadka, a Muslim offering of coconut, rice, and money for the poor as an offering for a safe journey. They estimated that if all went well, they would be in Jammu by morning. Ganesh was instructed to call from Anantnag and stop for tea at Deogal. Leaving Srinagar was without problems, as most police *chowkys* received gifts from the pandit family on holidays as was a customary practice in India. The first one-hundred-kilometer drive was an easy drive, as it cut through the plains of the Kashmir Valley. Once they entered the hilly terrain, the strain on the truck was evident, as Ganesh shifted into low gear as the truck negotiated a mountainous, steep terrain. At the back of the truck in his hideout, Mustafa could smell the diesel fumes of the Tata Mercedes truck as it climbed the mountainous terrain. He could feel the vibration of the rear axle and the rattling of the gear as the truck shifted into lower gears. The back was warmer than he had anticipated, mostly because of the heat generated by the exhaust under the carriage. He was relatively comfortable but could not sleep, as the memory of his family kept on returning, and he was acutely aware of the coffin-box-sized space where he lay. At some point, he must have fallen asleep but awakened by a backfire of the truck as the driver shifted to a lower gear. He thought it was a gunshot, but as the truck jostled on, he realized that it was just a backfire. The stop at Awantipora was a brief pit stop for a cup of *sau mile ki chai* (a hundred-mile tea). At various tea stands, the driver would routinely ask for tea, relating it to its mileage potency. At Anantnag, the police checked the back of the truck and were satisfied to see the bales of sandalwood, rugs, and saffron and also the fact that it was a pandit truck.

The driver called the pandits as planned to inform them of their progress. Bishma had already established contact with the checkpoint at Anantnag and Deogal, informing them of his truck's arrival. The driver understood why the checkpoint at Anantnag was hassle free. The stop at Deogal was short and only consisted of a check of the driver's ID and consignment papers.

For Mustafa, the back-of-the-truck passenger, time seemed to move at a crawling pace. Many thoughts came to mind; he remembered the day his sister was born and how he started calling her Fizza from the first day, even though she was not named until six days later. Fizza was not only his sister but also a friend, who shared so many great childhood memories. The Sheikhs had gone through tough times, and only in the recent years, they had reached financial comfort to afford a new home on the west bank of the Dal Lake. Mustafa's mum was always complaining that he was not attentive to his schoolwork even though he did well in school. He remembered how she taught him not to be ashamed of crying when he felt sad or to laugh when he was happy. She taught him to be sensitive and attentive to the needs of the sick and distressed.

She was inwardly religious and recited the *Yassin* from memory and treated his friend Krishna with the fondness and sensitivity of a mother. She learned of the *Mahabharata* and *Bhagavad Gita* from her Hindu friends and respected their ardent beliefs without any reservation, a quality that she also inculcated in her children. As he lay in hiding, he remembered the chanting his dad had taught him as a child when he was scared during dark nights. He started chanting the Kulma— "La illah illa Allah Mohammad-ur-Rassol-ullah Ali un Wali ullah and the Ahl-e Bayat also know as Panj-Tan-Paak- Allah, Mohammad, Ali, Fatema, Hassan and Hussein.—and saying the *Kulma* repeatedly just as he did in the past when he was scared or challenged. Then he started reciting the *Yassin*—'Yassin el kuranul hakim, ina kalaminal'—just as his mother did before she put him to sleep when he was a little boy. Reciting the scriptures was always magical, as it gave him much comfort.

He must have fallen asleep, as he did not hear the driver call his name, and awakened only when he heard the tarpaulin covering the back of the truck being opened. The driver said, "Dr. Sahib, we have reached Batot." As he crawled out of his hiding, he smelled a wood fire from a nearby *dhaba* and the smell of *nan* cooking in their tandoor. The smell of food always made him hungry, and he had not eaten much since he left the EKG class that evening. The driver told him that the *dhaba* was famous for its *nan* and chicken and asked if he would join him for a quick meal. They washed their hands and faces at a nearby hand water pump and sat down on a rough-hewn wood bench made from local timber, most likely walnut or pine, which was relatively abundant in the area. The *dhaba* waiter, a young Kashmiri boy, recited the menu—dal paneer, dal masala fry, mirch masala, chicken masala, chicken sag, and various other items—in a single breath; and the Ganesh his driver ordered one chicken masala with green mirch, one dal *makhni*, two *nans*, one Bisleri (local bottled water), and one local tap water. The food arrived very quickly, and it was amazingly tasty. They cleaned out the dishes to the last morsel, paid for the food, washed, visited the urinal, and returned to the truck, only to find some locals standing by the truck.

Indian long and short blades

Ganesh instinctively told Mustafa to walk close by his side as he reached in his jacket to feel his Indian long blade. He opened the driver's door and asked Mustafa to slide into the front passenger seat, without taking his eyes off the three guys. He slid into the driver's seat with the deliberation of a seasoned lorry driver, greeting the guys with "Salaam Alaikum," and started the truck and did not say a word until they were off on the road. Then he said, "They were mujahideen." Most likely, the ordering of a Bisleri bottled water was a giveaway. He made a mental note to be careful at the next stop, hoping that they did not note the registration number of his truck.

Once a few miles from the *dhaba*, Ganesh pulled off by the roadside, asking Mustafa to return to his haven at the back of the truck. Mustafa was intrigued by the intuitiveness of his protector and how he moved in the presence of the mujahideen, almost like a tiger establishing his territorial rights, not taking his eyes off the three as Mustafa and he moved to the truck. It was all about body language, Mustafa noticed. Mustafa understood the need to be more vigilant in the future, at least until the time he was at a safe distance away from his homeland and harm.

He settled in his cocoon and lost a sense of time; the jostling of the truck, the smell of burnt diesel fuel from the exhaust, and the sound of changing gears after some hours of travel seemed mesmerizing, putting him to sleep. He was awakened when the truck came to a stop just outside the first tunnel. The air was already thin, as they had climbed to a higher altitude. He heard a hooting of the white Himalayan owl, a double *hoo-hoo* with a few seconds' pause before the next *hoo-hoo*, a sound he had heard often and recognized. According to a local folklore, the white owl announced impending danger.

There were about ten vehicles ahead of them, awaiting clearance to enter the tunnel; the tunnel security was manned by Indian Army personnel, all armed with automatic rifles and night-vision gear, and another group of the forces was with trained dogs and electronic equipment for detecting weapons. Ganesh walked slowly to the back of the truck, opened the tarp, and asked Mustafa to slowly slide off the back and follow him. They walked to the roadside, and Ganesh opened his fly to relieve himself and asked Mustafa to do the same. As the two did *mutri* (peed), Ganesh asked that Mustafa sit in the front through the army checkpoint, as the patrol would most likely have heat sensors that would sense his body heat at his hiding place. As they were finishing the act, they heard somebody ordering them to return to their truck. Ganesh replied, facing the direction of the sound, "We just got off for *mutri*, Captain Sahib." There was a short wait time, as the tunnel was closed to civilian traffic until eight in the morning. They had travelled about three hours since their start from Srinagar, about sixty-eight miles. The remaining distance to Jammu was about 117 miles.

The check was very thorough, and they did a thermal check of the carriage and went over the truck with sensors to detect bombs and weapons. Once satisfied of safety, they asked a few questions and opened the barricade, signaling the truck to move on. The travel in the tunnel was slow; only approximately 150 vehicles were allowed through the tunnel each day, and fortunately, their turn came within the first few.

The tunnel between Banihal and Quazigund, a distance of about 1.6 miles, was short, but travel was very slow. *Banihal*, in Kashmiri language, meant "blizzard," which was appropriate for the area, as it experienced very frequent blizzards in the winter months. It was situated at about nine thousand feet above sea level, a high point in the Pir Panjal Range. In the very snowy winter months, the tunnel remained closed for a few weeks because of avalanches in the area. The tunnel travel was slow, and the short distance took approximately two hours. The tunnel was well designed to remove exhaust fumes made by diesel trucks in the tunnel.

Once the tunnel was crossed, the road to Jammu was relatively comfortable. Mustafa sat in the front with Ganesh during this latter stretch of their journey, as they had reached a safe zone; Mustafa remembered the epic story when Hanuman, also referred to as Bajarangbali and Pavanputra and with 106 other names, removed all obstacles for Ram (called *Maryada Purushottam* because of his very exacting and high moral standards) as he travelled to Lanka in search of his wife, Sita. Ganesh was also revered by all Indian religions as a universal god. Mustafa thought, *how appropriate*. Ganesh Hanuman indeed lived up to his name, as he was entrusted to take him to safety just as the mythological character Hanuman did for Ram.

As they entered Jammu, it was coming alive; the vendors were already pushing their handcarts to the city, laden with fruits, vegetables, and handicrafts for sale. Ganesh proposed that they stop at Shalimar Hotel and use the facility to freshen up and eat breakfast. Mustafa picked up the local paper and walked to the café, where he sat awaiting Ganesh, but Ganesh was nowhere in sight. He walked back to the reception and asked the front desk attendant if he had seen Ganesh. The Anglo-Indian receptionist remembered Mustafa as he spoke in very fluent English when he arrived at the hotel. He politely asked if Mustafa was inquiring of his driver.

"Yes, yes," he replied, "his name is Ganesh."

"Sir," he said, "he is at the driver's café left of the entrance."

He saw Ganesh, sitting with his back to the door. He put his hand on his shoulder, requesting him to join him at the other café, and Ganesh said, "I am fine here, Sahib," so Mustafa pulled a chair and sat across, as he abhorred the class difference practiced in his country. Ganesh felt very uneasy and said, "Dr. Sahib, you cannot sit here." Mustafa persisted, so Ganesh reluctantly agreed to go with Mustafa to the other café—*Sahib's Café*—and Mustafa mused at the class difference that was still prevalent in his country. As he crossed the front desk, the Anglo glared at Mustafa, but Mustafa's piercing green eyes and his Aryan built were a sufficient message for the Anglo receptionist to back off. They sat down at Sahib's Café, and Mustafa ordered for both. Ganesh was obviously uncomfortable using the cutlery, so Mustafa picked the toast with his hand and ate his sunny-side-up eggs using his left hand and a knife as a shovel in his right hand, something Ganesh picked up easily. Ganesh was very grateful for his kind gesture and followed suit. They ate the breakfast and ordered more chai, following which they washed up and went back to the truck.

As they walked to the truck, Ganesh said, "Dr. Sahib, *Dhanyawad*," meaning "thank you." "We are now in the safe part of Kashmir, so you may continue sitting in the front seat." Once they were settled in, Ganesh told him that the five hundred or so kilometers ahead would take about ten hours to reach the outskirts of Delhi, and thereafter, the drive to their destination may take as much as two hours because of rush-hour traffic. He said that he would continue on National Highway 1, also known as NH 1, and follow the Great Trunk Road all the way to Delhi.

Ganesh eased the truck onto Hospital Road and turned left to Shalimar Road towards Tawi Bridge, taking the second right to NH 1. The chai and breakfast but mostly the comfort of the well-padded front seat of the Tata Mercedes eased the tension and discomfort he had felt in the back of the truck, where he was confined to a coffin-like space. He started nodding off; Ganesh prompted him to put on the seat belt, as the road to Delhi had its fair share of road traffic accidents. He told him that many truck drivers drove continuously for twenty hours without sleeping, and they smoked ganja (marijuana). He went on to tell Mustafa how different parts of *Cannabis Indica* were utilized for its hallucinogenic properties. He informed him that the hairy part of the female flower of the cannabis, known as hashish, was the most expensive of all cannabis products and also the most potent, as it contained a very pure chemical; he went on to say that the leaves were the cheapest variety of ganja but may be processed in two ways. The dried, crushed leaves were the cheaper form and easily available at every bus stand, but when the leaf was crushed and sieved multiple times, it was more potent and a little more expensive than the leaf ganja, and everyone who has celebrated *Shivratri* knew of the sap collected in a little earthen pot, known commonly as bhang; however, he went on say that the bhang sold on the street was a crude preparation made from grinding the leaves and flowers of the female cannabis plant into a pulp.

He continued his monologue; he said truck drivers were a completely different subculture of the human race. They were responsible for the spread of gonorrhea and other sexually transmitted diseases because they routinely slept with different women at each stop during their road travel. Ganesh kept up the monologue even as Mustafa dozed off completely, snoring loudly. When the truck jerked sideways, Mustafa awakened, and Ganesh said a bus was swerving towards them and lane wavering, so he jerked away to avoid it. He said, "Sahib, the Great Trunk Road was one of the oldest marvels of road travel that extended from Bengal in the southeast to Peshawar in Pakistan to the northwest," and continued to talk about the ancient civilization of Mohenjo Daro of the Indus Valley civilization. The monologue continued even though his listener went back to sleep and was audibly snoring. When Mustafa woke up, he said, "Sahib, I bored you to sleep with my talking, did I not?" He went on to say that talking kept his concentration and focus on driving, a habit he learned from another driver.

Mustafa was impressed with Ganesh's knowledge of India and also trivia, and he complimented him; that's when he told him of Musa Khan Baba, who had driven trucks on almost all Indian roads and had travelled to Peshawar when India and Pakistan were one country. He was the most faithful driver serving Krishna's *Dhada* (grandfather). He said when he was a youngster and just out of school, he accompanied Khan Baba to Delhi many times, who was quite a historian. He said that Khan Baba knew the terrain so well that he could predict where the road was rough or bumpy much before the point was reached. He said even the inspectors at the various checkpoints respected Khan Baba and treated him with respect, partly because he was a big man—just over six feet tall and wide chested, like Little John from fables of Robin Hood of Sherwood Forest—and Khan Baba had an uncanny ability of remembering everyone, especially the children, and their need for books from the city made him a popular driver travelling the roads of India. He said Khan Baba picked up supplies for the *Chowky* workers from Delhi, and they all trusted and adored him, and the children loved his stories.

On the way to Delhi, they stopped only for food or to relieve themselves as necessary. As the distance away from Srinagar increased, the feeling of despondency decreased. Even Ganesh seemed at ease. They stopped for food at a roadside *dhaba* and for a 'fifty-mile' tea (*pachas-mile ki chai*) twice. The congestion on the road increased as they approached Delhi, and the housing also changed from flat-roof homes so prevalent in Punjab to houses with slate and clay-ceramic roofs. Even the smells changed; the fresh smell of earth was muted by the smell of cooking and the sulfide smell from open wastewater gutters and animal waste. Once they got nearer to the center of the city, the buildings changed again; there were more red stone houses with more organized yards and an occasional dog on a leash.

CHAPTER 3

New Delhi

Mustafa had some family friends in Delhi who he believed may help with a medical school transfer admission or a research job at a hospital. He turned to Ganesh and asked if he had suggestions of where he could spend a few days, and Ganesh said, "Sahib, I would like to invite you to stay with me at my *rakhi* sister's house. She is married to a *Havaldar*, a noncommissioned soldier stationed in Delhi. I called him from Jammu, informing him of our itinerary, and he is expecting us. I hope you will not mind living with him. I chose him for an added security of the army barracks."

As they neared the army barracks, the houses got smaller, and all were very identical and similar to bread boxes placed next to each other in neat rows. They stopped at a barricade, where Ganesh got down. He called his *rakhi* sister's husband from the barricade, who rode his Rajdoot to the barricade, where he submitted the pass for an entry into the barracks. The keeper of the barricade viewed the papers, carried out a customary search of the truck, and lifted the barricade, allowing a passage. The roads in the barracks were paved with red bricks, and on its either side were neatly trimmed hedges. The houses were all identical with small attached courtyards and some with unkempt gardens that had mostly browned. They reached the end of the road and stopped just short of the Rajdoot travelling in front of them. The officer got off his bike and opened the passenger door of the truck, helping Mustafa to get off. He told him that Ganesh had explained the whole situation and that he would be absolutely safe in the barracks and went on to tell him that he had applied to his senior for family leave for a week so that he may take him around to all his appointments and interviews on his Rajdoot. The *Havaldar* had modified his Rajdoot, as it sounded more like the Royal Enfield, the famous British bike whose logo was a cannon, depicting its motto of being made like a gun. Once they were inside the house, Ganesh called Srinagar to inform Bishma of their safe arrival to Delhi, and Mustafa was able to hear an audible sigh of relief. After the phone call, Ganesh took Mustafa to water the sacred Tulsi plant in the courtyard as is customary in India after a safe journey.

They washed their face and hands and sat down on the floor on short four-legged wooden stools to eat puri and potato curry, followed by *gajrela-gajar halvah* (carrot halvah). They sat down and chatted for a while but were disturbed by a call from Srinagar. The call was from Krishna; he had collected all the medical transcripts and letters of introduction to contacts in Delhi who may help Mustafa with an admission to a medical school in Delhi. He said that the documents were being delivered by a courier, along with a suitcase of some of his personal belongings and books he had collected from Mustafa's room. One of the names cited was Mia Mohamed, a very famous Kashmiri physician, who was the dean of the Mualana Azad Medical School a few years back. Professor Mohamed was renowned internationally for his original work on bone healing. After talking for a while, their host, Nirmel Singh, showed them where the two would sleep and gave them fresh towels to wash up. He said that they could bathe at any time of the day, as there was no problem with the supply of water in the barracks, unlike in other parts of the city. He said that the water was very cold in the morning, so they should switch on the geyser before bathing. In the bathroom, there was a tube of red toothpaste and black Monkey Brand tooth powder; some fresh short branches of neem,[3] also known as *Arishtha* in Sanskrit, used in India for brushing the teeth; a small bar of Sunlight soap; and a spare toothbrush still in its original wrapper.

After freshening up, they put a *dari* down on the floor and went to sleep. When Mustafa awakened to go to the bathroom, Ganesh was not where he was sleeping, so he quietly slid out of the room when he found Ganesh sleeping just beside the front door outside. He assumed that he must have moved outside when he was asleep. He quietly returned to the room where he was sleeping and went off to sleep. When he awakened, it was already seven in the morning but did not notice it, as the window was draped. He went to the bathroom, brushed his teeth, took a shower, and changed into a clean shirt and Terry cotton trousers. When he entered the

---

3   Neem tree is a sacred medicinal plant. The soft new branches are harvested for use as a toothbrush. It is believed that its medicinal property prevents gum disease known as pyorrhea.

---

front room, everyone was ready and waiting for him for breakfast. Whilst they were having a breakfast of *ande ki bhurji* (scrambled eggs cooked with finely diced onions and green peppers and a touch of coriander) and *double roti* (bread), Ganesh told Mustafa that he would go to the city to deliver the goods he was carrying, and Nirmel Singh, their host, would take him to Mia Mohamed at Mualana Azad; and hopefully, the courier from Srinagar would be in Delhi by afternoon. Ganesh said that he had arranged a rendezvous with the courier at India Gate. Mustafa could not understand why the courier could not drop the packages to the barracks, so Ganesh explained that it was best that no one from Srinagar knew of his whereabouts for safety reasons or even the fact that he was in Delhi. Mustafa appreciated Ganesh's street smarts; he obviously had a lot to learn. He called Prof. Mia Mohamed's phone and talked to his PA to request an appointment that morning. The PA said that there was a cancellation for 10:30 a.m. for a thirty-minute appointment. He looked at Nirmel, who nodded an OK, so he took the appointment.

He sat on the backseat of the Rajdoot, and they were off. Nirmel wore a helmet, but Mustafa as the passenger did not wear one as was customary in India. During his work in the Casualty Department of the Srinagar Hospital, he had firsthand knowledge of the incidence of head injuries in non-helmeted motorcycle riders. He was also aware that motorcycles and scooters were the most common mode of family transportation. He was not amazed to see more than two people traveling on a bike—a child sitting on the petrol tank in front of the rider and the passenger in the backseat with one or two children on her lap. The traffic, he noticed, was much heavier here than in Srinagar, and the bikes were bobbing and weaving between cars. Nirmel was very comfortable on his Rajdoot that he weaved effortlessly through the traffic and cars that were at a standstill. As they left the city, they moved towards the suburbs and soon in the south extension towards the hospital. When they entered the medical school campus, it was about 10:20 a.m., about ten minutes ahead of the appointment.

Mustafa entered the ex-dean's office and introduced himself to the receptionist, and the PA appeared from the back room and invited him in. The PA said the doctor was running late. He asked Mustafa if he would like a chai, and he declined. The professor, dressed in a crisp, starched white doctor's lab coat, came to the office a while later and smiled as he came forward. He invited him to the inner office and asked him to sit down in one of the two padded leather captain's chairs made of Kashmiri walnut. Once the formalities were done, Mustafa shared information of his unusual predicament that brought him to Delhi, and the professor listened without interrupting.

15

The professor then said, "Your dad and I share the same philosophy, and I have read all his articles. You should be very proud of him, and yes, I will try my best to help relocate you, but I will need all your premedical and medical transcripts."

Mustafa said that if all goes well, he should have the required documents by afternoon. Whilst they were talking, the professor called his PA in and requested him to call a close colleague at the All India Institute of Medical Sciences (AIIMS), also known as the pride of India, for a personal conversation. As he was conversing with Mustafa, his PA came on the intercom to inform him that the requested party was on the line. He wished, "As-salaam Alaikum," and said that he had a top-notch student displaced from Kashmir whom he would like him to interview for a third MB position. When all was said and done, he turned to Mustafa, asking him if he could meet the professor at AIIMS tomorrow; and Mustafa smiled and said, "Of course." The ex-dean turned back to the phone, inquiring, "Is it 11:00 a.m. at the Medical Science Building, room 606?" He repeated his greetings to his friend on the other end of the line and asked if Mustafa could meet him at 7:00 a.m. with all his transcripts before his 11:00 a.m. AIIMS meeting. Mustafa nodded yes and graciously said, "I will be here at 6:30 a.m." As he left the dean's office, he was very touched with his kindness and his willingness to help a destitute like him, and and thankful of the coincidence that he had read his dad's gazette articles and also shared his philosophy.

The next day, he arrived at 6:15 a.m. and waited outside Dr. Mia Mohamed's office with a file of his transcripts and recommendations, as well as copies of his award certificates and the description and bibliography of the research he assisted. Even though Mia had scheduled a 7:00 a.m. meeting, he appeared just after 6:30 a.m., stating that he got in early. He went over the documents and let out a little wow, saying that he was impressed. He walked Mustafa to the cafeteria, where he ordered two black coffees and a sweet bun for his guest. At the café, he just talked about his research and how he had travelled from Kashmir about forty years ago to pursue medical education in Delhi. Once the coffee was done with, he got up and clasped Mustafa's hand firmly, wishing him the best with his interview at AIIMS.

When Mustafa left Dr. Mia Mohamed's office, Nirmel Singh was waiting outside, straddled on his Rajdoot. He asked him of the meeting and looked at his wristwatch. He said, "It's 9:00 a.m., so we have time for a chai and a sweet bread." He took him to AIIMS, parked the Rajdoot, and walked to the cafeteria at AIIMS allowing enough time for the meeting.

After the chai, Mustafa thanked the soldier and went to the designated meeting on the sixth floor, room 606.

He arrived at room 606 just a little before 10:00 a.m. and waited outside the dean's office, sitting on one of the two hardwood chairs. At 10:30 a.m., a young medical student appeared at the office and introduced himself, telling him that the dean had asked him to meet him before his meeting. Whilst they waited for the dean, the student told him of the campus, the curriculum, and the rigor of medical education at the premier Delhi medical school.

The dean arrived at the designated time; he looked very commanding in his rimless glasses, crisp white shirt, bow tie, and white coat. He apologized, stating that he came straight from the grand rounds and wished that he had asked him to join him but went on to say that there would be much time in the future for grand rounds, almost telling him that he was going to be part the premier medical school.

He asked how he knew of Mia, and Mustafa said that he met him for the first time yesterday and the second time today. "Sorry, I did not introduce myself. I am Prof. Kayum Khan and also a student of Prof. Mia Mohamed," he said. "He called me to make me aware of your transcript, and he also told me that he had called Srinagar Medical School and talked to your professors, all of whom sang high praises. They are sad that you were forced to leave."

"Sir, I am deeply saddened too and doubly sad, as I lost everyone in the family—my sister, mother, and father. Sir, I am completely alone," he said.

"Son, take courage, and only look ahead henceforth," Professor Khan said. "Life is ahead."

But Mustafa could not control his tears, which dropped like large pearls smack on the table. The professor pulled out a few tissues and said sorry and asked him to gather courage. He read through the transcripts and nodded with his signature infectious smile, showing a row of pearly white teeth. Mustafa was impressed with his good dentition, as dental hygiene was not a priority amongst many, even on the medical school campus. Professor Khan said, "You are fortunate, as I lost a final-year student recently."

"I am sorry, sir. What happened?" asked Mustafa.

"Motorcycle accident. He was riding shotgun without a helmet." He did not say anything more, and Mustafa did not pursue the topic. "Tell me, son, can you start tomorrow? I have no doubt that the medical council will accept you, and I do not want you to lag behind. Mind you, this is not Srinagar. We have the cream of the crop, so you will be competing with the very best medical students from all over India. There's only one other medical school that stands up to AIIMS, and that is the oldest medical school in India, the Grant Medical College in Bombay, but we are the second best."

"Yes, sir, I am aware, and I promise you that I will never give you reason to regret your decision."

He called on his intercom, and his PA appeared from the back office, and a few minutes later, the third-year medical student did so too. He instructed the PA to get the paperwork done and told the medical student to take Mustafa to the warden to allocate a room in the students' hostel. He turned to Mustafa, telling him not to worry about the fees, as Mia will cover it through a Pfizer research grant, which will also give him a stipend to cover other incidental expenses, and in return, he will help the professor with his research.

He looked over the transcripts, nodding his head and smiling, volunteering that he had talked with his friends at the Srinagar Medical School, and everyone talked of his excellence. He turned back, saying, "They tell me you have a mind for medical research. You recently did a paper on the patterns of trauma at the Srinagar Hospital casualty room that was very well accepted and one that offered solutions to ease the congestion in the casualty room. May I have a copy of your paper for my viewing?"

As they were talking, he called in his receptionist, asking her to make five copies of the medical transcripts, and handed her the transcripts and recommendations. Mustafa said, "Sir, I have an original of my trauma paper, and if permissible, I could make a copy for you right away."

He replied, "Ask Chandani, my receptionist, to make two copies so that you may take one for Mia."

His dad always told him that there were many good men in the world, and he could not quite understand his philosophical view, but he now understood its true meaning; indeed, there were good men and women on Terra, our blue planet (which is also personified by names such as Gaia[4] and Mundus), who would go out of their way to help even total strangers as in his case.

As he left the office, he was amazed how structure was so quickly returning to his life, and he wondered how Krishna was faring in Srinagar, as the two spent all their free and study times together. As he got off the elevator, he saw Nirmel Singh waiting for him, but he did not have to tell him the good news, as he sensed it right away. He said, "Dr. Sahib, when you work at AIIMS, do not forget us in the forces, as we need doctors' help the most." *How perceptive*, Mustafa mused as he walked towards him and

4   Mundus and Gaia, the Greek goddess of Earth.

embraced him; he wondered if his ability to perceive beyond the spoken word was because of his being in the forces, where they saw comrades fall in the line of duty and where they intuitively communicated on the battlefront, or if it was a natural, God-given gift.

He gave him the good news and told him that he will call for him to pick him up for a ride back home to the barracks once the admission and housing formalities were completed. As he walked away, he heard the firing of the motorcycle, the sound of the high-powered seven-port, two-stroke parallel 350 engine of the modified Rajdoot as it moved away.

The medical student in charge of taking him for the orientation was tall, and he guessed about six feet tall, kind of "huge" for an Indian. As they walked to the hostels, the student said, "I am Rajender, and my friends call me Raj. I am from Jullundur, where we have a family farm. During my earlier days at school, I drank fresh milk, and all our food came from our farm, so that may explain my large built, just in case you are wondering. I am a merit scholar at AIIMS, and other than hitting the library, I play left wing on our field hockey team and run middle distances and cross-country. Do you do any sports?"

"Not really, but I enjoy debating and other scholastic activities," replied Mustafa.

Raj responded, "You may want to try running cross-country. I believe it is the best stress reliever on campus, and you do not need company to go for a run, plus you can do it in the middle of a busy day and pump endorphins back into the system."

Mustafa responded, "I am certainly going to give it a try."

They crossed the greens, and Raj said, "That is the ladies' hostels. Beware of the call of the sirens, as you will be living next to our aggressive dames. They will soon have you write their assignments and, before you know it, introduce you to their mothers." Bang! He clapped his hands and said, "That is how you may lose your independence. Watch out, guru."

The allocation of a room was quick and efficient; he was provisionally allocated a guest room, which was larger than a regular hostel room, but the drawback was that it was next to the dining room, kind of a noise magnet. But it worked out to his advantage, as he made friends with the chef and the kitchen staff and, in no time, received room service even when the dining room was closed. In reality, he got to love the location and requested the warden to allow him the pleasure of occupying the room for the rest of the term. Mustafa preferred *not* to study late into the night but to awaken very early in the morning, at most times at two, a habit from his early days at school in Srinagar. At the wee hours of the day, the hostel was quiet, as a large majority of students were fast asleep, and he also believed that he was able to retain information with greater ease when he studied during the early hours of the morning. His routine of awakening in the wee hours of the morning and jogging around the campus got him to know the feisty Gurkha, the night watchman.

In his first year at AIIMS, he was already a contender for the coveted Belly Medal, which was given to a student who demonstrated academic excellence in the final year of medicine. His friends in the class believed that he was a genius, mostly because he was asleep when the remaining students were hitting the books, but they were not aware that he awakened to study in the wee hours of the morning when all of them were still sleeping.

He spent three to four hours each day at the animal lab, helping Dr. Mia Mohamed with his research on bone healing of long bone fractures in white rabbits. The thesis of his research was on fracture healing using a mammalian model, namely, rabbits, which they injected with centrifuged blood products at the fracture site. The early results were encouraging in a group of rabbits injected with the frothy white part of the blood centrifuge. They coined the agent as "bone stimulator healing protein" or BSHP. The hours of lab work were paying off, as healing in the injected group was significantly enhanced, compared to the control batch that did not receive BSHP. Healing was studied with X-ray evaluation (radiographic healing) and also with microscopic study of fracture healing of specimens obtained by a needle biopsy at predetermined intervals. The enhanced healing was statistically significant compared to controls that did not receive a blood product injection. Even early reports showed a promise that Dean Mia Mohamed was on to something that may help enhance fracture healing. Mustafa was aware of Professor Karim's research on prostaglandins at the Mkerere University in Uganda, which made him wonder if a protein in the supernatant blood substrate had bone morphogenic potential (bone growth potential). Mustafa was absolutely thrilled with the undeniably positive outcome of the research. They were contemplating on extrapolating their research of injecting the BSHP to fresh human fractures and to those patients suffering from nonunion or delayed union of fractures. The human study was going to be straightforward, as the patient would receive their own blood product and therefore the research would not require a special approval from the National Institute of Health and only require an informed consent from the patient for the procedure.

The summer that year was exceptionally hot and dry in Delhi, and the small pedestal fan was insufficient but the only defense against the searing heat. Even the air-conditioning in the library made little or no significant difference. Mustafa kept a moist towel in front of his fan to cool down the fanned air, which helped a little. However, his ingrained habit of getting up in the wee hours of the morning paid off, as the night temperature dropped a few points in Delhi. During the very hot summer nights, most people in Punjab slept on beds placed on the flat roofs of their homes, as it was comparatively cooler than sleeping indoors in a house that was baked through the day like a tandoor (a clay oven). During the hot summers, he took frequent showers to cool off; so did other students. There was a line of students waiting for their turn to shower. The final-year examination was twelve weeks away, and most of the class had broken into study groups, but Mustafa preferred to study alone, as he was able to focus and retain information better alone than when in a group. The only group study activity he did was with his batch, which consisted of three boys and seven girls. The group depended on him for his vast knowledge and his ability to tutor them throughout the year.

CHAPTER 4

University Grant Commission Seminar

Dean Mia Mohamed summoned Mustafa to his office, a frequent invitation since the outcome of the research was being readied for publication. This time, it was for a different reason. Professor Mia announced, "Mustafa, I have proposed your name as a student representative in the University Grant Commission's conference on the introduction of social sciences to the medical core curriculum." Mustafa asked the criteria for his selection, and he was told that the selection was based on academic excellence. He was told that there were two other names from Delhi, one Baltej Singh from Mualana Azad and a lady student from the famous ladies' college Lady Hardinge Medical College. There would also be student invitees from Madras, Bombay, Pondicherry and other medical schools.

"When is the conference, and what is entailed of me?" asked Mustafa.

Mia answered, "Next month and your opinion and input on the introduction of the study of social sciences in the medical core curriculum."

"Meaning what? What are social sciences?" asked Mustafa.

"I believe the study of social habits, cultural practices, and other social behaviors that may affect health. There is much literature on pregnancy, attitudes and practices during pregnancy, child-rearing, and infant feeding, and if you research, you may come across a myriad of material, mostly originating from the United Kingdom and the United States," Mia replied.

He was obviously excited and privileged to be one of the seven students representing the entire nation's student body—a distinct privilege, he believed. In a few days, the word got around the campus; most of his immediate friends, especially the seven girls in his study group, were absolutely thrilled and happy, but there were a few others who were jealous and envious of his selection. These few ganged up on him at every opportune moment to dissuade him from accepting the assignment, and one of them even suggested that he may lose opportunity to top the merit list of the final-year students. He relented and shared his concern with his mentors, Mia Mohamed and Prof. Kayum Khan, both encouraged him to believe in himself. Professor Khan went on to tell him that even if he stopped preparing for the finals this very day, he would still pass with the highest merit, albeit he informed him that judging from his performance thus far, he was likely to break the university record set twenty years ago by none other than Mia Mohamed himself. He left Professor Kayum's office with a spring in his feet and music in his ears. He was rejuvenated.

Mustafa owned two pairs of white trousers and two white shirts made of cotton, which were always starched and pressed, and a navy blue blazer, which he received from the athletic committee for being the best all-rounder athlete (He had followed Raj's advice and taken up running to pump endorphins between study hours, which led to a selection on the track team). He kept his whites spotless and always well pressed. He used to keep his trousers under his mattress on top of a plywood board that he had placed under the mattress to avoid sagging of the flimsy cotton mattress. This was a trick he learned from other students who maintained a sharp crease in their trousers without a need for frequent ironing. He polished his shoes to an army shine— something he learned from his dad, who was an immaculate dresser—and used the spit-and-shine technique he learned from the *Havaldar* Nirmel Singh. His dad used to tell him, "Know the character of men you meet with the grip of their handshake, shine of their shoes, and their ability to look into your eyes as they speak. A person with a weak spaghetti like handshake cannot make strong decisions, unkempt shoes tell you that he is sloppy, and when he does not look at you in the eye, he is hiding something." In a few words, his dad had given him a wealth of education on showcasing himself. Even as he went through the very hectic schedule, he did not forget to say a short prayer each day, thanking his maker for offering him the privilege of having his dream come true.

He got up early the next morning and put on his "whites" and the blue blazer with the insignia Mens Sana in Corpore Sano[5] bearing the *rod of Asclepius*.[6] His shoes were polished with spit and brown shoe polish.

---

5   *Mens sana in corpore sano* means "healthy mind in a healthy body."

6   The rod of Asclepius depicted by a rod and a single serpent is the proper symbol for health and healing as it was held by Asclepius, the Greek god of healing, and not the Caduceus, the staff of Hermes, which is erroneously used by many health-care industries.

He walked to the bus stop just outside the college, and as he approached the gate, his Gurkha friend was waiting for him. He had with him a bowl made of traditional pipal leaves with halvah in it. The Gurkha offered him the halvah, saying, "Sahib, I have brought you *prasad* from Shiv Mandir for your success." The Gurkha fed Mustafa with his own hand and blessed him, later accompanying him to the bus stop. The bus arrived at its usual Indian punctuality, but there was no place in the bus to ascend, so he stood on the step platform, holding on to the handrails. It jerked away from the stop, kicking a lot of dust and a bellyful of diesel smoke, which made Mustafa wonder of the toxic limit of this noxious carbon-monoxide-steeped exhaust fumes ejected into the atmosphere by these ill-maintained vehicles that the people were forced to breathe each day of their lives.

His bus passed Panchkuian Road and stopped in front of the gates of the Lady Hardinge Medical College. He got off the bus and asked the *dhurban* (gatekeeper) for direction to Professor Anand's office. As was his usual practice, he reached the office early, so he waited outside the office for the scheduled 8:00 a.m. meeting. He was not aware that the professor was already in until the time a peon appeared from an adjacent room. He stared at Mustafa for a good minute and asked him what he was doing there. Mustafa told him of his meeting with Professor Anand, and he replied, *"Acha, Gorababhu,* he waits for you," and escorted him to the professor's inner office. He wondered why the peon called him *Gorababhu,* a word usually used for a white man, but quickly remembered a similar past incident when he was mistaken for a white man because of his fair Aryan complexion and green eyes. The professor was very casual but immaculately dressed in a blue blazer, a blue striped tie, and grey trousers. He noticed his shoes were polished to a glossy shine, the grip of his handshake was firm, and he looked right into his eyes as he smiled, showing a pearly white row of teeth. Mustafa was absolutely stunned by the professor's total presence. His memory took him to the movie *Sound of Music,* a recent movie that he had seen, as the professor looked very much like the lead actor; he could not recollect the name but believed his movie name was Captain von Trapp.

It seemed the two were staring at each other, and the professor broke the silence by saying, "Did you just arrive?"

Mustafa replied, "Sir, I came in thirty minutes ago. I like to be on time, so I usually arrive early."

"I am impressed," said the professor, "as I appreciate being on time myself. Honestly speaking, I believe that you missed your calling, as you should have been a movie star. How tall are you? And the green eyes tell me you are a Kashmiri."

"I am not very tall, sir," he answered. "With shoes on, I am just about six-plus tall. My green eyes speak of my Aryan heritage. And may I be as honest too, sir? You remind me of Captain von Trapp. I believe the movie was *Sound of Music*."

Professor Anand smiled, once again showcasing his perfect pearly white teeth. "Yes, so I am told, so you are not the first one. The name of the actor is Christopher Plummer."

He beckoned him to sit down and asked if he would like to drink a soda or chai. And once the formalities were done, the professor asked if he wondered why he had scheduled the meeting. Mustafa responded, "Sir, I am here as you requested, and I am truly thankful for the opportunity to meet you. Sir, I read of your research work at Johns Hopkins in Baltimore."

"Touché," said the professor, "And I of your recent research on fracture healing, which is truly intriguing, and if you continue with cutting-edge research, you may someday get a call from the Nobel Committee. Both Dean Mia Mohamed and Kayum Khan hold you in high esteem. I scheduled this meeting to go over the agenda so that we may discuss and plan how best to optimize the participation of the elite group of students selected from all of India. The planner's expectation is for the student participants to help structure the guidelines for a seamless introduction of the much needed education of social sciences in our medical core curriculum. What are you views?"

Mustafa had discussed the subject matter with his two mentors and also with some of the students, following which he researched the medical core curriculum in major Western medical schools, from which he had derived some information. He responded, "Thank you for asking my opinion. However, my knowledge is limited and therefore may not be cogent, but I do feel that there is a very strong need, as knowledge of social sciences would offer a physician a broader and more in-depth idea of wellness and disease, thereby equipping him or her with a more complete knowledge of combating diseases."

"Very profound," Professor Anand responded, "and very much with my train of thought."

Now that he knew the reason for the meeting, Mustafa felt at ease, which was obvious, as he sat less upright on the padded chair and let his buttocks sink into the cushion. Just as he was getting comfortable, a very alluring young female entered the office, and Professor Anand smiled, saying, "Good, CM, that you came. Meet one of our star students from AIIMS, who will be on the student team at the conference." Mustafa could noticeably not take his eyes off the young lady student. Mind you, he was used to being in the presence of lady students, as his study group was made up of seven girls and two boys, but CM just took his breath away. Professor Anand came to his rescue, saying, "CM, please give him copies of my research on the subject, and please team up with him to prepare a presentation at the conference. Oh, I am sorry. CM, Mustafa Sheikh. Mustafa, Chander Mukhi Kasturba. CM is a star MD student at Lady Hardinge Medical College." Mustafa mused, "*Hum, brains and beauty in one single package*" and inadvertently smiled, a spontaneity that Professor Anand observed immediately.

Professor Anand waved his hand, gesturing a good-bye, and the two walked away from the office towards the library. CM asked, "Have you ever eaten our Panchkuian samosas, world famous in New Delhi? Hopefully not, as I am yearning for one right now."

She walked him across the campus and a side street to a small hole-in-the-wall shack with large *kadays* (deep fryers) with boiling oil and a smell of spices and fried dough. There was a long line of people, both young and old, waiting their turn to order and others waiting for their samosas, which he observed were served in earthen pots. Mustafa relished tandoori delicacies and not fried fritters or samosas, but the present company made even eating samosas on a street corner exceptionally wondrous. Mustafa was worried, as he had just enough rupees for his bus ride back to AIIMS. Fortunately, she insisted paying for the order, kind of forward for an Indian woman, but he liked the quality, as it espoused independence and, more importantly, he was broke. The street was crowded, and she sensed an uneasiness in Mustafa eating on the dusty street, so she suggested they walk back to Hardinge.

They walked across the campus to the cafeteria, which was about two or three notches below in comparison to the one at AIIMS. They sat at a far corner, away from the gazes of other girls in the cafeteria. Mustafa felt that the two were the topic of conversations judging from the giggling and over-the-shoulder looks they got, and the belief was confirmed when a very pretty young girl walked to them.

"Sundri, who is this *paraya*"—meaning outsider—"at our cafeteria?" she inquired. "Won't you introduce him, or are you going to keep him to yourself?"

Sundri? He wondered. He thought her name was Chander Mukhi.

She responded after a long stare and a deliberate pause, "Oh, he is just another student from AIIMS. Please excuse us, as we were just leaving." Mustafa could feel an irritation in her voice and felt that she did not take the interruption well for some reason.

She walked him to the library and ran down information on the importance of teaching social sciences and all relevant literature, enough reading to keep Mustafa busy for the next two days. When all was said and done, she said, "I'll walk you to the front gate." This time, she led him by his arm. As they parted, she asked if he would be interested in seeing the sound-and-light concert the next evening at the *Lal Kila* (the Red Fort); and without even thinking, he said, "Sure."

"Well then, see you at 6:00 p.m. at the gate."

That night, Mustafa could not sleep. So many confusing thoughts kept him awake. He did not quite comprehend this new feeling he felt; he even felt a sense of guilt, but the excitement of seeing 'CM' again was enough to keep him thinking of her most of the day. This was very unusual for him, as he never felt that way in the presence of his female batch mates or, for that matter, any other female before.

That day, he was to meet S. Subash, a student who had traveled from Madras for the conference and with whom he was to share a room at the Nalanda House in the famous Delhi IIT campus, where the conference was scheduled. That afternoon, he met S. Subash, who was a live dynamite, very intelligent and very forward but about pint-sized. As they sat in the cafeteria, Subash mentioned that he met a very pretty young medical student when he went to see Professor Anand. He described Chander Mukhi, even mentioning the glint in her eyes, her mischievous looks, and her hot-pink nail polish. Subash went on to say that he was going to date her before the conference was over. Mustafa remembered that they were to go to the *son et lumière*[7] show at the Red Fort that evening, so he turned to Subash, saying, "Let us have a little friendly wager. Whoever dates the Lady Hardinge girl first, the other has to do his bidding."

Subash was excited, as he obviously loved challenges. He said, "Certainly. Be prepared to do my bidding."

The remaining day passed very slowly, but the evening found Mustafa at the Lady Hardinge gate exactly at six. She beat him to the punch, as she was waiting for him in the company of the *dhurban*. She was wearing a peach flared bell-bottoms, an alluring kurta on top, a scarf instead of a *dupatta*, a very small red dot on the forehead, and a single diamond nose stud on the flare of the left nostril. *An unusual combination for that generation*, he thought, and he said, "I like the eclectic combination of a bell-bottom and a kurta."

She responded, "I hate the mundane. I like to make my own fashion statement." *Ah*, he thought, *she has spunk.*

They hailed an auto-rickshaw, which puttered away on its two-stroke Vespa engine, spurting dark smoke from its exhaust, which rose upwards in

---

7   *Son et lumière* is a sound-and-light show of the Mogul era enacted at the Red Fort in Old Delhi.

rings, just like a smoker blowing away rings, polluting Delhi's atmosphere. By the time they reached the *Lal Kila,* he was less aware of the acrid smell of burnt petrol, enjoying the joy of a gentle fragrance of early jasmine emanating from CM. The close proximity in the cramped-up space of an auto-rickshaw and the jostling, a bonus offer from Old Delhi's potholes, and the long ride were enough to awaken yet unknown senses that Mustafa had never experienced before. *A very confident and good-looking young man,* CM thought, little knowing that he was spellbound.

The concert was an open-air affair that lasted about three hours, and the night air was chilly. Mustafa was wearing a half-sleeve shirt and a khaki trousers, which he bought for the outing. Her arm touched his, and she said, "You are freezing. Don't you know how the temperature drops in the night?" So she asked him to come closer so they could share her pashmina shawl she usually carried in her bag. She said, "This shawl is warm, especially as my mother has woven it with her own hands from virgin pashmina wool." Indeed, he felt an immediate warmth, but he was not sure if the warmth was from the shawl, his adrenaline that was pumping an overload in his system, or the warmth of her body. The show was the best he had ever seen; even though it was just for three hours, it was an eternally pleasing experience.

After the show, they hopped into a tempo, which carried them back to Hardinge; on the journey back, they shared CM's shawl. As they entered the gates, she said, "I will walk in alone. Please take the tempo to Nalanda House and take my shawl, but do not forget to return it to me tomorrow at the conference as it is very precious to me."

When he entered the room, he shared with Subash at the Nalanda House. Subash was awake and working on his presentation. "So what's up late, eh? I can smell a scent of a woman. Is it jasmine? And that shawl, where have I seen it before?"

"Well, you, *Madrasi,* I won our wager. I went out with Chander Mukhi, and this is her shawl. Your memory serves you right, as she was probably wearing it when you saw her at Hardinge, I assume."

"That's right, and I know that perfume. You did it. You beat me, you *Delhiet.* Well, what is your wish, as I will do your bidding?" Mustafa did not have to think hard; he knew exactly what he would make his roommate do.

The next morning when Nalanda House awakened, Subash ran around the campus in his birthday suit, a sight that may be ingrained in memories of many of the participants for eons to come. Subash's rear end was the topic of conversations at breakfast, and surprisingly unabashed, Subash came to breakfast wearing khaki pants and a brown herringbone tweed jacket. The guy had spunk.

The conference came to an end much too quickly, but a friendship with Chander Mukhi was sealed. However, there was a problem: Chander Mukhi was a daughter of a Himachal Khettry, who traditionally did not marry their daughters outside their religious sect and most definitely not to a Muslim and a complete outsider. Both Mustafa and CM understood the complexity and the problems of a Hindu-Muslim marriage. Not even a few months back, a Muslim boy who married a Gujarati Hindu girl was beaten almost to death by a gang of Hindu thugs in Ahmedabad.

The two kept on meeting at regular intervals through the remainder of the year. The conference was well received by its audience, and the University Grant Commission (UGC), which hosted the conference, chartered a directive for an implementation and adoption of the study of social science into the core curriculum of the Department of Social and Preventive Medicine.

CHAPTER 5

Final MBBS Examination

The UGC conference had eroded significantly into Mustafa's study routine, so he decided to shift into a more intensive study routine. There was also a discussion within the group of top contenders to simultaneously appear for both degree examinations, MBBS and MCPS. The MCPS examination was a few weeks prior to the final MBBS examination, and Mustafa thought it would serve as a dry run, as many of the examiners overlapped, and he believed he would be able to impress them during the MCPS examination.

CM and Mustafa met less frequently, mostly because of their preoccupation with the final-year examination. Both studied much of the night, literally burning the midnight oil, as electricity went out frequently in Delhi. CM read until the wee hours of the morning.

Sudhir was a frequent visitor to Mustafa's room and tried to see all that he was reading, as they were competing for the top seat in their final year. Mustafa changed his routine back to early morning study hours, mainly because of Sudhir's frequent "investigative visits." He also spent more time in the library, reading the latest papers on the advice of his mentors, professors Mia Mohamed, Kayum Khan, and D. Anand. He spent time with his mentors, who honed his answering skills for the viva voce (oral examination and case study). His mentors advised against taking two examinations simultaneously, as they believed it would be exhausting, but Mustafa had made up his mind, mostly because Sudhir, his die-hard competition, had also registered for both.

He met CM over cappuccino whenever he visited the Hardinge Library, which at times seemed to be just an excuse to see CM. The *dhurban* at the hostels got to know him well not only because of his visits but also because Mustafa always brought food for him when he came to Hardinge. The two, CM and Mustafa, kept in touch. The amazing thing Mustafa noticed was that the days he met CM were also his best study days; he believed the endorphins were responsible for an increased retention of materials read.

The next months passed quickly, as the MCPS examination preceded the MBBS examination. Mustafa had gone into a complete scholastic hermitage. He was sleeping in snatches and reading, researching, and reciting in most of his waking hours. The coffeepot was always on the ready for a fresh cup of acrid black brew that would have kept awake even Rip Van Winkle for a full decade.

The three-day MCPS examination was a breeze academically, and Mustafa felt that his performance was good, as he was singled out in the oral examination, and the examiners seemed to know him. Nonetheless, the intensive and long study hours spent in preparing for the examination, shortened sleep hours, and poor eating habits had taken a toll on his health and well-being. After the last oral examination, he decided to take a cab back to AIIMS, mainly because he felt exhausted. The cab left him just outside the hospital campus; he paid the cab fare and walked a few steps towards the gate, and his legs buckled. When he came to himself, he found the cabby splashing water on his face, and a crowd had thronged around where he lay on the paved sidewalk; he felt a throbbing on his forehead, where he palpated a bump on the frontal part of his skull, where he must hit the pavement when he fell down. He could barely comprehend what the people surrounding him were saying.

"Take him to the hospital. He has fainted," one said.

The other added, "Do not move him. He may have broken something."

And yet another added, "He may have some ID in his wallet."

Their words resounded in his mind like echoes in a domed structure. He felt he was in a dark tunnel; he could hear the echoing voices but not able to see much even though he believed his eyes were open. Someone later said that he had a glassy look, eyes gazing but not seeing. By the time they came to a decision on how to proceed, he was compos mentis and aware of his surroundings. He got up, and he was able to stand up and keep his balance. He said, "I am fine, thank you. I will manage. I am a student doctor at AIIMS."

One kind soul said, "I will walk you to the hospital so they may check you out."

They sat in the casualty room for about an hour, and then one of the aides recognized him and called the doctor of the day, who gave him a quick look over and a clean bill of health; he left him with the advice to take care of his health, which he promised he would, and pinned a clinical diagnosis of concussion.

He walked to the hostel and to his room, and he believed that he had slept for eighteen hours flat out after that, he had truly lost concept of time. When he awakened, he was famished. Whilst sitting in the cafeteria and talking to a fellow student, he found out that Sudhir had applied for the MCPS examination but backed out. He informed Mustafa that Sudhir confided in him that if Sheikh goes for the MCPS examination, he will be fatigued and not able to perform well in the final MBBS examination. *How conniving and how extreme*, Mustafa thought, but he knew that he could not take anything past Sudhir. That evening, he went to his mentor at AIIMS, who was not surprised by Sudhir's scheming plan to oust him as a major contender for the first place. He advised him to rest and eat well and asked him, as a matter of fact, ordered him to report to his house each evening for supper. By the time he arrived to his dorm at the boys' hostel, there was a bearer awaiting his arrival. He was carrying a package of *massub pakh* and a mug of almond milk from Prof. Kayum Khan's wife, whom he addressed as Auntie. By evening, Mansoor, a close friend who lived in the neighborhood and a commerce college student, was at his door. They were often mistaken as brothers, as they looked alike, and they both enjoyed practicing judo. Mansoor said his famous phrase as he entered the room, "Mustafa, you are so stupid." He went on to tell him that the guy who had helped him walk to the casualty room after his fall outside AIIMS worked in his dad's glass shop, and he told him all about his collapse. "Now you pack your bag, as you are going to stay home with me." Mustafa was able to convince him to allow him to continue his stay in the dorm instead, with a promise that he would take great care of his health. As the days passed, Mustafa slept a good six to eight hours each night and spent the remaining time in the library or with his study group. Sudhir's ruse had only strengthened his resolve to do his best. He spent some evenings with his professors, who coached him and gave structure to his study program.

The written MBBS examination was not difficult except for an essay question on amoebiasis, which he felt he did not answer well. He believed that he was stumped, mostly because of his inability to answer that one question well. All that he wrote about amoebiasis was from remote past knowledge, but he sketched diagrams of the human cycle of the parasite and quoted research papers as references. He was depressed that he had lost the chance for the first seat. It was only during the oral examination that he found out that he was singled out, as his answer to amoebiasis question was discussed by the panel of examiners, who had given him a distinction for his nonconventional essay. The oral examination went well; Dr. D'Souza, his external examiner, was extremely encouraging, as after his segment, he walked him to the next examiner, telling him to go for higher-distinction questions, as the young man was an extraordinary student. Providence seemed to be in his favor, as Dr. D'Souza had a reputation of being the most difficult examiner. It was fabled that he had once literally kicked a student out of the examination hall, telling him to find another vocation.

All the three major oral examination segments went off pretty well, and it was only after he met Dr. Ganjawalla that he found that the panel of oral examiners had decided to shave marks off his final score, stating that no student had ever scored that high a score in the final MBBS oral examination before. However, Professor Ganjawalla believed that the real reason for deducting the marks was to favor university chancellor's daughter from a competing medical school who was also a contender for the first seat. Mustafa was worried that he was caught in a political situation, but fortunately, his performance in the written examination gave him a distinct and insurmountable lead, making him the overall highest scorer in all three clinical subjects. He was sad that the panel of oral examiners had deducted points from his score but decided to let it slide, as he had no control of the situation. Mustafa, having scored the highest, was the valedictorian and the person to carry the university flag at the convocation, but he opted not to attend the convocation. The reason for boycotting the degree convocation was to register a protest against favoritism in places of higher learning.

Chapter 6

Internship

His high scores allowed him to pick choice rotations for his internship. He planned it well, allowing him to spend more time with CM. On the AIIMS campus, he was a celebrity, as the word went out that he had scored the highest in the viva voce examination in the fifty years of the university and written the best essay on amoebiasis.

During his internship, he continued working on research with Professor Mia and did some additional work in Professor Kayum's lab. In spite of the busy schedule, he was able to find time to spend with CM, especially during his SPM (social and preventive medicine) rotation, as he was a lead for a study on immunization at a local slum population. He constructed a questionnaire, which the rest of his class helped in completing by visiting and interviewing the slum community. Once the raw information was collected, he compiled the data and cross-referenced it with the national data, concluding on how to improve the slum vaccination program. The KAP (knowledge, attitude, and practices) study, to the chagrin of some in the SPM Department, brought to the forefront some previously unknown variables that were adversely affecting the slum vaccination program. A few months after the completion of the vaccination study and the presentation of a grand round, he found out from Professor Kayum an insider information that his name was proposed for a presentation of his data to a group of visiting physicians from the United States.

With CM's help and his professor's guidance, he prepared an illustrative presentation, which drew compliments from a lead pediatric doctor from the famous Boston Children's Hospital. He was pleased with the recognition, a feeling he confided and only shared with CM, and she succinctly stated, "I had all the confidence in you." She always had the last word and was always proud of him. The relationship between the two was gradually strengthening, and unlike a relationship based on lust, their relationship was based on acknowledging each other's strengths and helping overcome weaknesses. They knew that they were soul mates; nonetheless, their religious differences surfaced at times. On one of such occasions, she asked, "What are you afraid of?" and he went on to discuss how the religious differences would affect their respective families and their subsequent progeny. She promised, *"You need not worry, as our children shall bear your family name and shall follow your religion, and we will make them universal citizens"* He remained very skeptical, mainly as he was a pragmatist who believed in reality and not a hypothesis of a perfect marriage, especially where the differences in religious ideologies were so wide apart.

The year of internship passed quickly, and time was nearing to decide on specialty residency. He was interested in pursuing pediatric medicine, but Professor Ganjawalla convinced him that he had unique surgical skills and a sound knowledge of human anatomy, a great primer for a good surgeon. He discussed residency with professors Anand, Kayum, and Mia, and all three felt that Mustafa should consider residency in general surgery and later specialize as he got more skillful. He discussed the prospect with CM and applied for a surgical residency with Professor Ganjawalla's department. The interview was only a formality that needed to be completed, as the professor had already expressed his desire to train him. Surprisingly, Dr. Ganjawalla called him to his office just before the residency interview and asked him the weirdest question, "Mustafa, once you are selected, you will complete the program, won't you?"

"Of course, as that is my decision, and I want to be the best," Mustafa responded.

He was selected. And it seemed that the interns knew of the outcome much before the formal letter came to him. He shared the news with CM and all his mentors, who were all equally happy; Professor Kayum announced a celebrative dinner at his house. That night when he returned to his lodging, a fellow intern informed him that some of his relatives from Kashmir had come to the hospital, inquiring of his whereabouts. That got him really worried because he had no living relatives in Kashmir, as all members of his immediate family were assassinated by the mujahideen. He decided to go to Prof. Mohamed's home instead. He discussed the information with his professor, who asked him to sack in his guestroom that night and that he would call his friends in the CID to look into the matter. That morning, the professor made the appropriate calls, and three Kashmiris were apprehended and taken into custody. All three had arrived from Kashmir in the past few days and looked like seasoned fighters, and a raid into their lodging revealed small arms, automatic weapons, hand grenades, and rounds of ammunition. They were obviously not relatives or well-wishers but assassins with an agenda to assassinate Mustafa.

It was now obvious that the mujahideen had found out that he was in Delhi and that his safety was at stake. Professor Mia called Kayum and Anand to discuss a course of action as he put it. All three knew of the cold-blooded feudalistic nature of the mujahideen directives, especially Professor Mia, who had lived his life in Kashmir and therefore aware of the seriousness of contract assassinations at the hands of the mujahideen. This was their signature "seek and destroy"; they were ruthless, very determined, and left no blood relatives alive so as to avoid later repercussions and revenge killings. Dr. Anand, who had lived most of his life in Delhi and also gone to Johns Hopkins, felt that Kayum and Mia were too melodramatic and overreacting and that Mustafa was in little or no danger, at least until Mustafa's friend in an adjacent room reported a break-in at Mustafa's room, where the watchman and warden found the room completely disheveled and photographs and pictures reaped and pulled off the wall, a wall he referred to as his memory wall. Mustafa was not able to bury his family or recite burial prayers required of a living relative, so the memory wall was his way to do *Ziarat*, a prayer for the departed souls. He recited his prayers whenever he was able to but at least twice, at *Maghrib* and *Isha* each day routinely. He also kept the obligatory *Ramzan* fast for a month, and interestingly enough, some of his Hindu friends did so too; a Sikh friend, Inder Singh, had been observing the *Ramzan* fast for the past two years and joined other Muslim students for the *Behori* (prefast meals). The AIIMS hostel was a very secular and nonsectarian campus without much mention of religious differences. It was the most perfectly integrated campus of student body, made of students from all walks of life and different parts of the subcontinent. It was so different from Pune, where the students at BJ Medical had inflicted bodily harm and imposed other religious rituals to their Muslim colleagues during a Maharashtra Hindu–against Muslim riots just a few years ago, and the culprits were not censured or reprimanded for their actions but actually praised! It was not surprising as Nathuram Godse, the man who assassinated Mahatma Gandhi, was a revered figure in Pune, where a cult named after Godse was still in existence, and some of the students at BJ were its followers.

The ransacking of Mustafa's room changed Professor Anand's belief and mind-set, who now understood that Mia and Kayum were more informed of the mujahideen than he was. The ransacking of the room meant that there were more mujahideen sleeper cells in Delhi, so they concluded that the best plan of action would be to transfer Mustafa to another college away from Delhi for residency and if possible to another country. All three had contacts in the United States and the United Kingdom, but such a transfer would take a year or more, time that they did not have. Mustafa had completed an ECFMG examination, a required qualification to join residency in the United States a few months ago. But his situation did not allow for a wait of a year or more, so his mentors believed that a provisional immediate lateral transfer to Grant Medical (GMC) in Bombay or BJ in Pune was the only viable option, as both institutions shared reciprocity with AIIMS. Both institutions would be pleased to receive a resident from AIIMS, *the pride of India*, and Mustafa was a summa cum laude scholar of his class. A few phone calls and faxed transcripts later, an acceptance was received for a residency at the pediatric institute of the Grant Medical College and allied hospitals under the tutelage of a world-renowned pediatrician Udani, who was friends with Dean Mia Mohamed. Until the time of his departure for Bombay, he lived with Professor Kayum, and Dr. Anand had already called CM to inform her of Mustafa's potential move to Bombay, mainly as he was aware that there was a friendship or a relationship between the two, as CM blushed at the very mention of Mustafa's name.

CM arrived at Professor Kayum's home within hours, and she was obviously crying, as her eyes told the story only too well. Mustafa and CM spent time in privacy and promised to keep in touch. Inder Singh, his fasting buddy, packed a bag of Mustafa's meager belongings, which he brought to the professor's home. The professor's driver carried the bag in his car whilst Mustafa, Inder, and CM went to the train station in a taxi. The ride was very long, mostly because of the distance and Delhi traffic but without any incidence. They arrived at the Paharganj railway station just in time. The tickets were all ready and paid for by his professors, and the driver carrying his bag of worldly belongings was also carrying an envelope of rupees in one hundred dollar bills from his professors and a letter of acceptance to GMC, letter of references, and instructions with personal contact numbers of each of the three professors. In his letter, Professor Kayum mentioned of his upcoming Bombay trip for a student lecture series at the combined medical program in Bombay in two weeks. CM too had a packet of samosas from the Panchkuian food stand, some nuts and dried fruits for the journey, and also the pashmina shawl they had shared during their first outing at the sound-and-light show at the Red Fort.

The parting, thank God, was short, as the train was about to leave, but CM could not help a constant dripping of tears. Mustafa remembered a dialogue from a movie they had seen together recently, and he said, quoting the movie dialogue replacing "CM" for Pushpa as in the movie, "I hate saline water, CM. Let us part with a smile and a promise to meet again someday and somewhere in the near future."

The steam locomotive train[8] was already blasting a long followed by a short blast of steam train whistle, warning all passengers to get on board, as it was ready to depart from the Delhi station. The steam engine chugged away with its chug-chug sounds getting closer and closer as it gathered speed. Mustafa stood hanging from the doorway until the ticket collector closed the door. CM stood at the platform, waving until the train was out of sight. As the train was leaving the station, Mustafa blurted out, "CM, if I ever marry, it will be a woman such as you, one with brains and beauty," and CM smiled a short but distinct smile. And she mused now that he was moving so far away and maybe to the United States; the possibility of meeting him again was remote.

The journey to Bombay was easy, mainly because of a group of union leaders who boarded at the next stop. They were jovial and about the same age as Mustafa. Mustafa was carrying his research material and was editing his paper that was to go to the *Lancet*, a British journal of repute. The five union leaders noticed this young green-eyed, fair-skinned man and assumed that he was a *chitta*, a white man, so they started talking about him in Punjabi, mostly critical of the British; as many in their age group were critical of the British Raj, as the two hundred years of white occupancy of India had left many with bitter memories, especially up north in Punjab, where Colonel Dyer had massacred scores of unarmed men, women, and children at the Jallianwala Bagh in Amritsar. Mustafa remembered a poetry on the massacre written by a doctor in Boston, United States. He mentally recited the poem and felt proud that he remembered it verbatim:

Jallianvala Bagh

*Brig. Gen. Reginald Edward Harry Dyer's[9] 45th Infantry Brigade marched
Sound of army boots echoed off Jallianvala's walls then cracked and parched
Within the walls 20,000 Indians gathered for a nonviolent pact
To implement ways to repeal an unjust Rowlatt Act[10]*

---

8   India had leftover British steam engines, which were gradually replaced by General Motors diesel engines; however, some steam engines, also referred to as iron horses like this one, still carried passengers to Bombay.

9   Dyer, a son of a barman, was a social misfit who was removed from home when he was just twelve very similar to Horatio Nelson who too was removed from his family at the age of twelve.

10 Bills passed to legislate control of the Quit India Movement.

British rifleman and two machinegun-armored cars blocked the garden
1650 bullet rounds fired on the gathering without a warning or pardon
Ear-shattering death cries and sight of the dying pleased Dyer
That April 13th, 1919, these men, women, and children had no savior

Hunter Committee discharged Dyer for 'a mistaken notion of duty'
He left India without equitable punishment or further scrutiny
Churchill and his British parliament rubber-stamped Hunter's proclamation
Thus the 'Butcher of Amritsar' returned to England without incarceration

In the quiet of each night, the dead gather here to congregate
Cries of the dying are still heard as you enter its gate
The Flame of Liberty reminds us of the ghastly atrocity
Now Jallianvala, a memorial for those felled in Amritsar city

The union leaders continued their barrage of small talk for the next few hours until the train jerked to a stop at a station. Mustafa was tired and needed a chai (made by boiling tea leaves and cardamom in water to the first boil and adding milk thereafter, bringing the mixture to a second or third boiling point) to keep him awake, so he hailed a *chaiwala*; as the tea bearer arrived, he talked to him in perfect Punjabi to the astonishment of the union leaders, who were criticizing him in Hindi and Punjabi since the time they had boarded the train. The tea was served in earthen *piala* (cup). He asked the union leaders if they cared for tea, once again in perfect Punjabi, and one replied back in Hindi, saying, "Dhanyawad," -thank you. Once the train left the station, one of the young men ventured to break ice and strike a conversation with Mustafa, apologizing for their critical remarks of him. Mustafa smiled, assuring them that they were not the first ones to mistake him for a foreigner. They remarked that he was too engrossed studying and wondered if he was preparing for an examination, and he explained that he was editing some medical research that was due for publication. From that point onwards, they did not bother Mustafa but also offered him *aloo paratha* and potato *subzi* they were carrying with them. The time in their company passed quickly and with a sense of security because, by morning, they were entering the suburbs of Bombay.

The hustle and bustle was surprisingly unique to Bombay and the smells of morning so common to India. The train slowed as it lurched into the Grand Central Station of Mumbai. Before the train had come to a stop, the luggage bearers wearing red tunics, each with a brass medallion strapped to their upper arm, were on board, ready to help the passengers off the train. One of the union boys asked him where he was going, and

Mustafa pulled out a piece of paper where he had written the address of RM Bhatt Hostel, where he was going to stay while at JJ Hospital. One of them said, "Perfect, I'll take you there, as my brother, who lives just a block away, is receiving me at the station."

The ride from the station to JJ was interesting because, for the first time, he saw trams that were running on the streets of Bombay. The tram brakes made a very metallic screeching noise, a very recognizable signature of the tram crossings. He also noticed *tongawalas* (horse carriages reminiscent of the British Raj), which he had only seen in the movies. The sights and sounds of Bombay were so different from Delhi, where you would hear sounds of *tempo* (motorcycle-drawn auto-rickshaws) and the three-wheelers. The ride from Bombay Central to RM Bhatt took not greater than fifteen minutes, mostly because of the early hour of the day. He was dropped just outside the gate, and he made his way to the common room, where he was to contact Gangawne, who was to show him to his room. Gangawne was waiting for him, and as he walked to the common room, he recognized Mustafa by the fact that he was lugging a beaten-up suitcase very similar to other students that arrived at JJ. He walked him to the hostel and helped him to the fifth floor, which was allocated to the PG students.

He parked his suitcase on the bed, wondering why the mattress was missing. He asked Gangawne, who replied, "Sahib, I have kept it out in the sun, and I'll bring it in once it has been in the sun for a few hours. Sahib, I also torched the metal bed yesterday to rid any *katmals* for your safety."

Different, he thought but later learned that the airing of a mattress was customary in Bombay. He asked the direction to the pediatric institute. The JJ Hospital campus was vast with an admixture of Edwardian buildings and modern buildings. The main hospital was huge. It had seven floors and was sprawled out, covering most of the campus. Just south of the campus was a ladies' hostel and behind it a field hockey field. In front of the hostel was a basketball court. The campus was green with coconut trees, acacia, and other deciduous trees, quite different from AIIMS, which had mostly modern architectural buildings with very little greenery. The library was housed in a very pretty Edwardian building, which looked more like a fort.

He crossed the main campus to reach the pediatric institute and Dr. Udani's office. Dr. Udani was expecting him, as Dr. Kayum had faxed him his travel schedule. Dr. Udani was a stout man, who spoke in monosyllabic English interposed with some Gujarati, but his assistant was a very pretty lady that looked like the famous Indian movie star Asha Parekh. He instructed the young lady, whom he introduced as Dr. Parekh; her first name however was not Asha, as he later found out, but Usha. Dr. Parekh took him around, introducing him to each matron and each assistant doctor. She had so many stories and knew everyone well and remembered all the minutia of the institute; she was truly a repository of a lot of information that one would not necessarily find in a hospital prospectus.

As they walked, she told him of the institute photographer who left suddenly because of a family emergency, and Dr. Udani was in a fix, as he was to photograph patients with significantly unique disease presentation. Amongst them was a child who had both chicken pox and herpes zoster, kind of a dual presentation of the chicken pox virus, and yet another child with cutaneous tuberculosis. Photography was Mustafa's hobby, and he had put a photographic exhibition entitled "Diseases of the Eye" at AIIMS. He mused at the opportunity to be of service; immediately after his orientation, he returned from his room with his Lyka single-lens camera that he won in a competition. He loaded a high-speed film so that he could photograph without using a flash. He first went down to the child with chicken pox and intercostal herpes zoster, also known as herpes zoster vars intercostalis, taking about ten shots at various angles, and next the child with tuberculosis sicca, affecting the skin and associated with enlarged groin nodes.

When all was said and done, he took the roll to the media center and developed the negative and, once dry, processed two copies of glossy prints. When he walked to Dr. Udani's room, Dr. Usha Parekh was with him, and he felt that he was interrupting something, as they were standing unusually close to each other. But when he presented the doctor the prized prints, Dr. Udani walked to him, shaking his hand, beaming from ear to ear. Obviously, Mustafa had hit a home run.

"My son, Kayum did not tell me of all your attributes and especially of this one. I do not know if you are aware, but I lost my very best photographer, and I am completely lost, as I have a presentation to WHO doctors next week. Son, you are a god sent to me, my boy." Mustafa wondered where Professor Udani had picked up the "my boy" thing. Its origin was British, he believed, or maybe a vestige of the very long two hundred years of British occupancy of India. He later found out that Professor Udani had received his postgraduate pediatric training and MRCP in England from the Royal College.

That day, Mustafa made a place for himself at the pediatric institute, which fostered a direct relationship with Professor Udani. As time went on, he learned how to make Diazo (Diazochrome or blue background) slides for projection to his professor's benefit. He was equally loved by pediatric patients in the wards, as he blew balloons out of examination gloves, on which he drew cartoon faces; he sat by their bedside, telling them stories of epic Indian heroes, and drew funny faces on their casts using color markers. He also became a favorite with the nurses, as pediatric patients listened to him and even allowed the nurses to inject them. One of his bedtime stories was of a fictional hero who closed his eye and counted to ten in face of pain, and the ouch disappeared with a poof. The hero story came in handy when a child was on injectables; even the nurses adopted his unique and unorthodox ways of cajoling pediatric patients.

About three months into his rotation at the pediatric institute, he was summoned by Ms. Parekh, who requested him to accompany the driver to the airport to receive a student who was going to assist the professor with an analysis of very complex statistics on childhood vaccination. Mustafa inquired of the identity of the student, and Dr. Parekh casually told him that the student was aware of the pickup and that the driver had a placard. At the Santa Cruz airport, the driver parked the car at the short-term parking lot and walked with him to the gate. When Mustafa inquired of the placard, the driver looked confused and unaware of a placard. He said, "Dr. Sahib had informed me that you know the arriving student." He tried to call the institute but was not able to get in touch with Dr. Parekh, so he walked back where the driver was waiting in anticipation of the arriving student. As the passengers started arriving outside the gate, he noticed a familiar face; it was CM, pulling a roll-away bag and carrying an oversized handbag, a signature he recognized instantly. He used to joke and tease her for carrying a handbag bigger than a school satchel. She walked right to him and gave him a long hug and a peck on his cheek, thanking him for picking her up. The driver took the roll-away bag as they walked back to the car. CM informed Mustafa that Professor Udani was doing a research with Professor Anand, and he requested her to travel to Bombay to help out in the compilation and analysis of vaccination stats. It was then when he realized that Dr. Anand was acting Cupid.

The two weeks of CM's stay went by very quickly, but they spent all available time in each other's company. Mustafa took her to the Gateway of India, the famous landmark of Bombay, and the Victoria Terminus; they walked the Fort and Flora Fountain and Chowpatty Beach, where they enjoyed the famous Bombay *bhelpuri*. He also took her for coffee at the old and famous Taj Hotel in front of the gateway, overlooking the Arabian Sea, where they savored the best crumpets ever. He took her several times to a small corner restaurant, Noor Mohamed's Restaurant, which served the best *paya* and *Nan* and *chapti-kebabs* at a rock-bottom price and where the JJ doctors received a subsidized price too. The food at Noor Mohamed's was similar to the food he had eaten with CM in Old Delhi near Jama Masjid. They took a day trip one Sunday to the

Elephanta Caves, where they ate Noor Mohamed's *chapti-kebab* rolled in *Nan*, which he had packed for their travel. The kebabs were extra spicy and just perfect. The chilled Mangola soda sold at the local soda stand was perfect to wash down the spicy food.

The two weeks went by too quickly, and it was time for CM to return to Delhi. As they drove to Santa Cruz, they sat in the backseat of the cab so close that they could almost hear each other's heartbeats. Both were sad, as they were aware that they may not be able to see each other for some time again. It was a humid day, and he could smell CM's body aroma, which he remembered from many past meetings. The traffic going down to Santa Cruz was heavy, but they were in time for flight formalities and departure, and fortunately, the flight was delayed for an hour, not unusual for India Air, giving them bonus time together. At the last announcement of the departure, she got up, straightened the roll-away bag, and slung her handbag over her shoulder; she instinctively stooped forward, giving Mustafa a peck on his cheek, and as he drew her close to him, she gently bit his earlobe, another signature that he had come to know well, her nibbling. As she walked away, Mustafa repeated, "If I ever marry, it is going to be someone like you, a perfect combination of beauty, poise, and brain." She instinctively laughed teasingly, and Mustafa added, "Do not laugh, as you may have to endure me for the rest of your life." She walked towards the gate, offering a peace sign. She disappeared into the gangway, but Mustafa did not leave the airport until her plane was in the air. He had a feeling of sadness deep down at the thought that they may not meet again.

When he returned, Dr. Parekh teased him, informing him that doctors Anand and Udani had arranged the meeting of the two. The two Cupids had conspired to arrange everything.

CHAPTER 7

The Beggar at the Azad Maidan of Bombay

Azad Maidan

All the JJ residents received training at various hospitals spread all over the city; Gokuldas Tejpal or GT Hospital as it was known to the residents was one such hospital where Mustafa spent a twelve-week rotation. The hospital was behind the Victoria Terminus (VT), but the nearest local train station from the hostel that would take him to VT was two bus stops away; therefore, travelling by local trains was not the most time-efficient way of getting to GT Hospital. Azad Maidan was across from GT, and a bus stop on the other side of the Maidan went straight to the Bhindi Bazaar gate of JJ Hospital, so crossing the Maidan on foot saved time and also offered an opportunity for a brisk walk across the twenty-two-acre park. Azad Maidan was a premier public sports facility with playgrounds for cricket, football, and field hockey. The Maidan was in the heart of Bombay, surrounded by majestic and historic buildings of Bombay and the iconic Victoria Terminus, a world heritage center. GT Hospital was a full-service facility, where Mustafa served under Professor Udani.

When walking across the Maidan one very bright and sunny Bombay day, when the temperature had soared to about a one-hundred-plus degree centigrade and not a cloud in the azure blue sky, he noticed a beggar sitting under a pipal tree, which shaded him from the intense heat. He had noticed him at other times too. He reached into his pant pocket, only to find out that he barely had enough change for his bus ride, so he could not spare change for the beggar. However, the very next day, he bought food at the cafeteria for the beggar on his way back to JJ. He crossed the trodden path to find the beggar sitting at his usual spot under the pipal tree. He offered him food and water and sat by his side until he had eaten. The beggar ate the food and put his hands together without saying a word, but his eyes expressed gratitude. Thereafter, each day after finishing work at GT, he passed by the hospital cafeteria to pick up rice and *dhal* to go. On his way back to JJ, he stopped to feed the beggar, who accepted the gift most graciously. He did not say much, but his deep-sunken eyes glittered, and the face broke into a smile, showing very deep smile creases on both sides of his face and a full set of pearly white teeth. This random act of kindness gave Mustafa a very unique feeling of happiness that he had not experienced before. The beggar never spoke a word but acknowledged the deed with a sparkle in his eyes and a smile, a signature of gratitude, which was most pleasurable. Mustafa believed that the beggar either had taken a vow of silence or was dumb, so he too enjoyed feeding him in silence.

The twelve weeks came to an end, and Mustafa carried the last gift of food with him across the Azad Maidan. This time, he also asked the cafeteria to pack two *gulab jamuns* as a parting gift. He gave the beggar his offering and started to walk away after he ate, but as he moved away from the beggar's pipal mat, he heard the beggar's voice for the first time in twelve weeks. He said, "Babujee therye," which means "Sir, please wait." Mustafa turned around in sheer amazement that the beggar, who had not said a word until now for the past twelve weeks, actually spoke. His voice was mature and very pleasant. The beggar signaled him to sit down on the woven pipal mat. Mustafa sat down in a lotus position on the mat. The beggar smiled and thanked him for his kind offer of food in the past twelve weeks and added that it was very thoughtful of him to bring him *gulab jamun* today, as he had been thinking of it since he awakened early that morning, hoping that he would bring him *gulab jamun*. He also shared that he had not eaten *gulab jamun* for about a year.

The beggar spoke of Mustafa's friendship with Krishna, telling him that he was doing well but missed him a lot. He told him that he had left India in pursuit of education abroad, and at this time, he was in a very cold country across the waters. Then he offered Mustafa condolences for his dead parents and sister. He recited verses from the Holy Koran in phonetically correct Arabic, followed by verses from *Bhagavad Gita* in Sanskrit. He told him of many incidences from Mustafa's past that he had not even told Krishna or his dad about, so he wondered how this ascetic sitting under the pipal tree knew so much about him. Mustafa was truly surprised, and a thought came to his mind that the mujahideen had found him, and as if through telepathy, the beggar said, "I am not one of them, but they'll find you again, so be careful and vigilant, but you will be safe." He cautioned him to be aware of his surroundings. He told him that he was going to travel out of the country soon, to a very distant land, very green and lush. He told him that he would be safe in the distant land, but his journey would not end, as destiny would take him to yet another country, where he would be recognized for his medical expertise and knowledge. He said, "When in these foreign lands, take care of your health, especially when you cross your fiftieth birthday, as it is a dark time of your life."

Mustafa did not believe in soothsayers or in one's ability to look into the future but was truly confused with the beggar's knowledge of his past, especially his description of things that were not known even to his best friend, Krishna, or his parents, like the time he had fallen off his Rajdoot motorcycle and scraped his knee and bumped his head, a fact that had prompted him to invest in a helmet and also to buy one for his best friend.

As he travelled back to JJ, he had so many questions and no answers. Was the ascetic clairvoyant? How could he have so much knowledge of his past? He remembered his warning that he would be traced to Bombay. The thought that the mujahideen would find him preoccupied his thoughts as he rode the bus to JJ. He would have missed his stop if it was not for the ticket conductor, who reminded him that his stop had arrived.

A few weeks later, he returned back to Azad Maidan. The ascetic had left for Mathura, he was told by the one who had taken his place under the pipal tree. He told him that the sage was of high heritage and had given up a life of luxury in pursuit of divine truth. Mustafa had wondered why the ascetic had a perfect dentition, something seen in people of means in India, and now he understood the reason from the information that the ascetic was of high heritage. He made several more trips to Azad Maidan, but the beggar never returned, and his replacement consoled him and asked him to cherish his memory, as he had obviously touched him, and his *Ashirwad* would always be with him.

CHAPTER 8

No Safe Place

He had completed nine months with Dr. Udani, and now he was accepted completely by the institute. Just like at his previous medical schools, he was a Johnny-on-the-spot for preparing presentations for visiting professors. Dr. Dhal, a professor from the United Kingdom, had arrived with his team of doctors from the Royal Eastern Infirmary in Glasgow to present his research at the institute. Dr. Dhal was involved in cutting-edge research on disseminated intravascular coagulopathy (DIC) with special interest in the pediatric population suffering DIC. His team was also researching on the incidence and treatment of mucopolysaccharidosis, a disease caused by the malfunctioning or absent lysosomal enzymes needed for the breakdown of long sugar molecules, known as glycosaminoglycan. There was a prevalence of the disorder in the Ashkenazi Jews, mainly related to inbreeding amongst this orthodox sect of Jews.

Bombay had a large population of these orthodox Jews, who essentially prayed the whole day and found India a great place to practice their brand of religion, mainly because of India's tolerance of all religions. Collaboration with the pediatric institute was sought; therefore, the team had travelled to India. Once again, Mustafa was requested to research a small sample group of Ashkenazi Jews for a pilot project. The team was to return in six months; therefore, there was less urgency, and the numbers required for the pilot study were small.

Once the questionnaire was agreed upon, the team left Bombay. Dr. Udani was the lead Indian investigator, who recruited Mustafa to collect the cogent information requested on the short questionnaire. As he approached the Ashkenazi, he quickly realized that the group disliked and mistrusted strangers, especially Muslims. Mustafa got his lucky break when one of the Ashkenazi female children sustained a fracture of her thigh bone. Her X-rays revealed thinning of the bone and a funneling deformity of the femur, known as an Erlenmeyer flask deformity, one of the classic findings of mucopolysaccharidosis. The child was admitted at the pediatric institute for treatment, which gave Mustafa an opportunity to make headway with the Ashkenazi Jews, as the child was a daughter of a senior rabbi. Though unfortunate, the fracture was a home run, as he was accepted by the Ashkenazi community, and a completion of the preliminary data was facilitated and a liaison built.

The little girl's name was Tina, so Mustafa called her "God sent Tina." Fortunately, Tina's femur fracture healed with treatment in traction, but during her admission, another problem resulting from deposition of the sugar molecules in her vital organs was found, making her long-term prognosis pretty grim. Mustafa felt very sad and spent a great deal of his free time with Tina. Tina loved to write poetry, and so did Mustafa, so they had a common thread. The mistrust of Muslim soon passed, as her family and friends realized that Mustafa was not any different from anybody else, so they learned to trust and love him.

The rabbi invited Mustafa after a Sabbath day prayer; this was perfect, as their Sabbath day was on a Saturday, unlike his own belief that Sunday was the seventh day of the week. The questionnaire was completed in a single visit, as he had not only the rabbi's blessings but also assistance from multiple members of the Ashkenazi clan. He returned to the institute that Saturday with a spring in his step. He spent the rest of Saturday and most of Sunday compiling the data, which he presented to Professor Udani on Monday. Prof. Udani was surprised that Mustafa had been able to reach out to the Ashkenazi, as all past attempts had been unsuccessful. In the next few days, the data was analyzed, graphed, and tabulated for transmission via mail to Professor Dhal in Glasgow. By the time the professor returned to India, he was considering an offer for a potential post as surgery department chief at Kenyatta National Hospital (KNH) in Nairobi, Kenya. He was offered an expatriate pay and a very lucrative bonus and, additionally, a completely equipped laboratory for his research. Professor Dhal was very impressed with Mustafa's work on the preliminary pilot project and offered him residency at the pride of Africa, the KNH, if he took up the position. To which prof. Udani responded, "Pal, stop stealing my residents." Dhal told Udani that the real bonus of his African job was an opportunity to visit all the game parks of Kenya and Tanzania. He invited Udani to visit him and promised to take him to Ngorongoro Crater to view the habitat and lakes Manyara and Magadi to see the pink flamingos of Kenya. Dr. Dhal's stay in Bombay was short, but during his stay, he got an opportunity to lecture the students on his research on DIC and the use of streptokinase to break isolated blood clots.

Mustafa's life was improving, as he was getting acclimatized to the high humidity of Bombay. Alphonso mango season had just passed, and he got to eat the world's most delicious mangoes, mostly gifted by Dr. Udani's patients. He was once again feeling safe and not looking over his shoulder or awakening in the night to the sound of a car backfiring or by the sound of firecrackers. He also once again started confiding in people. He was initially treated as a white boy because of his fair complexion and green eyes, and actually, it was a bonus in Bombay, as he often overheard whispers, "He is so gorgeous." He mostly focused on maintaining a most impeccable impression at the hospital and in the department. Some of the ladies he worked with thought he was gay, mostly because of his aloofness, high intellect, and sweet mannerism, which were thought to be gay attributes. He truly did not care about changing their opinion. Some fellow-residents remarked that he had more *rakhi* sisters than most other residents in the hospital, but he was not bothered. All the female residents loved him, mostly because they trusted him and were aware that he would never make sexual advances. Some also requested him to walk them to the bus stop after a late night at the hospital. Life was assuming normalcy. He was unable to talk to CM, as he could not afford the cost of long-distance telephone calls, but he kept regular correspondence with her over Indian mail. He was always fascinated by the very fruity scent of perfume when he opened her letters. He even asked her once if she was spraying perfume on all the letters to him, and she remarked that it was her *kushboo* (personal fragrance).

One day when he returned from the institute, he found his childhood friend Krishna waiting for him in the cafeteria. He was surprised but very pleased to receive his friend. He had come back to India to visit his parents in Kashmir and on his way back to U.K. he decided to take a connecting flight from Bombay. That night, they sat up until the wee hours of the morning, talking about Srinagar, common friends, and professors. Krishna was carrying with him spiced walnuts, dried apricots, milk cakes, and other goodies sent by Krishna's mother. Krishna's visit was very pleasing but brought back a flood of memories. Krishna had brought with him photographs of friends and mementos of the medical school and also photos of the burial ceremony of Mustafa's family and photos of their gravestones. As he looked at the pictures, he said Surah al-Fatiha, "The Opening." (The first chapter of the Holy Quran) and ate a piece of the milk cake. He was not able to control a flood of tears as he remembered his family. Krishna told him that at each *Rakhi* day, he bought a *rakhi* that he tied on his wrist, even when in the United Kingdom. Mustafa was very touched by his friend's sentiment and spontaneously hugged him. He said, "You are my only family, and I love you most dearly."

The next morning, Mustafa took him to the institute and introduced him to his professor, Dr. Parekh, and the nursing staff. He also rounded his patients with him. Krishna observed and remarked that Mustafa had adopted everyone he came in contact with as his family. Dr. Udani was full of praise and remarked once again that Mustafa was god sent.

Krishna left after two days, but before he left, he told him of his plan to take up a house job and prepare for the MRCP examination. Mustafa felt a vacuum on his going and did not return to his room until late that night. He spent time on the pediatric floor with his patients. There was this one child with Ewing's sarcoma with metastasis in his care, who he believed was in a predicament worse than him, as the child had absolutely no lease on life, and at least Mustafa was given a second opportunity. He felt connected with the child, as he had been given a second chance, mostly by providence.

One night after visiting his Ewing's Sarcoma child, he returned back to his hostel; the *dhurban* told him that his brother and cousins from Kashmir had visited the residents' quarters when he was away and waited for good two hours and left, promising to return the next day. The information frightened and worried him much, as it brought back the memory of the mujahidin's pursuit and of his run from Srinagar and once again from Delhi. He remembered the ascetic's warning and his prediction of his travel away to foreign lands. The mujahideen had found him and traced him to Bombay, he believed. He wondered if Krishna was followed to Bombay.

He did not go to his room but returned to the institute instead, where he spent the night on an empty bed in the ward. He waited for Dr. Udani to arrive the next morning, describing the incident. Dr. Udani had very peripheral knowledge of the modus operandi of the mujahideen, so he called his colleague Kayum in Delhi for advice and information. Kayum listened to the whole case scenario and told him that he would call back after conferring with Mia. About three hours passed, three hours that seemed like a lifetime to Mustafa. He felt cornered, with nowhere to go. He had no place to run; he wondered where he would go now. The phone rang a single ring, and Professor Udani picked it up ahead of his secretary. At the other end was Mia, who talked to him for a long time. Dr. Udani cradled the phone and turned to Mustafa. He said that his driver was going to take him to his house and asked him to stay put there. Mustafa said, "But, sir, I have nowhere to hide and nowhere to go. I will just have to face my odds. Sir, I cannot keep on running." Professor Udani held him firmly by his elbow, encouraging him that he would help him resolve the impasse. Mustafa remembered the ascetic of the Azad Maidan who had forewarned him of the mujahidin's return.

The driver was waiting for Mustafa in the garage below the institute. He took him straight to the professor's home at the Bandra Bandstand. He had been to the house many times during the past months at the institute, mostly going over patient stuff and research data. Mrs. Udani, whom he referred to as Auntie, was motherly as always and even more when Dr. Udani informed her of his predicament. She had prepared some of his favorite food for lunch. After a sumptuous lunch, he slept for a while, as most of the previous night he had spent cramped up in a pediatric bed. When he awakened, Dr. Udani had returned and had also brought a suitcase of his life's belongings, which included his passport, which he had in safekeeping at the institute with the professor. Udani had talked with both professors in Delhi and had also called Professor Bwibo in Nairobi, who said that he would only be too pleased to accept Mustafa in his M. Med (master in medicine) program once he cleared an acceptance examination that he believed Mustafa would ace.

"But, sir, I cannot afford the travel," Mustafa objected.

"Well, son, no matter, it is all arranged. Kayum, Mia, and I owe you for your help and loyalty. We have combined our resources to pay for your flight to Nairobi," he responded. He went on to say that he had already called his travel agent, requesting the first available flight out of Bombay to Nairobi. The next morning, the agent called back to inform the professor that Mustafa was booked on a British Airways flight to Nairobi, leaving Bombay at 7:00 p.m. Dr. Udani had treated the Kenyan ambassador's child who had sickle-cell trait and mild anemia, so a Kenyan visa was processed with urgency as a personal favor to Prof. Udani. He just had to send the passport to the consulate, which was stamped whilst the driver waited.

Mustafa was feeling depressed and defeated; he was sad at not being able to talk to CM before his departure. At about two o'clock, the phone rang, and Auntie called him to receive a phone call from Delhi. He picked up the phone wondering but recognized the voice on the other end. It was CM; she told him that she was calling from Professor Anand's office. Mia had called him to give him the news of his impending travel. They talked for the next thirty minutes, saying their good-byes, and towards the end, CM said, "If I were to marry, it would be someone like you, with brains, good looks, and a phenomenal personality. Good-bye, my friend. You will be missed." The phone call was rejuvenating, as he felt that there was a light at the end of the tunnel, and maybe providence was taking him down this path. He was very thankful for all the help he received from his professors and friends who helped him overcome his problems. He mused maybe this was his final run, as his enemies would lose trace once he is out of the country.

He touched the feet of his professor and auntie, and they both gave him their *Ashirwad* (blessings). Additionally, Auntie tied a saffron thread on his right wrist. She said that she had brought the thread from the Shiv Mandir and that Shiva would protect him from all evil.

CHAPTER 9

Bombay to Nairobi Flight

The flight was on time; Mustafa's professor came to leave him at the airport. He hugged him like a son hugging a father, and he noticed that his professor's eyes were moist. Mustafa was leaving behind all near and dear to him; he was leaving his *janambhumi* (motherland) for Africa. He wondered if he would ever get a chance to return to India, if he would meet CM again. So many confusing thoughts came to mind. For him, going to Africa was like going to Mars—different people, different languages, different food, and different climate. He was tired, so very tired of running; he was being displaced for no fault of his making. So many questions ran in his mind with very few answers. He had never traveled in a plane, so this was a different experience. The plane was a Jumbo Jet 747, a state-of-the-art aeroplane at that time. Bombay's Santa Cruz seemed bigger than when he picked up CM, but then he remembered that he had done so at a local terminus and that he was traveling on an international flight; therefore, the international terminus was not only bigger but also better appointed and much cleaner but with the same smell of formaldehyde floor cleaner, which was used in all Indian termini, as well as at the train stations. The way to the gate was through a very glittering area with signs of duty-free products. He was surprised that they even had Old Spice aftershave, which was advertised in many Western films, and also Benson & Hedges cigarettes and other paraphernalia. There was also a candy store with walls of Cadbury chocolates and triangular Toblorone chocolates. Mustafa was completely amazed; he was walking through a wonderland of earthly goodies, sold duty free.

The air hostesses walking to the various planes were very pretty, walked with a straight back, and wore shiny black high-heel shoes. Some wore hats with a gold wing at its front, and some wore a scarf of a British flag or some other insignia. The air hostesses were exactly as seen in some airport scenes in the Western movies. As he walked on, there was a walkway that was moving; he watched others and got on the mobile walkway. As he was getting on, a speaker repeatedly announced, "Watch your step." He followed other passengers to reach gate 5A, which had a large sign, NAIROBI 7.00 PM. He had about one hour before the departure with not much to do, so he just walked around, absorbing the whole airport scene. It was amazing.

When he returned to the gate area, an older man wearing a suit and a skullcap with very intricate embroidery was reading an Arabic book, so he struck a conversation with him. He was a Somali living in Nairobi, and he was reading *Yassin*, the core of the Holy Koran. As they talked, Mustafa started reciting the *Yassin*. "Yassin al kuranul hakim, inna kalaminal mustakin, al seratical mustakin." The gentleman was surprised and impressed with a white boy reciting the heart of the Holy Koran without even looking at the verses. He complimented him and shook Mustafa's hand firmly. Mustafa observed that he had a rather large hand, but the skin of his hand was soft and the fingernails well-manicured, suggesting a sedentary profession and an individual who took great care of himself unlike others he had met before. The skullcap, he later found out, was a Somali skullcap, which most in his community wore. This was different from the skullcap worn by the Jews in India, who wore a miniature version known as the *yamaka*, also known as *yarmulke*, which at times had a Star of David embroidered on its center, and the Parsi (Zoroastrians) men wore a more elaborate headgear called the *Paghdi*, very similar to a Persian turban. The Somali wore a well-tailored double-breasted pin-striped suit with a perfectly folded silk hanky in the breast pocket. The Somali gentleman was visiting some friends in Bombay and was returning to Nairobi, where he was born and where he owned a motorcar dealership. He told Mustafa of the Kikuyus, Indians, Luhyas, and several other peoples of Kenya. He told him of Kenya's first president, Jomo Kenyatta, and his freedom struggles and a lot about the country, its people, and its customs. He told him of the flora (vegetation) and fauna (animal life) of the Rift Valley and that the Rift Valley was a fault line in the African tectonic plate, much like the one in the West Coast of the United States of America, which ran from California to the British Columbia in Canada. The gentleman was a geography and a history lesson intertwined. He informed him of trivia, such as the *Magadi Soda*–saturated Lake Magadi, a lake in Kenya, which was the reason for the unique deep pink hue of the Kenyan flamingos who fed on the fungus that grew on the brackish waters. This was the first Somali Mustafa had met, and he was truly impressed. The gentleman, who identified himself as Mohamed, was of Muslim heritage; his skin had a very dark hue, and the nose and his facial structure were that of an Indo-Asian heritage. His hair, even though fashionably long, was salt-and-pepper with a tinge of henna, which gave it a red highlight in the fluorescent airport light.

Just as the conversation was getting interesting, a person at the gate announced priority boarding for the first class, and Mohamed got up to proceed for the boarding. Mustafa was not aware of class discrimination in flight, so he got up to stand alongside his Somali fellow traveler, only to be told to await a boarding announcement for economy class passengers, so he sat down with a feeling of an obvious embarrassment. After the first class was seated, people requiring assistance and families with children were permitted to board, followed by economy travelers, who were last to board. He found his 15B window seat and settled in. It took him some observation to figure out how to put on a seat belt. The seat was very comfortable and made of plush leather and nothing like a train or a bus seat, and it could be moved to a reclining position. All this information was a first for him. Just as he was settling in, there was an announcement of safety instructions, and the plane lurched. He observed that the front of the plane was harnessed to a vehicle that pulled it away from the pedestrian bridge. The thudding noises he had heard from the belly of the plane before it moved was from the luggage that was being placed into the luggage compartment of the plane, he inferred. All these mundane observations were trivial but a new experience for him, as he had never been on board an airplane.

Once the plane was away from the gate, the tow vehicle disengaged. The engines of the plane fired, and as he looked out, he saw two very large turbo engines extending from about the inner third of the wing, and he also observed that the wing had flaps that extended with a whining noise. The wings widened very much like a bird extending its feathers when taking flight. The plane moved towards the center of the runway, where he saw a few other planes awaiting their turn to proceed to the large, long central runway for takeoff. As the plane turned its nose on the straight runway, the roar of the engines got louder and the bumping of the tires on the tarmac more discernible and in quicker succession. He noticed that the wings widened even more, accompanied by what he later researched to be the noise of the servo opening up the wings for a takeoff. As the speed increased, he heard a distinct thud, and the nose of the plane rose away from the ground, and after a few minutes on the runway, the massive plane was airborne. There was some turbulence as they climbed upwards into the clouds and above. The clouds looked like fluffy balls of cotton and the houses below like small dollhouses; the vehicles on the roads below looked like toys moving in both directions. From up there, he could clearly see that Bombay was surrounded by sea, except in areas of land bridges to the mainland. He briefly saw the reclamation land south of Bombay just beyond Marine Drive and the lights skirting the drive, giving it a look of beads of pearl from that vantage point, understanding its reference as the pearl necklace. Bombay was a phenomenal city, a conglomerate of many cultures and races. He wondered if he would ever return to his beloved India to once again experience its sight and sounds. The song "Dharty Wantanki" (The Soil of My Homeland) came to mind as his thoughts travelled in rapid succession just like the plane taking flight.

Just as he was settling in his little space, an air hostess approached him to inform him that a friend in the first class had requested him to join him if it was OK with him. As he got up, she asked of his hand luggage and guided him across a curtained section to the first class, where most of the seats were not occupied. Mohamed smiled as the air hostess brought him to the seat next to him and placed his backpack in the overhead bin. As he sat in the seat next to Mohamed, the air hostess brought him a warm washcloth, followed by a bowl of warm nuts and a piece of delicious creamy chocolate. Mohamed said, "I was feeling lonely, so I requested the air hostess if she would agree to upgrade you to join me, and as there were so many empties, she graciously agreed to grant my wish."

What a great guy, Mustafa thought, and as if he was thinking aloud, Mohamed said, "Requesting an upgrade for you was the least I could do for my namesake." For a moment, he did not comprehend his remark, but it came back to him that he was named Mustafa, as he was born on the birthday of prophet Mohamed-ul-Mustafa (SAW), so in reality, he and Mohamed, his fellow traveler, were both named after the prophet.

The history, geography, and African trivia lessons continued as fresh fruit arrived, followed by a three-course dinner. Mohamed had requested a nonvegetarian Muslim meal for both. The young air hostess was obviously attracted to this near-six-foot-tall green-eyed hunk of a man, who, to her chagrin, did not even notice her, as he was preoccupied with his thoughts of CM somewhere down there, somewhere far away in India. She continued to approach him frequently, so much so that Mohamed remarked, "She likes you, Mustafa. Do not be surprised if she gives you her Nairobi telephone number before this flight ends." And as if a prewritten dialogue, she approached him as he was waiting in the galley to use the restroom, where she gave him a slip of paper with her Nairobi address and telephone number, saying, "Allow me to show you around Nairobi. It is a great city, and I am a great guide." Her action did not slip Mohamed's observing gaze, and as Mustafa settled back into his seat, he mentioned, "Eh, so she did give you her address, and did she not also propose to be your tour guide in Nairobi?" Mohamed was obviously worldly wise and a good specimen of a human being, and Mustafa had a gut feeling that he may have been approached by many sirens, as his facial expression and poise told a story of his charm loud and clear.

Mustafa remembered a poem from the book *Mind's Eye* on maturity. *The poem described Mohamed so well,* he thought. He closed his eyes, searching his memory bank, and started reciting the poem verbatim:

Each step unfolding its own story
A man who has achieved fame and glory
Voice mature with years of phonation
String of words in precise expression

Facial creases and gentle gestures
All telling of a multitude of past adventures
Spring and fall past and gone
But winter lives not just skin and bone

Gentle snowflakes melting on the silver grey hair
Dripping down the furrows of his face
Brown eyes expressive of life that has been fair
High spirit and gentle grace

Each season leaving its mark
Not affecting the soft interior beneath the seasoned bark

Indeed, facial creases and gentle gestures spoke a multitude of past adventures. Mohamed mused, saying, "Penny for your thought," and Mustafa recited the poem to him, and he smiled with a hint of agreement.

The pretty petite hostess returned with sliced alphonso for the two, and Mohamed smiled knowingly. The first-class section was very comfortable. The seat reclined more, and there was a lot of legroom. Each passenger was given a small pouch, which contained foot covers, a toothbrush and toothpaste, a comb, a hand lotion, and an eye mask. Mohamed slept for some time, which gave Mustafa quiet time, during which he worked on his research due for publication. He must have dozed off when the cabin was darkened. When he awakened, the television screen showed that the plane had entered the African airspace, leaving about two hours in-flight time before reaching Nairobi. The hostess went around, handing customs and immigration forms. Mustafa was an Indian citizen but had a student-work visa, and he was not carrying any farm products or dutiable articles, and his belongings were mostly used personal items and photos, so completion of the form was simple.

The landing was flawless to a relatively small but modern airport. The plane touched down without a lurch, and he once again noticed the noise of the servo and the thud of the landing gear prior to the landing.

The first-class passengers were allowed to come out before the economy passengers. The air hostess was at the door, and as he passed by, she gave a quick squeeze on his upper arm and a very noticeable wink, making a sign with her little finger and thumb to telephone.

Unlike the Bombay airport, the airport smells in Nairobi were different, and the lingering smell of formaldehyde did not reach his nostril as it did in Bombay. As he walked the corridor and reached the restroom, he noticed that it was cleaner and without copper rust stains on the sink. The immigration and customs procedure was quick, as the flight was not booked to its full capacity. His worry of reaching the Kenyatta National Hospital (KNH) was resolved by Mohamed's offer to drop him there on his way home to his Upper Hill house, which was a ten minutes' drive from the hospital campus.

As they came out, his driver was waiting at the exit door, and he had a luggage boy with him, who helped carry their bags to the car. The way from the airport to the city was a dual carriageway with acacia plants on both sides, which were covered with flame red flowers. The flame red flowers were in full bloom on the acacia, adding a great contrast to a clear blue backdrop of the sky. Mohamed followed his gaze and intuitively remarked, "They are referred to as the 'flame of the forest' because of its vibrant red color."

The car pulled into the medical campus and stopped at the administrative building. He lugged his suitcase in with the driver's assistance into the medical building. The doorman guided him to Professor Bwibo's office. He waited outside as the secretary went in to announce his arrival. The waiting area had paintings of Indian motifs and sceneries and statues, and the inner office was adorned by more of the same. Professor Bwibo was about five feet and eight inches tall and somewhat stoutly built. He had curly hair and a small area of balding at the crown. He dressed casually and did not wear a tie. His handshake was firm and fairly warm. He asked him to sit down and requested over the intercom for his secretary to bring in coffee. He went on praising Professor Udani, informing Mustafa that he had received postgraduate training under him when he was in the United Kingdom. He went on to say that he was aware of Mustafa's predicament and that he would try his level best to make his stay in Kenya and work at the department as exciting as it was in India.

After the coffee, he called his office bearer to accompany Mustafa to the residents' quarters. As they walked out of the hospital and across a fenced area of identical houses, the bearer guided him to a house on the far right corner and up a single stairway. He opened the door to a relatively plush sitting room with an attached dining area. There was a small kitchen next to it, and as they walked down the corridor, there were three bedrooms, a huge difference from his hospital room in India. The house was freshly painted and very clean. The sitting room and the adjacent bedroom opened to a balcony facing a wooded area and, beyond that, the city of Nairobi at a lower level than the hospital campus. The bearer informed Mustafa that Dr. Bwibo had paid him to bring groceries that would serve his immediate needs, and he had also hired a house help to assist him with cleaning and cooking. Mustafa was not used to such luxuries, as at the hostel in Bombay, he ate at the cafeteria and lived in a single-room residence. This was a new experience for him.

As the bearer was showing him around, his new house employee arrived. He spoke in broken English, stating that his name was John and that he was a Kikuyu. John was about twenty-eight years old and very thinly built. He went on to say, "Bwana, I know how to cook Indian food, as I have worked for an Indian doctor in the past. I can make chapati, chicken curry, rice, lamb curry, bhendi, yogurt, biryani, and many other Indian dishes." Mustafa was completely amazed and speechless, as he had never experienced that sort of hospitality in his previous years of residency. He asked John where he would live and he was informed that he had a room in the servants' quarters, a short walk from his house.

As soon as Mustafa had opened his luggage, John took over and hung his clothes and kept his underclothes in the closet. He took his toiletries, keeping them in the bathroom. Mustafa obviously thought that he was getting in the way, so he decided to walk to the hospital to acquaint himself with the pediatric floor. On his way out, he wondered how John would lock the outside door, and John told him intuitively that he had a key to the house and that he should not worry.

The pediatric hospital was not attached to the main building of the Kenyatta National Hospital but a short distance away. When he entered the main building, he inquired and he was informed that a local transport vehicle would take him to the pediatric institute. The driver took him there, and the drive was about five minutes. The pediatric institute was somewhat quaint and was housed in a stucco building with a red-tiled roof, which looked like a house rather than a hospital. The corridor was wide, and on both sides were large open areas with interspaced pediatric beds. There were four separate wards. One of them had multiple beds with transparent canopies, on which he noticed trickling beads of moisture. The matron approached him, as he was in a special part of the institute, and after an informal introduction, she said that this was their croup ward, and the tents over the cribs were to supply oxygen and humidity. She casually asked if Mustafa had suffered from childhood measles, and he said he had not, and she suggested vaccination.

As he was walking over and reading various charts, Dr. Bwibo walked in with another physician, who was the chief resident. The physician was from Canada's famous McGill University on a sabbatical. Dr. Bwibo informed him that Stephen would orient him, and be his immediate senior physician. Stephen was excellent and spent a great deal of time showing him around. The patient history was much shorter in Nairobi than at the pediatric institute in Bombay. The charting of patient data was also quite different, and each chart had a problem list in its front, and the back of the chart was a treatment list, which was chronologically charted. Color coding was utilized to differentiate charts from different wards. Mustafa quickly memorized the differences so that he would be able to start his work with a running start. After Stephen had orientated him, Mustafa hung around to get to know the staff, the patients, and also the charting system.

The nurses were quite helpful. Most of the head nurses were referred to as matrons, and the nurses were referred to as sisters. This was much like the system in India, which had derived its roots from the British. The hospital floors were apparently cleaned with formaldehyde, as there was the telltale lingering smell of the chemical in the wards. The children were from indigent local population, Kikuyu, Luhya, Luo, Kalenjin, Kamba, Kisi, Meru, and some Kiswahili. They all spoke Swahili, but Mustafa unfortunately did not understand a word. He knew that he would have to learn the language and was encouraged by the fact that Stephen who was also a foreigner in this country spoke Swahili, and if he could care for the patients and learn that language, Mustafa would do the same or better. As he sat at the pediatric floor looking over the charts, one of the younger nurses came about and gave him his first orientation in Swahili. She taught him his first words, *Jambo* and *Habari Gani*, meaning "hi" and "how are you?"

He stayed at the institute until jet lag got the better of him, but he could not comprehend why he felt so tired and sleepy even though it was daylight. He had never traveled across time zones, so he had no idea of a jet lag. He later understood it after discussing his lethargy with Stephen, who told him that it may take a couple of days to get his bearings back. He called it "acclimatization," advising Mustafa not to sleep during the day, as it may only take longer to acclimatize. He tried his best to keep awake during the day, and over the next two days, he was back to normal. He also noticed that he drank more fluids during the time, and his bowel movement was not as regular. As he acclimatized, his system also started getting back to normal.

John, his home servant, was very resourceful and was his personal teacher, who taught him most of his Swahili and took him around town, showing him different shops and cinema halls. Mustafa spent more and more of his time in the hospital, and he got to know many physicians of Indian descent, who were professors, residents, and medical students from University of Nairobi, working at the Kenyatta National Hospital. Over time, he noticed that the majority of the doctors were of Indian descent. This was very comforting, as he did not feel homesick. Many of them went out of their way to invite him home for meals and socializing. The Department of Surgery had a provisional chief, as the prior chief had to leave, mainly because of his unprofessional conduct with female staff and his history of alcoholism. It was common knowledge that he kept a bottle of black label in his bottom drawer, from which he took frequent swigs. It was also fabled that he had fathered at least twenty children with different Kikuyu women, even though he was married and had a family of four with his own wife.

As time passed, Mustafa was able to communicate with his patients in Swahili and picked up enough Kikuyu, Luo, and Kalenjin to be able to gather pertinent medical information. Once again, he was most comfortable with his pediatric patients, whom he cared for diligently and whom he also made examination-glove balloons for and recited stories to. He spent a great deal of time at the institute, and the nurses became aware of his dedication. In comparison, they felt that Stephen, his chief resident, was essentially in Africa to spend his time at various wild-game resorts. Most of the patient-care work was done by Mustafa now, even though Stephen took credit for it. In the process, Mustafa developed a tremendous acumen in medical diagnosis of pediatric diseases. Within a few months, his knowledge and attributes were well-known on the KNH campus.

The interesting part of the Kenyatta National Hospital campus was that it had an international staff. The intensive care unit staff and also the respirators were mostly from Japan, the pediatric staff from the McGill University, the surgical staff from Scotland, and the internal medicine staff from England. There were also quite a few African doctors trained in the

Soviet Union. For some reason, these doctors were great orators but poor physicians. This was a fact that was well-known on the campus. Many of these Russian-trained physicians had married Russian women, who were treated badly, as their husbands were violent and also had African girlfriends on the side. This was an unusual experience for Mustafa, whose cultural attributes were so different and so Indian.

As time went on, Dr. Bwibo recognized Mustafa's dedication, his love for his pediatric patients, and also his ability to work and respect the ancillary staff at the pediatric institute. About eight months into the rotation, Dr. Bwibo summoned him to the office, asking him if he would like to receive postgraduate training in pediatrics at the Nairobi University. Obviously, this was a great opportunity, but Mustafa was not sure if he wanted to pursue a career in pediatric medicine. His mind was set on surgery since his long discussion with Dr. Ganjawalla, his mentor at AIIMS who wanted him to do just that. However, he did not think that it was appropriate for him to give Dr. Bwibo an immediate reply, so he promised to think about his offer. Over time, Dr. Bwibo was able to convince him that pediatrics was his calling. Mustafa continued his house job and essentially took over most of the work that should have been carried out by Stephen. Stephen loved him for that and often complimented that he was a 'quick study.'

During his time at the institute, he accumulated a large photographic collection of diseases and also pictures of various people and their customs. This was a paid job, and as his needs were few, he was able to save enough money to buy an old VW beetle, with a rear engine. Buying a car was most essential, as he was able to get around and also travel short distances to places like Limuru in the Rift Valley and a local game park. He got a great buy from Mohamed his Somali friend who was a motorcar dealer. He continued his friendship with Mohamed, who introduced him to Somali cuisine and his family. Mohamed had eight children, and his wife, Fatema, was a wondrous housewife. Mustafa loved her goat curry and leavened bread, which was cooked over an earthen pot. He also loved *Matoki* made with goat meat and plantains and *Mogo* (cassava cooked in coconut milk and goat meat). He enjoyed African cuisine and many a times ate *Sambe* (boiled maize flour in water and eaten with soup, like chicken or meat curry) with his man servant, John, who also liked to be called Juma. John also made *Marage* (kidney beans cooked in coconut milk or boiled in water and sautéed with onions, tomatoes, and tamarind). This was an amazing experience, which he would never have gotten anywhere else in the world. His Swahili improved over time, and many of the locals did not believe that he did not grow up in Africa, as his pronunciations, eating habits, and gestures were as African as any of them. Even Dr. Bwibo remarked that he was most likely an African in his previous life and that he must have done some good karma to return to Africa. Dr. Bwibo continued to convince him to take up pediatrics as his vocation, as he believed that it was truly his avocation.

The Department of Surgery was still without a chief. All the free time Mustafa could find away from the pediatric institute, he scrubbed on cases with Dr. Sanjalya, an Indian surgeon trained in Bombay and well-known at the Kenyatta National Hospital for his great knowledge of anatomy and unparalleled surgical skills. His suturing technique was very unique and meticulous. Mustafa loved spending time with Dr. Sanjalya, whom he also assisted at the Aga Khan Hospital at times. He realized that he enjoyed doing surgery and was quickly getting good at it. He continued reading pediatric medicine and also surgical medicine. As time went on, he was invited to present cases on surgical grand rounds but mostly presented at the pediatric grand rounds. He spent a great deal of time in the library, which was extremely well stocked with the latest journals, even though it lacked a collection of recent surgery and pediatric textbooks. The library was also a great place to spend hot, sweaty African summer days indoors because it was air-conditioned.

He had made friends with a radiologist, Dr. Adamali, who took him to a local Indian gymkhana, where he played badminton with other Indian professionals and enjoyed Indian cuisine, mostly because of Dr. Adamali's hospitality. Most of Nairobi was run by Indians, like the shopkeepers and also the teachers at various schools. This truly made up for his being away from India and being homesick. Adamali also loved playing squash at the Nairobi Gymkhana, so Mustafa learned squash and enjoyed the game as he got more proficient, giving Adamali and others a run for their money. The good thing about playing squash was that they could play at odd hours, such as after the second shift in the middle of the night when the courts' times were not booked out.

He kept a steady postal communication with CM, whom he wrote every Thursday, as a letter when mailed before Friday would be received in New Delhi on Monday at the latest. The correspondence continued, and they shared stories of each other's lives and their progress in the medical arena. CM was nominated with a few other students for a short study fellowship in Hawaii. She had mentioned that there was a good chance of her winning the fellowship. That would give her an opportunity to travel abroad to the island of Hawaii in the United States. She seemed very excited at the prospect. Eventually, she did get the opportunity but was reluctant to travel. Mustafa, however, convinced her to go ahead with her plans, as the opportunity would open greater vista. For her, this was an amazing opportunity, as she had never ever traveled outside India or even been on board a plane. When he got her letter informing him that she had decided to go ahead and accept the fellowship, he celebrated. After buying some sweets, he distributed them in the department as a note of celebration. That weekend, he drove his car to Limuru so that he could introspect in the quiet wilderness of the Rift Valley.

Time went by, and Mustafa started receiving mail first from Taiwan and later from Honolulu in Hawaii. It seemed that CM was initially homesick but quickly found friends and fun things to do whilst in Hawaii. She wrote that she had bought him colorful ties and a pair of cuff links made out of sea corals, which she would mail to him on her return to India. A package arrived, and the ties were indeed colorful and cuff links gorgeous, but unfortunately, all his shirts were button-on shirts with a single cuff. He showed the cuff links to Dr. Adamali, who asked him to bring some of his favorite shirts to him, and he would get his tailor to modify them for cuff links. When all was said and done, he now had shirts that allowed him to wear beautiful cuff links on special occasions.

CHAPTER 10

New Chief

Dr. Sanjalya brought the news to Mustafa that a new professor was selected to head the Department of Surgery and was on his way from the United Kingdom. He also told Mustafa that they had selected an Indian professor from Glasgow, who was well published and a great surgeon.

A few weeks later, the word was out that the new head of Department of Surgery was none other than Prof. Dhal, whom he had met during his time with Professor Udani, and he also remembered the study on mucopolysaccharidosis in the Ashkenazi Jews, which he had helped collect data on when he was at the pediatric institute. He had overheard his conversations with Udani and wondered if the coincidence of having Professor Dhal as the head of the Surgery Department was ever going to materialize. He had forgotten that the professor had mentioned of the possibility and also offered him a job but thought nothing of it at that time, as he thought that he was just joking.

Dr. Bwibo mentioned that the professor to head the Department of Surgery was finally selected and that he was also of Indian descent but had grown up in the United Kingdom. Dr. Dhal arrived the following weekend and assumed office on Monday. Since the time he had seen him in Bombay, the professor had grayed significantly and put on nearly twenty pounds. He had managed to bring with him some of his lab staff and also an assistant, with whom he would be researching his work on intravascular coagulopathy. Dr. Sanjalya invited Mustafa for an inaugural lecture by the professor. The lecture theater was filled to the capacity, and he saw that Dr. Bwibo was also in the audience. The professor gave a very detailed and educative explanation of his research. He also introduced his staff and his assistant, Dr. Zainab, who had accompanied him to Nairobi and was affiliated to the Department of Surgery. That evening, Mustafa spent time in the library, reading all of Dr. Dhal's recent publications, and noticed that Dr. Zainab was cited in every study. He realized that she was an integral part of his research team.

After a few weeks, when Mustafa was assisting Dr. Sanjalya on a complex surgical case requiring bypassing of the biliary tube, Dr. Dhal walked into the surgical suite and gave Mustafa a long look, inquiring, "Haven't I met you someplace?"

Mustafa replied, "Sir, I had the distinct privilege of working with you at the Bombay pediatric institute of the JJ Hospital when I was at the Grant Medical College, working with Dr. Udani."

"You don't mean the study on mucopolysaccharidosis. Of course, I know those green eyes, and you are the Kashmiri genius, aren't you?" the professor replied.

Mustafa replied, "Guilty as charged but hardly a genius."

The professor was curious to know what he was doing in Kenya and why Professor Udani allowed him to leave his department, as he knew that the professor thought a world of him. He left the operation theatre, asking Mustafa to meet him after the case. Sanjalya was kind of surprised that Dhal remembered Mustafa and also somewhat envious.

Mustafa showered as was his practice after a surgery case and put on his street clothes; on his way to the pediatric institute, he passed by Professor Dhal's office. As he walked in, Professor. Zainab was in the office, and the two were discussing the restructuring of the department, as it had fallen into disrepute. They were obviously charting a new course for the department. As Professor Dhal saw Mustafa walk in, he said, "Come right in, and thank you. I am intrigued and curious to know why Dr. Udani agreed to let you come to Nairobi. He was very pleased with you and felt that you would one day take over his work at the pediatric institute."

"Sir, I loved working at the institute. However, providence charted my life differently." Professor Dhal was curious, so Mustafa related his life story, beginning from Kashmir to New Delhi to Bombay and ending in Kenya. He looked at Mustafa with a fatherly look, telling him that he was aware that he was a Kashmiri and that he himself was a Kashmiri and that his dad had migrated to the United Kingdom as a chef to an Indian restaurant in London and later branched off to own several eateries all over the island. His specialty was the Kashmiri *Raan* cooked in a clay oven. Mustafa remembered how his mother marinated the leg of a lamb over eight hours in yoghurt, spiced with fresh ginger, chilies, cumin, cloves, and cinnamon. "Yes," he said, "I know of *Raan* only too well, as that was my mum's best tandoori dish."

"Well, we are both displaced Kashmiri, and as I am older than you are, I have the right to be your mentor and you my study." He turned to Dr. Zainab, introducing her as the third Kashmiri in the room. In the months that passed, Professor Dhal and Mustafa got closer. They cooked Kashmiri dishes, spent time together, and talked about Kashmir at length. Dhal had never been to Kashmir and yearned to go there one day. Mustafa cautioned him not to hurry, as there was a lot of discord in their land, and it had been turned from a heaven on earth to hell by militants and insurgents from a neighboring country.

Just before Christmas, Dr. Dhal asked Mustafa if he would be his best man at his wedding to Dr. Zainab, and of course, Mustafa was delighted with the privilege. The two were living together and were two peas in a pod, so marriage was the next most logical step, especially so as some in the department were talking of their intimacy. Christmas was just wonderful, as the two got married not in a church but with a justice of peace, as Dhal was a Kashmiri pandit and Zainab a Muslim. Religion did not matter to the two, and their life together was mostly the romance of their shared medical research. They usually spent time and energy crouched over a microscope or adding droplets of various chemicals on a petri dish or injecting animals in their lab. This was one couple that was meant to be together. Mustafa later learned that Professor Dhal was married to an English *Maam* (woman) and that their life together was less than pleasing—a nightmare, he once said. His wife was gallivanting, flirting, and as some believed warming other men's beds whilst the professor worked hard to literally bring the bacon home. The marriage broke up within the first few years, and his wife walked away with his house, car, and much of his earnings, but he did not care, as it was a good riddance of an absolutely bad marriage. She was looking for more, as she kept up her amorous and luxurious lifestyle, which prompted the professor to move out of England and as far away from her as possible. Taking a job in Kenya was the perfect solution compared to living a life steeped in acrimony in the United Kingdom. He was very happy with his work in Kenya and also found a second chance at marriage. Mustafa wondered if he and CM would be as well matched as Dhal and Zainab.

Professor Sanjalya not long after, asked him to go to his office after completing a case of gastrojejunostomy and resection of the nerve of Laterjet. He was surprised with the request, especially as the professor did not give him reason for the meeting. When he went to his office, he asked him to close the door behind him and sit down. He said, "Professor Dhal had requested that I talk to you, as he wants you in his surgery program. He believes that your surgery skills and knowledge of human anatomy would make you a great surgeon one day." He went on to tell him that he could very easily notice his ease and comfort even in very stressful situations, a prerequisite of a good surgeon—to be calm under fire. This discussion set a dilemma because, on one hand, Prof. Bwibo, who had given him an opportunity to leave India when his life was threatened, wanted him to apply for M. Med in pediatrics and, on the other hand, Prof. Dhal was requesting him to enter the surgery program. He verbalized his concern and the feeling of obligation to Prof. Bwibo, and Prof. Sanjalya asked him a very succinct and cogent question, "Tell me what gives you the most job satisfaction, and let that be a determining factor. If you truly believe that you are going to be happy treating pediatric patients, day in and day out, then that is what you must do, and if surgery is your love and avocation, do not shortchange yourself. Make a wise choice, and then be your best in what you do."

Mustafa promised Dr. Sanjalya that he would give his suggestion a serious thought and not make any rash decision. When he reached home, there was a letter from CM, in which she mentioned that she had mailed him a treatise in surgery that he always yearned to own. *How appropriate*, he thought. CM must have heard or sensed his inner voice. Before he slept, he thought of his conversation with Professor Sanjalya. Next morning, the book arrived, and he started reading it immediately and carried it to work. At lunch, he was reading the treatise when Professor Bwibo arrived. "Great book, it seems. What are you reading with such great engrossment?" he asked, and Mustafa handed him the book. Prof. Bwibo smiled as he handed him his book back, but he also got to read CM's inscription on the first page, "To the World's Greatest Surgeon - Sundri."

The very next day, he called him to his office. He said, "I hear of your surgical skills from various sources, and even the OT nurses are talking about you. After leaving you yesterday, I went to talk to Prof. Sanjalya and thereafter went to Dhal's lab, and all of us believe that surgery must be your only option even though I believe that you will make a great pediatric physician. After yesterday and after reading the inscription on the book you were reading, I started thinking. Tell me who is Sundri?"

Mustafa told him about CM in one short sentence, "My soul mate, sir."

He told him, "I have arranged an appointment with Prof. Dhal for 3:00 p.m. Be punctual as always. Best wishes."

When he entered Professor Dhal's office, Professor Sanjalya was already there, and so was Professor Zainab. They all smiled, and the professor said, "Welcome to the Department of Surgery. We are ready to launch yet another great future surgeon."

CHAPTER 11

Surgery Interviews

Mustafa Sheikh was a high achiever and absolutely dedicated to health care. His academic performance during each year of his academic learning, right from his early school days and later in medical school in Srinagar to his internship at AIIMS in New Delhi, to his pediatric residency in Bombay with Professor Udani and now in Nairobi under Professor Bwibo, spoke well of his ability to outperform his peers. He was acknowledged also for his public-speaking ability and performance on the field-and-track varsity team. (He had taken cross-country running at AIIMS and very quickly got into the varsity team.) He had coauthored a few papers with Prof. Mia Mohamed and had extensive lab experience under Professor Khan at AIIMS. All told, he was a sure pick for one of the five surgery residency slots for the M. Med (surgery) postgraduate training program of the KNH-Nairobi University. His above average height, athletic built, green eyes, and most of all polite and unassuming demeanor added to his presence during an interview.

The interviewees were judged under three broad criteria modeled after the criteria followed at the Royal Infirmary in Glasgow. These were structured to achieve an unbiased and quantitative evaluation of each candidate. It accurately assessed the candidates, and each evaluation was scored independently on a 0–10 point score by each of the five interviewers, and the information of the scores was not shared by the group in an attempt to remove bias. The academic and research performance of each candidate was the first criterion; the second criterion was the overall ability to perform under very tough situations required of a grueling surgery residency, and as one of the surgeons proudly mentioned, "We make Spartans"; and the third was the preparedness to interact with a variety of mock emergency surgical/medical situations.

Even though each candidate was identified by a number, all the candidates were known to the hospital campus, as they had worked at KNH at various times during their employment with the Ministry of Health. Mustafa was the only person of Indian heritage in the group, and the remaining were black Africans; Professor Sanjalya did not believe being an Indian was a deterrent, but he was not on the interview board. Professors Dhal, Karyuki, Miller, and McMasters from KNH and Professor Salim, a Kiswahili from the Coast Province, were appointed to interview the prospective candidates. Mustafa believed that his performance during the interviews went well, a feeling that he confided to Professor Sanjalya. He carried copies of his medical transcripts, publications, and letters of praise written by his professors and patients, and certificates of achievement on the track, swim, field hockey, and football teams neatly bound in spiral binders, which he presented to each of the interviewers. Later that evening, Professor Sanjalya met him in the hospital corridor, congratulating him for scoring the highest with each of the five interviewers. He told him that Professor Dhal was truly pleased with his performance, especially as he scored well in each of the three criteria with each of the five interviewers.

A month passed after the interviews, and even though each candidate was informed that they would hear from the board in about a week, no information on the selection was shared with any of the candidates. The university's academic term was to start in three months, leaving the candidates very little time to arrange for housing and moving families, as many were married and had small children and some posted in district hospitals away from the capital city, Nairobi. Professor Dhal seemed apologetic, and Professor Sanjalya, for some strange reason, did not offer any information and only encouraged patience when Mustafa inquired about the results.

Just four weeks before the medical school academic year, he received a congratulatory letter informing him that he was accepted in the first batch of the premier M. Med (surgery) postgraduate training in surgery at the Nairobi University. Attached to the letter were various documents needed to be completed. He was already living on campus at KNH, so he did not have to complete forms for housing. He met Professor Sanjalya that day and later Professor Dhal, who was busy operating most of the day. Both said that he had scored well, and they were proud to have him on board.

January brought in a hectic schedule at the hospital and the department, where most of the lectures took place. The list of books was extensive, but unfortunately, most books were unavailable in Kenya at that time. He asked Dr. Sanjalya's help, only to be told to go and visit Professor Dhal before buying or ordering books by mail. The following day, he scheduled the first available appointment with Professor Dhal, which was after the workday at 6:35 p.m. When he arrived at the scheduled time, professors Zainab and Sanjalya were also at the office, all in a celebratory mood. There were *Shami* kebabs, famous Bohora meat samosas, and *Sheer Khurma*—which he later learned was Professor Zainab's specialty—all spread out on the round table that Professor Dhal used for "sit-down talks" with the surgeons on his team. There was also a bottle of champagne in an ice bucket. Professor Dhal was the first to congratulate him and spontaneously hugged him and kissed him on each cheek, a traditional Kashmiri greeting. Professor Sanjalya shook his hand, and Professor Zainab gave him a quick hug.

Professor Dhal opened the bottle of Dom Pérignon with a loud pop as the cork flew out. "I have kept this bottle from my wedding for a special occasion, and none can be more appropriate than today," he said. He poured it in each of the four fluted glasses and raised a toast, "To Mustafa, who is now an official member of the surgery team." Mustafa was in a way surprised at the jubilant tone of his toast, as he was not aware of the reason for his jubilation until later when Professor Zainab confided that Mustafa had scored ten with four interviewers and an eight with Professor Karyuki, a fifteen-point margin from the second best candidate, a Kiswahili from the Coast Province, who received his medical degree from Makerere University in Uganda, the pride of Africa, south of Sahara, but Mustafa was being denied admission to the program only because he was Indian. Mustafa's discriminatory deselection, even though he was the best candidate by far, angered Professor Dhal, who submitted his resignation to the university upon hearing news of the deselection, and his resignation ultimately prompted Mustafa's acceptance by the ministry. Mustafa now understood the reason for the long delay for the announcement of acceptance.

The Makerere University opened as a technical school in 1922 and later, in 1963, became the University of East Africa, offering general degree courses under the University of London. In 1970, the East Africa University split into Makerere University in Kampala, Uganda; University of Nairobi in Kenya; and University of Dar es Salaam in Tanganyika, as the three countries became independent nations after the imperial governance of Britain left the shores of Africa. Obviously, if he had to worry of competition, it would come from the Makerereian, who was well trained and very confident but humble and soft-spoken, so typical of his Kiswahili heritage.

Otolo, a female interviewee, had scored very marginally and would not have made the grade, but she was selected, as she was the only black female applicant for surgery at the university. She and the other two of her compadres had received their training in Russia at the Patrice Lumumba University, which was founded in the USSR in 1960 as the Peoples' Friendship University (PFU) mainly to train Africans and also Asian students who were unable to secure a seat for medical education in their own country because of an intense competition. The policy of educating students from developing countries was a Russian strategy of spreading Russian influence in Africa during the Cold War. In 1970, the PFU was renamed Patrice Lumumba University in honor of the Congolese freedom fighter and the first democratically elected president of independent Congo. It was rumored that the Russian university produced communist comrades, who had greater political acumen and very limited knowledge of medicine or engineering.

Professor Dhal had instinctively poured very little champagne in Mustafa's glass, being aware that Kashmiri Muslims did not relish alcoholic drinks, but this was a day to celebrate so the exception. Following the toast, Mustafa's eye feasted on the delicacies on the table, but he hesitated to be the first to fill the plate. Professor Zainab picked a plate, adding two of each delicacy until the plate was full, and handed it to Mustafa, saying, "Let me have the pleasure of serving our best student." He knew that she did so because he would have left the office without doing justice to the *shami* kebabs, a fact she understood from a previous time after marrying Professor Dhal when she had invited him home. She had given him a carry-home bag, as he did not do justice to the food on the table. He was pleased with her concern for him, as it reminded him of his own mother. He even told her once that her show of kindness took him back to the days of his childhood, when his mother fed him all her wonderful home cooking. And she told him that it was a maternal instinct, which was most likely genetically embedded in the X chromosome of every female. As if to validate that as a fact in his mind, he remembered that his sister used to save her share of their favorite food for him even when he was living in the medical students' hostel. He wondered if it was truly genetic, and if so, every male child with his XY chromosomes also to a lesser extent carried the trait just as females with their XX chromosomes.

He must have drawn deep in his thoughts when the professor brought him back to time zero as he handed him a work-study schedule and a cardboard box, which contained books. He said, "All three of us have collected books that will broadly cover the core curriculum, and the journals in our departmental library and the medical school library will offer additional current and up-to-date knowledge." He parted with a very full stomach, a load of books, and a feeling of everlasting gratitude. He was blessed, as all his teachers and mentors took excellent care of him wherever he went.

Chapter 12

Master of Medicine (Surgery)

All the lectures were held at the new departmental lecture hall or in the hospital, which had state-of-the-art auditoriums, as the hospital was mostly built with foreign grants and designed by top notch Indian and British architects.

Each day started very early for Kenyan standards, as the core curriculum was very extensive and fashioned on the British surgery fellowship program, since the two programs shared reciprocity, and was also designed to offer Kenya a world-class training program. Most of the textbooks required for medical study curriculum were unavailable in Kenya and very expensive because of the lower value of the Kenyan shilling compared to the British pound and also because of the fact that foreign exchange was not easily available, except after a permission from the central government. The box given to Mustafa by his professors contained most of the books, and as the library had not received the consignment of new books, Mustafa suggested an evening study group after the lectures were done. A study group proposal was welcomed by Barraza, the Kiswahili from Makerere, but the three Russian-trained graduates did not believe in a need for a study group, reasoning that the lecture series would suffice, and they were very verbose and over confident of their superior training. The self-exclusion by the three Russian-trained students gave Mustafa an opportunity to know Barraza better, as they spent evenings and most weekends together, studying. He also got to know Barraza's family and enjoy the Kiswahili delicacies that his wife cooked for them on weekends. He specially loved *Barrazi* cooked in coconut milk, *Matoki*, and *Mogo* cooked with goat meat. She also made flatbreads very similar to the ones he ate in Bombay, making him wonder if the Kiswahili coastal cooking was influenced by eons of travel and trade between India and East Africa.

He had read in Cynthia Salvadori's book *Through Open Doors* that it was a Kutchi Indian sailor who helped Vasco da Gama, the famous explorer, to ride the monsoon winds to cross the Indian Ocean from East Africa to reach India, validating a prevalent belief that there was travel and trade between, India and Africa, much before the German or British occupation of East Africa.

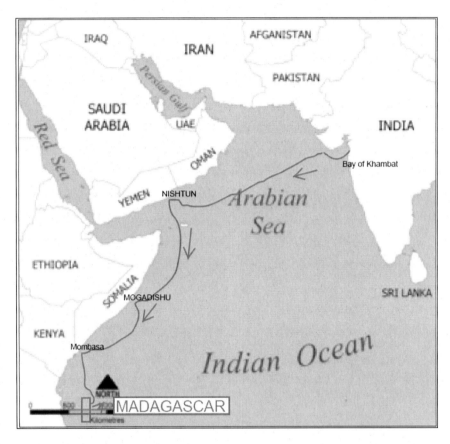

Indian Vahan rode the Trade Winds from Bay of Khambat to East Africa. Trade between India and Africa predated British Occupancy

Kapasis and Karimjees were already riding the trade winds in their long boats with a triangular sail, they referred to as *Vahan* (derived from the Sanskrit word *vahana*, meaning "vehicle"), from Khambhat (Bay of Cambay) in India to the east coast of Africa and all the way to Pemba, Zanzibar, and Madagascar, whence they brought back to India copra, cloves, cinnamon, and vanilla, a pod of an orchid plant that grew in Madagascar. It is even fabled that the British explorer Henry Morton Stanley, who arrived in Zanzibar in 1871 to seek out Dr. David Livingston, was assisted by an Indian trader, who helped organize about two hundred porters for his journey to Ujiji in Tanganyika, furthering the belief that the Indian presence in East Africa predated the British, albeit the currency prevalent in East Africa during the British Raj was an Indian rupee. *So much for history,* he thought, and truly, the people who wrote history made omissions and additions to flavor and favor the times of their existence, no different from the British version of the massacre at the Jallianwala Bagh, which omitted the fact that Colonel Dyer assassinated a group of unarmed Indian, men, women, and children in Amritsar, telling the world that they were violent and armed.

Getting back to Barraza, they became inseparable friends, a friendship that helped both of them in their future endeavors. The first term paper was to be submitted in about a month. It was structured to measure baseline knowledge of the group so as to help the course instructors to structure their courses, the test was akin to a litmus test. As in the United Kingdom at that time, the examination questions were essay type and mostly covered basic sciences in medicine. Mustafa and Barraza performed well and beyond the expectations of their lecturers, mostly because of the fact that they both received their education in a very structured and a competitive environment, as both Makerere University and Indian universities were very competitive, and only the cream of the crop was admitted to both medical colleges, like a preselection, as opposed to a random selection of candidates at the Patrice Lumumba University, which even accepted students who had not matriculated from high school. The challenge was obvious; the lecturers had to cater to the bottom of the barrel, as well as the cream of the crop. The excuse given by the three Russian-trained graduates for their lackluster performance was that the library did not have books, and they were not given textbooks by the university, but in reality, Nairobi University had a lot of books at its library that amply covered basic medical sciences. The Russian-trained graduates, Mustafa realized, were very verbose and combative and trained to argue on any scenario, an attribute that came in handy during a hospital strike organized by the residents and mostly spearheaded by the Russian comrades, who knew the exact protocol and procedures for organizing a protest, a training that he later found out was a requisite of the Russian core curriculum, as they were training these students as future ambassadors of change in Africa and Asia, with a belief that the group would take over governance and finance in Africa and owe their loyalty and allegiance to Russia, where they received their training.

The lecturers provided an option of after-class study to 'round up' the batch, but the three Russian-trained doctors mostly excused themselves from the extra hours of work, and when they were approached by the department, the Ministry of Health intervened. A situation arose where

Barraza and Mustafa were castigated by the three Russian-trained doctors for their better performance in each subsequent test. The department invited help from Scotland, who provided external lecturers, but once again, that effort failed mostly due to a lack of compliance, combative attitude, and lack of diligence by the three Russian-trained doctors. Even to these foreign lecturers, Barraza and Mustafa showed excellence.

Mustafa spent his spare time on photographing medical cases and African flora and fauna and at the hematology lab, helping in researching sickle-cell disease and filariasis, also known as elephantiasis, a parasitic disease spread by mosquitoes and black flies, which blocked the lymphatic system. Sleeping sickness caused by the tsetse fly that transmitted a protozoal parasite called trypanosome and malaria, which was dreaded by anyone traveling to the tropics, were other topics of great interest to Mustafa. Elephantiasis was a fascinating disease caused by an infection of a threadlike parasite known as *W. bancrofti*, which infested the lymphatic system of the body, causing a blockage in the flow of the lymph, thereby causing the affected body part to become swollen and huge.

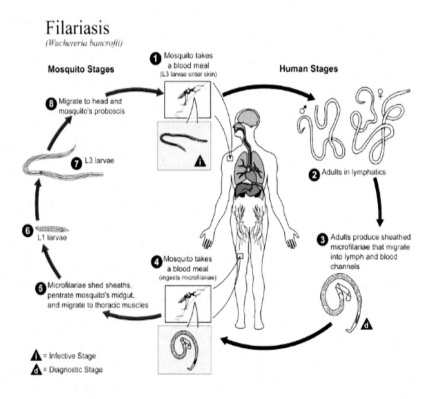

Cycle of W. Bancrofti parasitic infection responsible for Elephantiasis

Kenya was a paradise for the study of tropical diseases, very much like India, something that fascinated Mustafa. Working in the lab was a discipline he had learned whilst in Delhi with professors Mohamed and Khan and later with Professor Udani in Bombay. The closed-space environment of a laboratory made him feel safe, which he believed may have been related to the fact that the mujahideen were in his pursuit over the past many years, and the fact that laboratory work could be done at any time of the day, as he could walk to the lab when he was tired of hitting the books or when he was unable to sleep. In a modern-day scenario, one could quite easily label his lab preference resulting from PTSD (post-traumatic stress disorder) arising from the stress of having his family massacred and from being on the run from the mujahideen.

Barraza was cut from the same cloth as Mustafa, as he too loved to spend time in the lab, especially as there was so much available time, and the two were leading the pack by a great distance from the three Russian trained. Also, Barraza was keen on outperforming Mustafa, an inbred quality of the Kiswahili, who were related to the Arabs travelling the coastal regions of Africa, just as the Indians from Khambhat and elsewhere. The belief was that the Kutchi sailors were adventurers, as they came from the Rann of Kutch, a desert with its share of deadly scorpions, forcing the Kutchis to be on the move—'hard to bite a moving target.'

There was a talk of extending the academic year by an extra six months, but fortunately, the directors of the Scottish fellowship program advised against it, as it would set an unusual precedent and reflect badly on their fellowship program, albeit if adopted, Kenya may have lost its reciprocity with the Scottish fellowship program. Two things came out of the long debate between the Ministry of Health that had requested the extra time, the university, the Department of Surgery, and the Scottish fellowship's board of directors: One was that the term would continue to be two one-year academic terms, and the second and more important outcome was to disallow a change in the core curriculum to facilitate the three slackers. This was what the heads of the Department of Surgery and Dr. Dhal expected, as he was the one who had negotiated and initiated the collaboration of the M. Med (surgery) program with the Scottish fellowship board.

During the debate and thereafter, Barraza and Mustafa kept a low profile and also suggested that the other three join in with the after-school study group, which got Otolo interested. She understood that she needed extra help and was ready to give it a shot, getting rid of a false belief that the Russian-trained graduates were better trained than their Indian and Makerere counterparts. The Surgery Department's observation was not unique, as the M. Med medicine and M. Med pediatric programs were also experiencing a similar disconnect with their Patrice Lumumba graduates. Once Otolo joined the study group, her performance improved, but the lack of knowledge of basic medical sciences was a severe limiting factor much to Barraza's discontent, as they were spending more time bringing her up to speed than learning new material, but Mustafa exercised patience and tolerance, a learned skill from his time in the medical school and residency in India. The first few tests showed a small but significant improvement in Otolo's performance, so they felt that they were making a headway.

In the months that came, the group fell into three distinct performance levels: Barraza and Mustafa in the first tier, Otolo a distant second, and the remaining not even making a passing grade. This set disdain and backstabbing amongst the failing students, who gelled together with other bad performers of the medicine and pediatric M. Med programs.

CHAPTER 13

Casualty Department

During his training at KNH (Kenyatta National Hospital), Mustafa was posted as a chief medical officer at the casualty room. As a chief medical officer, he was in charge of a group of medical students from the Nairobi University and interns from various medical schools, including Patrice Lumumba University. He took his responsibility very seriously and, with help of the Surgery Department, set up a curriculum for the trainees. When he joined the Casualty Department, the staff lacked basic knowledge of cardiopulmonary resuscitation guidelines, so patients in near-death situation brought to the casualty room had little or no hope of survival. Those who encountered better trained interns or even students from Nairobi University were lucky, and those who did not, died without even a fighting chance of survival. Even the nurses, some expatriates, and locals who had trained in the United Kingdom noted the discrepancy of care. Mustafa discussed the problem with his immediate superiors, who structured CPR training classes for everyone working in the Casualty Department, and others in the surgery program were invited to make it incumbent on all comers. Each week, a group study on basic sciences of electrolyte balance and basics of CPR, including establishing intravenous access, airway access, combating acidosis, and the use of various medications to 'jump-start' the heart, was organized in the Casualty Department, and all were invited. The participation was voluntary.

During his free time, Mustafa with a team of keen medical students collected data on the type of trauma treated at the Casualty Department and structured a questionnaire similar to a study he conducted in Kashmir but covered a much wider base. He planned to use the data to better understand the pattern of trauma seen in the Casualty Department of the KNH, the rate of DOA (dead on arrival), the treatment, and the basic medical triage in the department, which he felt was imperative in channeling its surgical emergencies appropriately. As the study took shape, he found out that there were two large statistically significant spikes in surgical emergencies seen in the Casualty Department each month. The two bimonthly spikes also coincided with an increase in admissions of alcohol intoxication and nearly obtunded patients in the Department of Medicine. Such spikes were, however, not seen in his earlier study in Kashmir, which he used for a comparative analysis. He found that on the fifteenth day of each month and again on the last day of the month, there were more stab wounds, RTA (road traffic accidents), and near fatal alcoholic intoxication. Puzzled at first, but Rita, a Kikuyu student working with him, had an insight. She said that it was funny that her father was obtunded on *pombe* (country liquor) on exactly the same two days of the month, which also coincided with his biweekly paydays. The payday coincided with an increased alcohol intake, more RTAs, a larger number of violent injuries from stabs, and even sexual violence.

He presented his preliminary findings at a departmental grand round meeting on Monday; and within a week, he was summoned to the office of the hospital superintendent, who commended his work and offered him an assistant to help him with his continued study. Dr. Dhal, on his trip to his alma mater in Scotland, presented the casualty findings that piqued an interest in a Scottish group doing RTA research in Scotland. On Professor Dhal's return, two from the group came to Kenya and spent just a few days with Mustafa, viewing his data, and spent the remaining weeks visiting the famous Rift Valley and the world-famous game parks and enjoying the sounds and sights of Kenya. They went back to Scotland very happy with their Kenyan visit, but Mustafa did not receive even a thank-you note from them, or their impression, or suggestion for an onward study. The study continued for his remaining term at the casualty room and also for the remainder of the M. Med program.

One morning, Mustafa walked in to an active CPR at the casualty room, where he found a doctor injecting adrenaline in the heart of a patient, who was in a near death condition, but on whom an IV access or an airway access was not established. He took over the resuscitation, following established CPR guidelines, but his arrival was too late for a favorable outcome. He later asked the supervising doctor who had injected the intracardiac adrenaline to meet him, but the doctor was rambunctious. He addressed Mustafa with both of his hands on his waist, saying, "And what is it that I am going to learn from an Indian graduate that I do not already know?" Mustafa was somewhat taken aback by his attitude but did not believe it appropriate to respond to the affront. Later that day, he received a call from the hospital superintendent, who advised Mustafa to let the matter pass, as the doctor in question in the casualty room fiasco, a Patrice Lumumba graduate, was the son-in-law of the health minister. He discussed the matter with his professors so as to keep them informed, and Professor Sanjalya advised him to let it roll off his shoulders, as it was the best strategy to follow in Kenya. Professor Dhal, who was British in much of his ways and so different from Dr. Sanjalya, was angered that the administration would condone such a malpractice, and Professor Miller, a remnant of the British rule in Kenya, shared his philosophy. Sanjalya reminded Mustafa of a very cogent Kenyan quotation, "When bulls fight, the grass suffers," meaning that the bulls were the Ministry of Health and the professors at the medical school and the grass all the residents, students, and the contracted doctors, such as Professor Sanjalya. Over time, Mustafa understood the value and philosophy of Sanjalya's advice but harbored a subconscious disdain with the double standards practiced in the democratic republic of Kenya.

The study on patterns of trauma was completed and the findings presented at a graduation day and the study was well received. Professor Dhal promised to help him publish it in *Lancet*, but it never came to pass, mostly because of an interplay of the time in Kenya and the fact that the study would reflect unfavorably on the state of health in Kenya, something the Ministry of Health would not allow or condone. The son-in-law of the minister continued his dysfunctional methods, which were mostly ignored by the staff, mostly because of a worry of repercussion in a country where it was important who you knew and not what you knew.

Mustafa's term in the casualty room passed without any further confrontations. When he left the casualty room, the matron, a British expatriate, baked a cake and cookies and, joined other nurses and university medical students in arranging a party. Rita, whose dad was drunk twice a month on paydays, brought in a pot of *Mogo* with a celebratory remark that her dad had stopped drinking alcohol, and her mother had made the *Mogo* just to thank Mustafa. He felt a lot of love in the room that day and an appreciation of the fact that he had gifted the casualty room a gift of knowledge in keeping with his dad's advice and ideology, *"Each of us is born in a world less than perfect, and it is the duty of each and every one of us to make it better when we leave it than when we entered it."* He did not understand the depth of his ideology until now, when he was leaving the casualty room, where his colleagues felt that he was an agent of much needed change. The best gift yet, was from a family of a DOA (dead on arrival) patient who survived because of the CPR guidelines, and the family offered a financial gift to Mustafa, which he graciously refused to accept, but he asked them to donate the money for the training of medical students and resident physicians rotating in the Casualty Department. The news percolated and flowed down the coveted halls of the Nairobi University and KNH, giving his professors another proud moment.

CHAPTER 14

Forced Mass Indian Exodus

August 1972, a forced mass exodus of greater than sixty thousand Indians from Uganda

In the earlier days of Milton Obote, the third president of Uganda, Idi Amin was a high-ranking army officer in Uganda, and the two, Idi Amin and Milton Obote, supplied Israeli-made arms to Patrice Lumumba in Congo in exchange for ivory and gold, but in the latter part of Milton Obote's presidency, Idi Amin fell in disfavor, which embittered him, prompting a military coup that ousted Milton Obote.

Idi Amin ruled a reign of terror and atrocity for eight years—from 1971, when he forcibly took over the government, to August 11, 1979. He is referred to as the *butcher of Africa*. In 1977, his health minister, Henry Kyemba, wrote extensively of the genocide in his book, *A State of Blood*.

Idi Amin was an educational dwarf, who, it is believed, did not complete even a fourth-grade education but excelled well in the KAR (King's African Rifles), a British Army contingent that quelled uprisings against the Crown, including the Mau-Mau apprising of Kenya. After Obote came to power, he promoted Amin to a major, but almost immediately after his takeover of Uganda in 1971, Idi Amin promoted himself to field marshal. He was a prolific womanizer, and it was believed that he had five wives and fathered thirteen known children and many others he may have fathered during his reign of terror.

After he overthrew Obote, he massacred more than five thousand Acholi and Lango soldiers who were faithful to President Obote. The International Commission of Jurists estimated about two hundred thousand murders directly related to Idi Amin, and Amnesty International upped the figure to about five hundred thousand. His inner circle was aware that he cannibalized those he killed so that they would not haunt him. He imprisoned anyone who opposed him, and he also imprisoned soldiers from his own army and other dissidents, who were bludgeoned to death by a hammer by recruited jailers to save on bullets.

Historically, Indians had been trading in Africa since the eighteen hundreds and beyond, and over the years, they had taken over the trade and finance of the East African countries. The latter generations of Indians were born in Africa, thereby making them birth citizens of Africa. One such family, the Madhvani family owned about 12 percent of the GNP (Gross National Product) of Uganda and controlled various sectors of business, agriculture, and manufacturing. After the death of the multimillionaire Jayant Madhvani, Idi "Big Daddy" Amin—who at the time already had three wives—proposed marriage to Jayant's green-eyed and gorgeous widow, Meena (Minacdave), and felt humiliated by her rejection, which led to the seizure of the Madhvani homes, vehicles, businesses, and holdings. Jayant's brother, Manubhai, was jailed in, what was then referred to as the *Singapore Block* of the infamous Makindye prison. President Obote was attending a commonwealth conference in Singapore at the time of the coup, and the Singapore block of the Makindye prison was reserved as Obote's return residence. The takeover of the Madhvani holdings and the imprisonment of Manubhai was the beginning of the expulsion of Asians from Uganda.

Mombasa was a British processing center for the expelled British Indians, so trainloads of Indians passed through Nairobi on their way to Mombasa. The processing center channeled the expelled Ugandans to commonwealth countries as refugees. Most arrived at the Nairobi train station in dirty, shredded clothes. The local Indian businessmen, medical residents, doctors, and medical students of Kenya arranged relief stalls at the train station to feed and clothe the destitute Indians and also other Asians from Uganda. Some amongst the expelled were some of the richest families in Africa; there were doctors, engineers, lawyers, and businessmen who now did not even have a clean shirt or a sari to cover their broken bodies. Many in the group were molested by the soldiers and hooligans as they left Uganda.

Mustafa spent an inordinate amount of time at the station, as he espoused a very personal bonding with these refugees. He too was a refugee displaced from Kashmir, his homeland, by tyrants who called themselves the mujahideen. Ladies in this destitute group had been crying so much that their eyes were dry and tearless and their lips parched from the African heat and lack of hydration; their unwashed faces were covered with the red ochre soil of East Africa, a testament of Idi Amin's atrocities. The exodus of Indians left a very distinct impression on Mustafa. He already knew that he was deselected from the M. Med program because of his ethnicity, and if it were not for Professor Dhal, he would not have been selected, discounting the fact that he had scored the highest points at the M. Med interview making him the best candidate by far by their own admonishment.

He saw the pain in the eyes of the refugees, and he also saw the humiliation suffered by the women; some of whom were raped by the soldiers as they left Uganda, and one suffered a gun butt injury to her groin. The atrocities he saw frightened him a great deal, as he saw no difference between the mujahideen and the Ugandan Idi Amin terrorists. Most of the refugees were born in Uganda and knew no other country of shared loyalty; many had Ugandan citizenship, but their passports, the only proof of their heritage, were burnt, depriving them of any proof of belonging to Uganda.

The exodus of Asians from Uganda was an awakening of what could happen to Indians in other African countries. He wondered whether this was a prologue of what was to come in Kenya or for that matter in any of the African countries that were independent, a situation of reverse discrimination. He mused on what would happen to the Afrikaans of South Africa when South Africa got its independence, when, at that time, white supremacy was the rule of the day. Were more atrocities to come?

CHAPTER 15

Children's Hospital, Boston

Mustafa kept in touch with all the professors from his medical school in Kashmir, his professors in Delhi and Bombay, and all the visiting professors he met. He kept in touch with Professor JH at the Children's Hospital in Boston, who had invited him to Boston.

The M. Med program was near its completion, and the final graduation examination was close. The study hours had intensified to a high level, so much so that Barraza and Mustafa were spending a lot of time in the library. Otolo was fading away and could not spend much time with the study group, mostly because of her new boyfriend, Nyamundi, who was demanding, leaving her exhausted in the daytime. Barraza consoled Mustafa not to worry, after a few unsuccessful attempts to get Otolo on board. Mustafa continued to harbor a feeling of defeat, as he had failed to convince Otolo of the progress she made in a short while in his study group.

The written examination extended over three days, followed by a short break before the oral examination. The written examination covered the core curriculum and nothing out of ordinary. Barraza felt it was a breeze; Mustafa did not say much as was his usual habit, not expressing his inner feelings publicly. The three Russian-trained graduates complained that the examination was not fair, as it did not showcase their real abilities as surgeons, and they even talked of boycotting the oral examination. The oral examination was very well organized, and the questions evaluated the candidates on knowledge, surgical ability, and response to staged surgical emergencies, similar to a mock trial in evaluating law students. The examiners were from the United Kingdom, so there was no sense of collusion or bias, and the examinees were identified only by a numerical identity. When all was said and done, the days passed, but the rumor lingered on the campus that the examination was rigged to discriminate against black Africans, discounting the fact that Barraza, a Kiswahili, was a black African too.

The results arrived to the department within a few days after the oral surgery examination, but the information was held from the candidates, and the university convocation went on without an announcement of the M. Med (surgery) results or degree. The rumor that trickled from the Ministry of Health was that the whole examination was scrubbed. On a Monday after the convocation, Barraza and Mustafa were called to the Surgery Department, where they received their diploma behind closed doors and without fanfare and where press was excluded, and the two were requested not to give press interviews, quite different from the university convocation a few days ago. Mustafa had performed well and about fifty points ahead of Barraza and, therefore, the first recipient of the Ethicon Prize for Academic Excellence. Barraza was infuriated not because he did not stand first, as he was aware that Mustafa deserved the first position, but by the closed-door convocation, depriving him of sharing the precious moment with his family. Barraza was the first child in a family of basket weavers to become a doctor, and now completion of the M. Med with distinction was a proud moment that he needed to share with his family and all the basket weavers of the Coast Province who helped in financing his education. He was their jewel.

Mustafa requested personal days off from the department mostly to recuperate from the stress and strain of the examination and also to avoid sarcastic remarks, like "*Muhindi* traitor." *Muhindi* was an African slang used to define Indians in Kenya. When he returned to the department after his days off, Dr. Dhal handed him a letter from Dr. JH of Boston. In the letter was an offer to join his research team as an orthopedic fellow to work with Dr. Simon on gait analysis on children at the famous Boston Children's Hospital. This was indeed a great opportunity to join a world-famous, hospital at the hub of the U.S. medical education, Boston. But he was aware that Dr. Dhal had put his resignation on the table when he was not being selected for the M. Med program notwithstanding the fact that he was the most eligible candidate for the postgraduate training judging from the highest scores in all the three segments with each of the five interviewers.

He discussed the fellowship offer with Dr. Sanjalya, who said he knew of it and asked Mustafa to discuss the matter with Professor Dhal. When he approached Dr. Dhal, he invited Mustafa for a private dinner.

During the dinner he told Mustafa that he did not want to discuss the JH proposal in the department, as most discussions in the department reached the ministry. Professor Dhal also informed him that the ministry had advised the examination to be nullified and retaken with all the questions set by the local surgeons appointed by the ministry. He went on to explain that the UK fellowship board did not agree with the Health Ministry's directive, which led to the late, closed-door convocation for the two passing students. At the dinner Mustafa found out that the ministry had recommended Dr. Dhal to relinquish the chair even though he had a five-year recurring contract. However, Professor Dhal was in luck, as his contract was secure with the UK fellowship board, which offered him back his chair in Scotland, along with a substantial raise and a personal research laboratory with a compliment of a dedicated staff.

Mustafa was very sad, but he was clear that his continued stay in Kenya was not the best option, viewing the injustice he suffered during his short stay in Kenya and also from what he learned from the Ugandan sacking of the Indian community. Some Indians in Kenya, however, felt that the lessons learned from Idi Amin's sacking of Indians may result in severe economic repercussions. Indians formed the foundation of the financial well-being of Uganda, not discounting the fact that the Madhvani family contributed to 12 percent of Uganda's gross national product. The Indian community in Kenya believed that the loss of the economic foundation may send Uganda in a tailspin, which it did within three years of the Indian exodus, prompting the subsequent president to invite Indians back on a silver platter.

The very next day, Mustafa completed the admission paperwork sent from Boston; collected recommendations from doctors Sanjalya, Miller, Adamali, and Dhal; and made copies of his transcripts and a copy of the ECFMG (Educational Certificate of Foreign Medical Graduate), which he had completed during his final medical school year. He mailed the package to Boston via priority mail, keeping two copies for himself.

Dr. Jh's office responded almost immediately. Within days forms for temporary licensing, a stipend for travel, and endorsed visa forms arrived. He was amazed with the efficiency of Dr. JH's department, as it would have taken a few months to get to that stage in Kenya, and that too after bribing a few officials down the road. It was quite obvious that Boston had mastered the system of seeking out their postgraduate students. Mustafa also called Dr. Dhal to put his mind at ease, assuring him that the process was underway.

Once all the papers were completed, he made photocopies of each document in triplicate and scheduled an appointment at the U.S. Embassy.

He had already requested and completed the appropriate forms for a student visa, in preparation for the meeting. His interview was with a female African American officer at the embassy. The lady had a very gentle voice, and she was much heavier than some of the Kenyan women, and Mustafa noticed that she was seated in what seemed like a custom-made chair, which was wide to fit her large size. After an extensive interview, she indicated that a medical examination by an embassy-appointed physician was a requirement, as the embassy would not accept an examination done at KNH. Mustafa smiled and said that he would comply and have the formality taken care of. Once he completed the medical examination and chest X-rays mostly to exclude tuberculosis, he scheduled a subsequent appointment at the embassy. The lady informed him that all his papers were in order but asked Mustafa his reason for not applying for a permanent resident visa in preference of a student visa that he had applied for. She explained the advantages of going to the United States as a permanent resident and also helped him with the paperwork for a resident visa, which she referred to as a "green card."

He discussed the green-card issue with Dr. Sanjalya, who showed concern, as Mike Ribeiro, an M. Med gynecology resident, was brought back from the airport and disallowed to leave, as Kenya believed his leaving was tantamount to brain drain. His passport was confiscated, and he was implicitly told not to leave the country. He cautioned Mustafa to avoid the problem, advising him to leave as a tourist.

Mustafa was very worried, especially after he talked to Mike, who told him that they had put him in the slammer, where he ate *margwe and donna* for the whole week and had to share a filthy toilet with other cellmates. The unfortunate thing was that his wife and son, who had flown about a week before him, were already in the United Kingdom, and he was stuck in Kenya without a travel document, almost in a house arrest.

Mustafa scheduled an urgent meeting with the very resourceful officer at the embassy to discuss the predicament and take her advice on changing his visa to a visitor's visa. She was very knowledgeable and also aware of repatriation on the grounds of brain drain prevalent in the country. She promised to help protect Mustafa from harm and promised to discuss the issue with her superiors. The very next day, she called Mustafa's home quite early in the morning, requesting him to meet her at lunch. She advised Mustafa to fly on a visitor's visa to Montreal, where his passport would be stamped for permanent residency at the U.S. Immigration Office at the Montreal airport, and his passport would be stamped for a visitor's visa when leaving Kenya. She assured that the process would not cause him undue concern.

He packed a small suitcase of personal items and photos and parked his car under the house, leaving the keys with a friend to keep for him in case he returned. He also left a full-month pay for John and some personal belongings as a present for him.

He passed by the department to meet professors Dhal and Sanjalya before making his way to Jomo Kenyatta International Airport. The customs and immigration process went smoother than he had anticipated, and he let out a deep sigh of relief when he reached the gate. The plane was on time, and his flight was to take him to Gatwick Airport in London, where he had a layover of ten hours and an onwards flight to Montreal. Once he was on board the British Airways Jumbo Jet, he felt safe. The plane left precisely at the scheduled time as was the routine with British Airways, true to its advertisement "On Time All the Time."

They reached London, and the flight was without incidence, and he actually slept through some of the time and refused the airline food, mostly because of the pungent odor of microwaved food. Gatwick was a relatively large airport in comparison to airports in Bombay and Nairobi, and he saw many Indian workers who helped to keep the airport spotlessly clean. He stopped to talk to a worker, who had come from Jalandhar in Punjab, who told him that he was a farmer in his country and came to London to earn money to pay for his sister's marriage. The stranger also offered Mustafa *aloo paratha*, which he had brought for lunch. Mustafa bought sodas for both of them and ate a*loo paratha* with mango pickle with him. He enjoyed the meal with the airport cleaner, and when he offered to give him a couple of dollars of the little foreign money Mustafa had on him, a gift from Dr. Dhal, Gurubir, the airport worker, folded his hands together in a *namaste,* saying, "You are my *mehman,*" meaning "guest." Mustafa was touched by the showing of signature Indian hospitality. He was reminded of the age-old saying "You may take an Indian out of India but never India out of an Indian."

He returned to his gate; his suitcase was booked for the United States so he did not have to worry of that until he was in Montreal, where he was to complete the immigration and customs formalities. He had a small rollaway bag, which contained his camera and reading and writing materials, but he did not find time to catch up on his reading and promised to try as they flew across the Atlantic from London.

The gate opened at the stated time, requesting business and first-class travelers to board, followed by handicapped and families with children. Mustafa boarded the flight almost towards the end, as he did not carry much to store in the overhead bin. Once he settled in and put on his seat belt, he opened his book *Recent Trends in Orthopedics* given to him by his professor to prepare him for his new job in Boston.

The flight took them over Iceland across the northern territories to Quebec and Montreal. He read during some of the time, and once again, his personality, tanned complexion, and green eyes had the hostesses going to his seat frequently. He was getting used to the attention and remembered his flight from Bombay to Nairobi with Mohamed, the Somali. Indeed, he had met some of the nicest people; even the lady at the embassy was a god sent angel and most caring of his welfare. He was lucky to have met so many wonderful people in the course of his travel' who had helped him in his struggles and study.

The flight had taken him through two time zones, but he did not feel fatigued or look like some other travelers who had a disheveled look from exhaustion. He had gone to the restroom a few hours before the arrival time and freshened up. The bottle of eau de toilette in the bathroom was empty, and the airline toilet was unkempt in comparison to when they took off from Gatwick; even the toilet seat cover dispenser was empty, not unusual for a Jumbo Jet carrying so many across the Atlantic, he learned later.

The Montreal airport was about twice the size or larger and much cleaner compared to Gatwick, making the latter airport look like a second-world airport. The hustle and bustle was impressive; he traveled from the gate to retrieve his beat-up suitcase and onwards to the U.S. immigration. The officer was not aware of any special arrangement for his visa, so he referred him to the chief immigration officer. The chief apologized for the inconvenience and proceeded to process his papers. The process was simple, straightforward, and efficient, just as the lady at the U.S. consulate in Nairobi had promised. Of course, he had completed the USA entry form; and he was not carrying any food, he had not been on a farm prior to or during his journey, and he was not carrying cigarettes, alcohol, or anything dutiable.

The Montreal airport had a multiethnic staff, among them an Indian employee he met at the Canadian Airways counter whose parents had migrated from Uganda during Idi Amin's expulsion of Indians. He described the exodus just as his dad had told him so many times and of the passage through Nairobi, where they were received by Kenyan Indians, and distinctly remembered a tall green-eyed Kashmiri who provided them food, water, and clean change of clothes. Mustafa smiled, musing how life brought people together, a completion of a circle, and pleased that the displaced Indians within a very short time had adapted to a new country and also done well.

Life, he felt, had many beginnings and ends, and he wondered about CM and if he would meet her again. CM had returned from Hawaii; her brothers, both younger than she was, were married. Her parents had already seen and interviewed a few prospective young men. They were impressed by an IAS (Indian Administrative Service) officer, who was unassuming, intelligent, and very humble. They thought that he would be a perfect match for their daughter. She agreed to meet him, and the two hit it off at the very first meeting. He was tall and had green eyes and even spoke her dialect prevalent in her mountain state. She was getting up in age, and this was a perfect match; he was also a Khettry Hindu—how could it be more perfect? She felt comfortable with him, and his demeanor was calm, and he loved to listen to her. But she was hesitant, her thoughts going back to her first meeting with a tall green-eyed Kashmiri. Over time, she realized that her life with Mustafa was not a viable option; there was the matter of family, tradition, culture, and, of course, religion, not discounting the fact that Mustafa was not even living in the same country. After meeting the boy's family, she was convinced that he was the more logical and viable choice for a lifelong partner. No questions of religion of their progeny, no pains resulting from cultural and religious differences. The choice was perfect, and of course, the happiness of the parents and family was paramount too.

The wedding was a three-day traditional affair with food served on *patal* (leaf plates) to guests who sat on the floor, eating handfuls of *bhat* and *jore* without even a drop falling on the *shervanis* and scooping vegetables and chicken with freshly fried bhaturas. Everyone complimented the *rasoia* (the cooks), who some referred to as *boty*, and, of course, the hosts for the extensive cuisine. The *mehndi*[11] ceremony was followed by *sangeet*. CM's parents had invited singers from Delhi, who sang traditional *qawwalis*, and Pahari singers from the mountains playing traditional string instruments. The whole affair was just perfect. The whole town was on three days of holidays. Two prominent families had come together. What a perfect match. The wedding followed a honeymoon in Manali, and then they were back to New Delhi, CM at Lady Hardinge and Prem Prakash at the office of the internal ministry. The days passed at work and evenings with friends and family, attending dinners or hosting political "who's who" visiting the institute. Two years of marriage without any progeny prompted the parents to go on *tirtha-yatra* to Yamunotri, Gangotri, Kedarnath, and Badrinath. Upon their return, they fed Brahman's food for three days and gave alms to the poor.

---

11 *Mehndi* is a painting of exquisite designs on the hands and feet with crushed *mehndi* leaves. *Sangeet* are teasing songs recited at the *mehndi* ceremony.

Coincidentally, the gynecologist had good news; she was pregnant, once again bringing to life an age-old Indian belief in the divine powers of the gods. The pregnancy was tough, as she was an older primipara; first bouts of nausea and vomiting were followed by preeclampsia, headaches, swelling of the feet, and finally a delivery of a daughter. The child was just perfect, a great admixture of the two. She grew up in a wonderful environment full of love and caring.

The flight out of Montreal to Boston was very short. The plane landed at Logan Airport. Professor Sanjalya had called a relative living in Boston to care for Mustafa and help him get situated in Boston. From the airport, he went directly to the hospital, where he met the professor. His accommodation was already arranged in Longwood Towers next to the hospital as with other fellows. The one-room studio was much smaller than his residence in Nairobi but very efficient. It had a kitchenette, a bed, a small table, a bookshelf, a refrigerator, a microwave, and a cooktop. There was a common Laundromat on a lower floor, just a perfect arrangement. Below, there was a food court, which sold subsidized food. After leaving his bag in the room, he thanked Om Patel, Professor Sanjalya's cousin, for his hospitality. He decided to walk to the hospital but was stopped by a security person, who requested him to show his identity badge. He was never stopped by a security guard at any of the hospitals he had worked in the past, so this was a confusing first welcome to Boston. He wondered why a security guard would have to screen doctors entering a hospital. *An oxymoron*, he thought. But he was saved by a fellow resident, whom he had just met at Longwood Towers and who knew the officer and explained of his recent arrival from Africa for a fellowship with Dr. JH. He showed him around, but the hospital was old, and the corridors ended in a maze of corridors, very confusing for a first orientation. He made a mental note of the corridors as he crossed them and also made a mental note of the way to the gait lab, where he would be spending most of his time.

The next few days were a little blurry, as he felt overcome with fatigue and lack of sleep, and at one conference, he fell asleep at a lecture. JH noticed that he had nodded away at the lecture. Later, he told him to go and sleep off the jet lag. *Jet l*ag he had felt when he came to Africa from India, he understood the penalty of crossing two time zones quickly. Once he found his bearing, he was back on track and felt at home in the new environment. He spent more and more time learning the American way of practicing medicine, which was different from the British, which he had seen in India and again in Africa. He was amazed that the physicians referred to bacteria as 'bugs' and antibiotics as 'bug juice.' In Kenya, he had adopted a system of marking the extremity or the part to be operated with an indelible marker after he learned of a wrong site operation by a visiting German doctor, so he did the same with his pediatric patients at the children's, but instead of making an X mark, he drew a funny face. This was a practice not in vogue in U.S. hospitals, so he was labeled as the fellow who was not able to remember the side or site of surgery. JH asked of this aberrant practice but accepted the logic of it, so he agreed to have his patients marked for site identity, a first at the hospital. Nonetheless, Mustafa continued to wear his new title of a fellow who marks the site of surgery but without concern, as he knew it was an additional measure of safety.

His work at the gait lab was very interesting, as a fellow resident used joint markers to study motion during martial art. After six months of studying children's gait pattern, it was evident that there was no fixed gait pattern in children. Some kids who were referred for walking on tiptoes over months reverted to a heel-toe progression as they matured, and other children with in-toeing gait over time walked normally. Various parameters were studied, including the rotation of the tibia, the lower leg bone, known to the medical doctors as tibial torsion, and the rotation of the femur as anteversion or retroversion. Having much to learn and new territories to explore fascinated him and kept his mind from wandering to CM or Kashmir.

On one surgery day, as he was observing his professor carry out a spine surgery on a child from Puerto Rico, he commented that the material looked similar to the caseous material seen in TB of the spine, and the professor commented, "When you hear hooves, think of horses, not of zebras," and one of the residents remarked, "But, sir, he is from Africa, so he is used to thinking zebras." Nonetheless, the professor requested an acid-fast stain of the material, and Mustafa's observation was verified as correct, as the boy had TB of the spine. Fortunate for him, news at a teaching hospital traveled faster than light, so by the next day, everyone in the department looked at Mustafa with renewed respect. He had already earned the name of an "iron resident" because of his omnipresence in the hospital, but the truth of the matter was that he was most comfortable in a medical environment, and Friday 'liver rounds' at a nearby bar did not entice him much. Nurses invited him to toga parties, but his idea of fun did not coincide with being draped in a white bedsheet or for that matter getting drunk at the end of the week and ending up in a strange bed. Thank God AIDS was not prevalent in those days, as many residents would have been the carriers, mostly because of their promiscuous lifestyle. Soon two groups evolved: one of the single residents and the second of married residents. The married residents did not involve themselves in the activities of the single residents, therefore a better company for Mustafa. One of the married residents also advised him to wear a fake wedding band to stop the nurses from constantly hitting on him, an advice that worked like a charm.

CHAPTER 16

Mission Hill Project, Boston

The old Mission Hill Project off St. Alphonso Street was a housing project for the poor Boston community, which had over time become a hornet's nest of crime, not unlike other housing projects in other large metropolis. Some Fridays, Mustafa walked to a nearby masjid[12], a walking distance from Longwood medical area, for evening prayers. On one such evening, as the days were getting shorter in the Northern Hemisphere, he finished his prayers and was walking back down St. Alphonso Street to Longwood Avenue, where he saw on the other side of St. Alphonso Street three young black kids, who were walking a little faster than him, and as he crossed the street, they intercepted him much before he reached Longwood Avenue. Two of his assailants held his arms, and the one behind him put a switchblade on his neck and reached in for his right back pocket, extracting his wallet, which had his hospital ID, two one dollar bills, and a few visiting cards of doctors he had met. The one on the left took his Rado watch, a keepsake he had won for medical research, and put it in his pocket, but he could not remove the fake gold wedding band, which he wore as a protection from aggressive female nurses, who were relentless in 'asking him out.' The one on his left casually suggested that they should cut his finger to get the ring. Mustafa was appalled and frightened at the prospect of losing a finger. He suggested to get it off for them, but the one in the back kneed him, saying, "You white dudes are the reason for bussing."

---

12 The word Masjid is used in preference to Mosque as the later may have derived from the Spanish word Mezquita that may have derived from the word mosquito during the time of King Ferdinand and the holy crusades.

The public school desegregation referred to as bussing program was instituted in 1974 by Boston Mayor Kevin White. The program heralded a tremendous and bitter black-white divide, as children, both white and black, were bussed out and away from their school districts in an attempt to integrate the Boston public schools. Both the whites and blacks took to the street very angry and violent, and many white families moved to the suburbs, such as Newton, Wellesley, Natick, and many other suburbs around Boston, only to find out that many of those schools too accepted bussed students from Roxbury, Mattapan, and Dorchester. Mustafa was just a victim of the times, and his fair skin and green eyes did not help, as he did look like a white man even though he was Indian.

He panicked when one held his hand and fingers, and the one on his back brought a knife to his hand. Mustafa instinctively did the stupidest thing; contrary to the advice he had received about 'muggings,' he moved sideways, bringing the assailant down over his left shoulder and down to the ground. He was free, and the knife was in his hand. He kicked the one on the ground a 'field goal kick' across his jaw and noticed blood spew out of his mouth. He gathered his stance and kicked his ribs, and the assailant let out a bloodcurdling scream. The other two backed off and ran away, leaving their friend writhing on the ground. Mustafa kicked the one on the ground once again and dragged him to a public phone next to the Spars Pharmacy at the corner of Longwood Avenue and Huntington Avenue.

The 911 response was quick, as a squad car appeared on the scene in minutes. A large burly white officer got out of the car and pulled his gun when he saw the knife in Mustafa's hand and a bleeding black teenager down on the ground. He shouted, "Drop the knife," and Mustafa dropped the knife. When the officer approached them, Mustafa explained the situation, and upon finding Mustafa's wallet and ID in the black teenager's pocket and even though the kid complained that he was assaulted, the officer slapped him across his broken jaw. The teenager was frightened, and in his fright, he volunteered the names of his friends and accepted that he and his friends assaulted Mustafa. All the three teenagers lived in the Mission Hill Housing Project. The kid was placed in the backseat of the squad car after completion of a police complaint. Mustafa thought and believed that the bad experience was behind him. He lost his watch but felt confident that the law would find it back for him, especially as the officer had all the names.

A few months passed, and a summon was served on him for assault and battery of a minor. He was absolutely surprised, as he had acted in self-defense when he was a victim of a street mugging. He reached Officer Sullivan to find out that he was also cited for assault and battery and use of excessive force. Mustafa consulted an attorney, who referred him to an attorney practicing criminal law. The attorney agreed to represent him after an initial payment was made. Mustafa thought the misunderstanding would be cleared in a short time, but to his chagrin, the matter went on for months, interposed by continuances and more attorney fees. He had spent all his savings, but without a resolution in sight, he was called for a hearing that was continued; obviously, the public defender assigned to the black kid was well aware how to fatigue the defendant into a submission and a plea.

On one such day after returning from a continued hearing, he was asisting Dr. Stuart with discograms, and during a break in the lounge, the doctor asked him if all was well. Mustafa shared his story, and Stuart asked him to call him at home that evening to discuss his case further. He called at the designated time; Stuart picked the phone, informing him that his wife, an attorney, was on the phone too. She mostly asked questions, which Mustafa answered, and at the end of an hour-long telephone call, she promised to review the matter and call him back in due course. The next day, just as he was having a sandwich, attorney Stuart called him; it was only at that time he found out that she was an assistant attorney general. She had pulled all the files with the help of all the elves working at the AG's office and contended that the case represented a miscarriage of justice and promised to seek AG's advice and assistance. In a few days, she came back with the news that the AG's office had supervened, and the case was most likely to be retracted. She had also discussed the case with his attorney and asked Mustafa to get in touch with him within the next few days.

Mustafa called his attorney who did not talk much on the phone but invited him to the office. He arrived at the office a few minutes before the scheduled time, and the attorney was gracious enough to get him in right away, unlike the previous times, when he waited for hours at a time in his waiting room. He clasped his hand, saying that he had good news for him. "I approached the AG's office and had the case dismissed." He said. Mustafa was surprised that his attorney was taking credit for attorney Stuart's efforts but just kept quiet for the sake of prudence. As he was leaving the office, his attorney said, "Dorothy has a check for you for the amount you paid me, as I have decided to offer you pro bono service." Mustafa was once again amazed by the gesture and wondered what situation may have compelled his attorney to transform from a shark to a pussy cat; he believed that attorney Stuart may have a lot to do with the transformation.

He left Dorothy's desk with a check in hand, going straight to the bank on the campus as if worried that the check may bounce or the payment denied. He deposited the total eight thousand dollars he had paid his attorney in the course of the case. The very next day, Sullivan came to thank him, as his job was on the line because of the gravity of the filed accusations. His advice, "Next time you come across a situation such as this, just drop your assailant in the gutter."

Mustafa learned that, in America, it was important who you knew and not what you knew, but whatever the case, it was no different from India or Kenya, and what mattered most was that truth and justice had prevailed. Once again, he thanked the angels who came to his rescue, something he was getting accustomed to over time since the beginning of his journey out of Kashmir. He thanked all his angels—Krishna and his family; professors Mohammed, Kayum, Udani, Dhal, Bwibo, Sanjalya, and Hall; and the lady in the embassy—in a special prayer that evening.

CHAPTER 17

Want to See the Real Doctor

In the early seventies, there were not as many Indian physicians practicing in Boston and even fewer at the Harvard-affiliated hospitals. These few were mostly Indian residents and fellows. The residents and fellows were not randomly selected but handpicked from recognized, top-notch residency programs of India by those who were already aware of the high caliber of Indian residents and fellows.

In the early seventies, there was only one Indian restaurant in Cambridge, the Natraj, named after the dancing god Shiva.[13] Natraj in Cambridge was an imitation of an Indian cuisine, and what invited Mustafa to spend his hard-earned dollars on a meal there was the *raan*, a Kashmiri leg-of-lamb specialty that was on the menu. He ordered the dish with great expectations, but the expectations deflated quickly with the first bite. It was indeed hurtful to leave food on the table, but honestly, the *raan* was an insult to the exponents of fine Indian cuisine. He also wondered why the restaurant was named Natraj, as it was serving meat dishes that he believed was a blatant commercialization of Shiva's name.

There were two other residents in Boston whom he had met in India, and both were at the conference on social sciences in New Delhi, one at a hospital in Worcester and the other one a fellow in the Pediatric Cardiology Department of the Children's Hospital, but the three rarely socialized, mostly because of an exacting residency and fellowship schedule, when

---

13 The biodance of Shiva, much like the biodance of the dervish, derives its inspiration from the environment.

———

102

social moments were rare, and travel was difficult, as none of them had personal vehicles.

Mustafa was invited to a radiology professor's home for an authentic vegetarian home dinner. He had marked the date on his calendar with the highest expectations. After a glass of *jal-jeera*, the professor asked Mustafa to accompany him to the Newton Center subway station to pick up his daughter, who was schooling at Tufts. He parked his car just outside the station, requesting Mustafa to go down to the subway station to bring his daughter to the car. The subway lurched in, and the daughter was just as the professor had described her, about five feet and six inches tall and looking like a fifteen-year-old even though she was twentysomething. He waved to draw her attention and walked her to the car. As they climbed the side stairway to the street, a young white boy overtook them, and as he passed them, he spat on her white dress. The boy muttered something that Mustafa could not quite understand but sounded like 'spic.' He made a motion to go after the boy, but the young girl held his hand firmly, shaking her head and saying, "Let it be. He is just an ignorant white kid. Time will teach him acceptance of all immigrants, not by a show of violence but by strength of character and a show of superior intellect." Mustafa was completely enamored with her profound constraint and wisdom. He wiped the spit with his hanky and dropped it in a nearby bin.

By the time they reached her dad's car, she had already shaken off the spit encounter and did not mention it to her dad, who she knew was very volatile, and such insults were intolerable to him. She had taken after her mother, who was calm, collected, and always chose her words carefully; she was very cerebral and quite a character, which Mustafa observed in the first hour of their meeting that day.

The dinner was absolutely amazing, and Mustafa was very shy of taking seconds, but Mrs. Nagaraj kept refilling his plate, bringing back memory of Zainab Dhal, who did the same, a memory from a geographically distant Kenya. He wondered how Dr. Dhal was faring at his relocation back to United Kingdom. After a very sumptuous dinner followed by *ras malai*, *gajrala*, and *gulab jamun* and a cup of masala chai, Dr. Nagaraj kindly dropped him all the way back to the tower on Longwood Avenue.

He slept well that night and had the best dreams ever. In his dream, he was back in New Delhi with CM. Her voice was always very calming; even in his dreams, she brought a very calming feeling. Just before he fell asleep, he remembered the words of profound wisdom that he heard at the subway station, "Let it be. He is just an ignorant white kid. Time will teach him acceptance of all immigrants not by a show of violence but by strength of character and a show of superior intellect." *A lesson well learned*, he thought.

Months passed, and Mustafa was on night call, covering the pediatric surgery floor that weekend. An eight-year-old Caucasian was admitted to the emergency room with a very nasty fracture of the elbow. Mustafa was called to the ER to evaluate and treat the fracture. Before he met the family, he studied the fracture on X-rays and approached the family. The mother gave him a look of disgust as he parted the curtains, entering the ER cubicle. He introduced himself and went on to tell the parents about the fracture and his opinion on the treatment of the displaced supracondylar fracture. The mother stopped him as he was discussing the fracture, options of treatment, and prognosis. She looked him right in the face and in her Boston Brahman accent ordered Mustafa "to get a real doctor," and she refused to have her child cared for by a colored man. And as he went on to explain his credentials, she interrupted his explanation by saying, "Don't you understand English? I will not have my child treated by a colored man." Mustafa apologized and left the cubicle; fortunately for him, the ER nurse was a witness of the mother's despicable behavior towards one of their star resident doctor. Mustafa called the private on-call doctor, who promised to come to the ER to resolve the problem. Most times and even in India, he was mistaken for a white boy because of his Aryan complexion and green eyes, but this incidence was different, which he believed was because of his Indian accent or maybe because he was a trainee.

By the time the on-call doctor arrived, the woman changed her tone and stated that Mustafa was abrupt, abusive, and unprofessional and that he could not speak English, and his pronunciations were not discernible to her. Fortunately for Mustafa, the ER nurse had already related the whole episode to the charge physician on call in the ER, who requested that she document the incident verbatim in the ER patient record. When the private doctor sidelined Mustafa to request an explanation for his rude behavior, the ER physician supervened, requesting him not to draw any conclusion without a complete knowledge of the facts, handing him the ER chart and the charge nurse's report documenting the incident. He read the report with great anguish, as he had already decided to write Mustafa up for unprofessional conduct following the one-sided discussion with the child's mother. After reading the nurse's report, he requested both the ER nurse and Mustafa to accompany him to the cubicle where he approached the mother with facts as cited by the nurse and Mustafa, essentially cataloguing Mustafa as one of their star fellows. The mother restated that she would not have a colored man, no matter how smart, care for her child. The woman opted to leave the hospital and take her child to another facility down the street. As she was leaving, Mustafa apologized for any inconvenience she may have experienced. She just ignored him as a nonentity and walked away in a guff.

The incident reminded him of the wisdom learned from a young girl at the Newton subway station. "Let it be. He is just an ignorant white kid. Time will teach him acceptance of all immigrants not by a show of violence but by strength of character and a show of superior intellect." *Yes indeed*, he mused, *time will teach acceptance of internationally trained physicians*. But he wondered whether the time would come within his lifetime.

CHAPTER 18

Surgery Residency

The fellowship at the Children's Hospital was great, as Mustafa met a lot of physicians at the very top of the medical pyramid, and he enjoyed the challenging academic medical environment. He was treated well by his professors, other orthopedic physicians in private practice who had admission privileges at the hospital, and fellow resident physicians. Towards the end of the fellowship as was routine, Dr. JH scheduled a meeting with his residents and fellows. He recommended Mustafa to stay on to complete an orthopedic residency in the United States.

Mustafa had received significant surgery training in Kenya, but the American Orthopedic Board required a minimum of two years of surgery training at a recognized U.S. program, so it was imperative for him to comply with the requirements, which was an impediment, as he had a substantial general surgical experience and training already. His mentor had already talked to department heads at Harvard and found a surgery residency slot. The interview at Harvard was a formality that needed to be completed, and Mustafa was posted at one of the Harvard-affiliated hospitals as a straight intern, about three years down the rung from his level of training in Kenya, but that truly did not matter to him. He started the residency in right earnest and fitted in quite easily, mainly because he had been working in a premier U.S. hospital the past months as an orthopedic fellow, which had helped orient him to the American medical environment. Of course, there were some difficulties during the residency not because of intellectual inadequacies but mainly because of personality clashes resulting from his superior surgery knowledge and skills honed during his past surgery residency in Kenya, where he was already carrying out most cases independently.

His chief resident was somewhat uneasy, mainly because Mustafa, as a second assist, was able to discuss surgery cases and options of care in greater depth, and his superior knowledge of human anatomy was easily evident and appreciated. He read most journals, mainly as he had a lot of free time that he spent in medical library at the hospital and some weekends at Harvard's Countway Library of Medicine in Boston. Unlike his fellow residents who were married and had additional responsibilities at home and to their children, he was not married and had all the free time in the world. He did not imbibe alcoholic beverages or frequent single's haunts, so time away from work was spent in the library. His study discipline and his ability to easily retain new materials helped his ability and performance in medical grand rounds, all this to the chagrin of the senior residents.

Routinely, the surgery residents chilled at a local bar each Friday evening; and the residents at the Mount went to Parrot Beak in Cambridge. Chilling out in a bar was not Mustafa's idea of relaxation, but on that particular Friday after a great case of gastrojejunostomy and resection of the nerve of Laterjet, which a high-ranking surgeon allowed him to do, chilling out, he believed, was fine.

His chief resident, who scrubbed as a first assistant, was sidestepped by the surgeon in charge of the case, allowing Mustafa to be the first assistant and also carry out most of the surgery. Mustafa had been doing similar surgeries in Nairobi on his own, and his expertise was quite evident, as he carried out the dissection and complex anastomosis (suturing of the stomach to the jejunum) very well, demonstrating a skill of a seasoned surgeon, contrasting with the surgery skill of his chief resident, who was a few rungs down in his surgery skills.

The chief was infuriated, as he was forced to second assist, but he personally invited him to the liver rounds as a showing of friendship, and he drove Mustafa to the Parrot Beak. They arrived much earlier than the remaining group of residents, who were still finishing evening patient rounds at the Mount, readying for the weekend. Westerly, the chief, sat him down away from the bar, and after the waitress brought salted peanuts and crackers, he told Mustafa of his disgust with his attempt to supersede him in the operating room. He informed Mustafa that he would be restricted to the floor where he would clerk in all new patients and also do all the 'scut work,' which was routine and menial labor allocated to the lowest on the medical totem pole. He was ordered never to step into the OR except when requested by him personally, or when he was on call, or when other residents were unavailable. Mustafa new better than argue; he remembered a pearl that one of the private doctors had shared, "Never get into a pissing contest with a skunk, as you may win, but you will come out stinking even if you win." Mustafa responded, "It would be my personal pleasure."

In an attempt to bury the hatchet, Westerly offered to buy him a drink. Mustafa informed him that his preference was a soft drink or anything nonalcoholic. By the time Westerly was back with the drinks, the rest of the group had occupied the remaining seats on the table. Westerly had two tumblers in his hands, one darker than the other. He put the lighter tumbler of amber fluid in front of Mustafa and swiped about a quarter of his drink in a single go. He brought his tumbler forward in a gesture of a toast. "Best of residency," and almost ordering Mustafa, he said, "Bottoms up." Mustafa took a sip of the bitter amber fluid and put the tumbler down, asking about its content. To that, Westerly said, "Of course, it is a soft drink. It's light lager." The remaining residents shook their heads in a combined accent. The rest of the group ordered a variety of drinks, and the conversation opened up as the drinks poured. Mustafa managed to finish his tumbler though with great distaste of the acrid bitterness but did so to 'fit in.'

As the evening passed, Mustafa felt an unusual carefreeness, and his conversation became glib and disjointed. The residents teased him a little, mostly because he was a favorite of the nurses, who frequently asked him to toga parties and dinner, and the privates, who preferred to *round* their patients with him. Two hours into the liver round, he needed to go to the restroom and staggered to stand up and wandered to his destination in the company of a fellow resident. He "peed" an unusually large amount, which smelled different and was clearer than usual, but he was *too happy* to comprehend the reason for the change. Once back to his chair, they were ready to wind down and head back home. Westerly dropped him at the Mount, where he managed to stagger to the lounge, where he sat down, cradling his head in his hands as it was throbbing. He felt nauseous, so he went to the restroom but noticed that someone had removed all the urine stalls, so he peed in the john and puked at the sink, vomiting some of the crackers and crushed peanuts, and as he was coming out of the restroom, one of the female staff entered, and it was only then he noticed that he had walked into the ladies' restroom!

He sat in the lounge, where he passed out, and when he woke up, his head was throbbing awfully, and a head nurse was standing by his side, taking his pulse. He asked the head nurse why she was taking his pulse, and she told him that a student nurse had observed Mustafa coming out of the women's restroom staggering, and when she came out of the restroom, she found him passed out on the lounge sofa. She returned back to check him out, and she reported to the charge nurse that he was out like a light. The head nurse asked if he was fine, and his first response was to look at his watch, only to realize it was about midnight, meaning that he had slept on the sofa for at least two or three hours.

He related his visit to Parrot Beak, where Westerly had bought him a bitter drink, claiming that it was a soft drink, and he had only very blurred memory of how he returned to the hospital. It was already past midnight, and the head nurse suggested that he sleep over in the on-call room. She accompanied him to the room, and on their way, she grabbed OR scrubs for Mustafa. Once safely in the room, the head nurse left. He wore the OR garb and plunked himself into the bed, only to be awakened by the ringing of the phone; it was a wake-up call from the head nurse. He took a quick shower and went to the floor to start his day as a floor clerk as ordered by his chief resident, but later remembered that it was Saturday.

Early Monday morning, the head nurse reported the incident to the chief of surgery; but when asked, Westerly contended that Mustafa was the one who ordered his drink and that he gave him a ride from the pub as a personal favor, as he was obviously drunk. The head nurse did not believe Westerly's story, as she knew from dealing with Mustafa over the past few months that he may be gullible, but he was most definitely not a liar. Mustafa continued to do all the *scut work* without noticeable disgust. Dr. Canzanali the surgeon he had assisted with the Laterjet case bumped into Mustafa on the floor a few days later as he was examining his patient; he remarked that he had not seen him in the operating room since the time he had helped him with the gastrojejunostomy a few Fridays ago. He asked a reason for his absence from the OR, and Mustafa told him of Westerly's conversation with him following the first assist on his gastrojejunostomy and also of the fact that he got him drunk by telling him that the drink he bought him was a soft drink and later dumping him back at the hospital absolutely drunk.

The very next day, Dr. Canzanali called the chief of surgery to request that Mustafa assist him with his surgeries that day. Dr. Canzanali summoned Mustafa to the operating room, but when he arrived, Westerly asked him to return to the floor, but Canzanali was waiting in the lounge, anticipating the interaction. He told Westerly that he had personally requested Mustafa to first assist, and the request was approved by the chief of surgery. Westerly threw his OR hood down on the floor in an act of anger and walked to the chief's office, only to find out that the chief had approved the request for Mustafa to first assist Canzanali. As he walked from the chief's office, he vowed to make the rest of Mustafa's residency *a visit to hell*. After the cases were done, Canzanali accompanied Mustafa to the chief's office, where he complained of Westerly's unprofessional conduct but mostly praised the level of Mustafa's surgery skill and knowledge of human anatomy. The chief promised to resolve the problem in an amicable manner.

A few days passed, and Mustafa received a call from the Harvard surgery program director. Mustafa thought that his residency would be terminated, but to his surprise, the chief complimented him, recommending a promotion to a third-year residency and an immediate transfer to the cardiothoracic service at the Deaconess Hospital. The transfer, even though flawless, was not without anxiety, as now he had to reorient to a different hospital and to a completely alien specialty. Fortunately, his new chief resident, who had come from South Africa, was very understanding and spent a great deal of his time to orient Mustafa to the new specialty. Mustafa was a quick study and easy to work with, contrary to Westerly's contention that he was below par and obstinate, "just a poorly trained foreign shit." The cardiothoracic chief enjoyed having Mustafa as his understudy, and over a short time, Mustafa was presenting cases at the grand rounds and liked by all on the cardiothoracic service. The promotion from internship to a third-year resident had an additional bonus as the American orthopedic board considered to shorten his surgery requirement of two years to one year, allowing him to join an orthopedic residency the very next year. He was interviewed at three of the most prestigious Boston orthopedic programs and selected by all three; two offered an entry the very next year, and the third offered a spot a year later. Mustafa had no intention of wasting a year even though it meant opting out of a premier program, and choosing to join another orthopedic program instead.

At a meeting with his orthopedic chief few months into the orthopedic residency, the chief confided that Westerly had called and visited him to dissuade him from accepting Mustafa in the orthopedic program. He told him that he selected him as his surgery staff, and both the surgery and cardiothoracic physicians on staff had highly recommended him.

Once again, he remembered the words of wisdom he had heard from a young girl at the Newton subway station. "Let it be. He is just an ignorant white kid. Time will teach him acceptance of all immigrants not by a show of violence but by strength of character and a show of superior intellect." Mustafa often wondered if Westerly ever learned not to be a bigot.

CHAPTER 19

Orthopedic Residency

Mustafa had gone through residency interviews a few times in the past, first in India, where it was extremely competitive, mainly because of many new graduates applying for choice residencies, such as surgery cardiology and orthopedics. At times, in India, an interview spread over a week, and the candidates were all amassed in one waiting area; but comparatively, Kenyan and American residency interviews were done individually, so the interviewee felt very little duress. Mustafa was informed that his interviews were spread all over Greater Boston, one at the Massachusetts Hospital and the others in Brookline, Jamaica Plain, Roslindale, and the combat zone area of Downtown Boston. The first interview was at the Massachusetts Hospital, where the doctor's office was very well appointed and the staff very friendly. He noticed a steady traffic of residents coming to the office with various inquiries. Dr Edwin, just over six feet tall and a very warm and pleasant person, put Mustafa at ease as soon as he entered his office. He made small talk, and when Mustafa told him that he was from Kashmir, he smiled, asking him of what he was doing so far away from 'heaven on earth' and quoted Mogul emperor Shah Jahan, "If there is a heaven on earth, it is here, it is here." He told him that he had gone to Kashmir several times mostly as a tourist and once on a medical mission with a flood relief team of doctors. Mustafa had made preparations for the interview, but this was nothing like his previous interviews, as it was casual and more like a conversation in an OR lounge. Dr. Edwin had read and checked out all the information on Mustafa that was couriered to him by the program director, and he shared some insider information of the program, which he believed may be useful during his residency, and also told him of the sought-after rotations, where he would have great hands-on experience.

The remaining interviews were about the same except for two, one at the medical center that was after-hours at eight in the evening and where the exhausted professor dozed off to sleep during the interview and a second one at a veteran's hospital that was conducted by a younger physician, who asked many questions and spent about ninety minutes interviewing Mustafa. All in all, upon completion of his interviews, for the first time, he was not sure if he was going to be accepted in the program, as one the interviewers had dozed off during the interview. When the envelope arrived, he was amazed and pleased and also truly surprised that the interviewer who had gone to sleep was also impressed as he later learned from the chief of staff.

His rotations were to start at a peripheral suburban hospital at times referred to as the MGH of the suburbs. This was an important rotation, as he also learned *how not to do surgery* mostly from an inapt surgeon, who had great and thorough theoretical knowledge of surgery and human anatomy but possessed terrible surgical skill. His demeanor in the operating room was condescending, where he was rude to the operating staff and residents. He even threw a blood-soaked sponge to the wall when he was given a wrong instrument by the surgical nurse. The incident prompted Mustafa to keep a diary of all the mishaps in the operating room, which he presented to the program director, redacting the names of the surgeons. His treatise was appropriately named "How Not to Do Surgery," which the chief read with great interest and commented that both how to, and how not to do surgery were equally important to learn. He said that good cannot be appreciated if one was not aware of the bad.

In Kenya and also in India, he had come across a preselect group of some of the top-notch surgeons, whereas in Boston's suburban hospitals, he came across a mix of surgeons. He noticed that the newly qualified surgeons trained at some orthopedic programs demonstrated superior surgical skill compared to those trained at another highly rated program, which he later found out was a result of the residents' receiving limited hands-on surgery exposure during their years in the program. He felt lucky that providence made him join this program as he was selected in all three Boston programs, but one residency was promised a year later, and he opted not to waste a year waiting for that residency program even though it was more prestigious. His learning continued, and even though a rotation at the center was highly rated, the learning opportunity and honing of surgical skills was much better at some of the peripheral hospitals; however, exposure on pediatric orthopedics was the best at the center mostly because of the vaster variety of pediatric orthopedic disease that were referred to the center.

In the latter part of his residency, the physicians requested him to first assist, which deprived his junior colleagues from an opportunity of learning newer and complex techniques. On one such occasion, where a surgeon was carrying out a very routine and straightforward major joint replacement surgery, Mustafa tutored a junior resident on the procedure, discussing options of care, templating X-rays for prosthetic implant selection, and also individual preferences and idiosyncrasies of the surgeon; and once assured that all checks and balances were addressed and he was certain of the resident's readiness to first assist, he did what a good senior resident should have done: he allowed the junior to scrub in as a first assistant but waited in the gallery above the OR, observing the progress, ready to scrub-in if needed. The case went off well, but the surgeon was annoyed that Mustafa did not scrub in to help him. When he saw Mustafa on the patient floor, he beckoned him with his index finger, no different from how a Brit would have beckoned an Indian with the bending and straightening of the index finger. As Mustafa approached him, he blurted out, "How dare you have a junior scrub on my case?" Mustafa apologized and asked if the case went off well and also inquired of the junior resident's performance. The doctor said that he was good and that the case went well. So Mustafa explained, "Sir, the junior that scrubbed on your case prides that you are the best there is, and the opportunity to scrub on a case with you was something he had desired from the first day of his rotation at this hospital. He was thoroughly couched for the surgery, and I personally went over every little detail so that there would be no hitch, and, sir, just for your information, I sat in the gallery, observing the whole surgery, prepared to scrub-in if needed. That was my decision as his senior resident, and I hope you respect the decision, as it was made with the best intent." The private did not say much and walked away, but later that day, he called Mustafa to his office. He clasped Mustafa's hand firmly and thanked him for his explanation and said, "From now on, I'll respect your decision to send a junior to my room, as I am now assured that the junior will be ready to first assist."

There was this one time when Mustafa was first assisting an orthopedic surgeon trained at a very prestigious Boston program on a simple intertrochanteric fracture of the hip at one area hospital. The surgeon lacked the most basic knowledge of fracture fixation. He wore size 12 shoes, so large that a single shoe cover did not fit his shoe, so he had to don one cover from the back and the second from the front and tape the two in the middle. After the patient was anaesthetized, the surgeon was not able to position the patient on a fracture table or position the image intensifier to view the fracture reduction. The surgeon's inability wasted an hour of anesthesia time, and the surgery was not even started until he allowed Mustafa to help with the placement and positioning of the patient. Routinely, with a surgical treatment of an intertrochanteric hip fracture, a closed reduction of the fracture had to be carried out prior to opening the skin; unfortunately, after an hour more of anesthesia time, now a total of two hours, the fracture remained unreduced. At an average, the total anesthesia time for a routine intertrochanteric fracture surgery was never greater than an hour; but in this instance, it had already taken two hours; Therefore, the anesthesiologist supervened, advising to awaken the patient and start afresh in the morning, when more help was available.

After a case review with the orthopedic department chief the following morning, the chief resolved that the surgeon in question may only book fracture cases between 7:30 a.m. and 3:30 p.m. and have another orthopedic surgeon available to assist with 'complex' cases, even though surgical care of an intertrochanteric fracture was deemed pretty routine and a high-frequency case in any busy hospital. In defense of the surgeon was the fact that he had published more articles in peer-reviewed journals than others in the department. That reminded Mustafa of another orthopedic surgeon at Children's Hospital who was well published, having greater than thirty original papers in peer-reviewed journals, and a great name in basic science research and who also had his own basic science research lab, but lacked surgery skills. Needless to say, most surgeons that Mustafa came across were great technicians and possessed a wealth of knowledge, and it was only because Mustafa kept a record of how not to do surgeries that he had case based knowledge of the less skilled surgeons.

Chapter 20

Chief's Office Meeting

Mustafa had completed two years of his orthopedic residency, but he did not have an opportunity to discuss his training with his departmental chief, except for cursory corridor meetings with the him. In contrast, other residents were called to the chief's office about semiannually. Every time a resident returned from one such meeting, he exalted on matters discussed and how impressed the chief was with his individual performance, so Mustafa was worried and also envious of those residents. Mustafa's work and his knowledge were praised by most privates, with the exception of 'the big-footed surgeon' at one of his earlier rotations, who attributed his own failure in treating an intertrochanteric fracture to a lack of assistance by his resident surgeon. However, a few years later, when Mustafa was an American Board certified surgeon, the big-footed surgeon invited him to join his department at one of the southern states, where he was appointed chief of an academic orthopedic program! That is when Mustafa realized that the surgeon was acting-out only because of the humiliation he suffered that night in the OR, when he was superseded by an anesthesiologist, and it had nothing to do with Mustafa. Mustafa was the sacrificial lamb.

On a bus ride to Maine to attend a grand round, Mustafa found courage to ask the orthopedic service chief the reason for his exclusion from semiannual meetings with the chief just like the other residents. The chief said that there was no reason for a meeting since his performance was great and that only those residents whose performance was questionable were reviewed and advised, some biannually and others quarterly. He said, "I am hoping that you will continue to stay away from my office for biannual meetings, but if there is a problem, please do not hesitate to schedule time with my assistant." That bus journey resolved the issue, and he understood why some residents were frequent visitors to the chief's office.

During the bus ride, the chief sat beside Mustafa and gave a summarized review of his performance. He also told him that Westerly, his chief resident at the Mount, had scheduled a meeting with him just prior to his selection for a residency to make him aware of Mustafa's incompetence and lack of basic knowledge; however, all his other chief residents spoke highly of him, and Peter from the Deaconess visited him to support his application, after learning of Westerly's meeting with him, who boasted that Mustafa will never be accepted to a residency, at least not in Boston. Peter had brought with him letters from all the surgeons at the Deaconess supporting Mustafa's application to the orthopedic residency. The chief acknowledged that the excellent recommendations that Peter brought with him and his personal effort to talk to him left a distinct impression that Westerly harbored a personal grudge. Mustafa shared with the chief his conversation with Westerly at the Parrot Beak and the fact that, instead of a soft drink, he had served him an alcoholic drink during a *Friday Liver Round*, which made him very sick since he had not taken an alcoholic drink prior to that, and also told him that the hospital charge nurse had reported the incident to the chief of surgery at the Mount, following which Westerly's conduct was questioned. He also told his deparmental chief how Westerly kept him out of the operating room and made him do all the scut work on the floor as a punishment for outshining him in the operating room. He informed the chief that the surgeons at the Mount petitioned to the chief of the surgery program to consider Mustafa's promotion to higher level of residency commensurate with his knowledge and skill, which was the reason for his promotion from an internship to a third-year residency.

Just as the bus entered the medical campus, his orthopedic program chief advised Mustafa to continue maintaining a low profile and his signature proficiency but to contact him if there was a problem.

The orthopedic residency training was without surprises until his third year of residency, when his chief resident, Marvelous, designated a second-year resident as an interim chief resident in charge of the residents during his absence when, rightfully and according to protocol, Mustafa should have been the designated interim chief. The program director advised him to discount it, as it was most likely an unintentional oversight.

In the three years of his orthopedic residency, Mustafa presented two research papers at an annual residency meeting—the first one "Patterns of Trauma at the Kenyatta National Hospital," which was a representation of the trauma and surgery admissions at KNH in Nairobi, and the second one on "Intramedullary Screw Fixation of Lateral Malleolus for Treatment of Bimalleolar Ankle Fractures." The two paper presentations gave him the extra brownie points needed to secure a much desired chief residency at the Veterans Hospital. The Veterans Hospital chief residency was much desired, mostly as it gave the chief resident a comprehensive administrative experience of managing a large pool of surgery patients who were in need of both elective and acute trauma orthopedic care, which was a great primer for chief residents wishing to embark on an independent private orthopedic practice.

The three years of residency came to an end in December, during the later months Mustafa had identified a prime medical office building in Brookline and rehabilitated it for starting a solo practice. He had applied for a part-time job at an outpatient Veterans Administration (VA) clinic in the city and also a part-time civilian orthopedic position at the Army Hospital at Fort Devon army base for supplemental income during early months of a new private practice, during which time he predicted almost no income from the private practice.

However his orthopedic chief had planned an academic career for Mustafa but without confiding with him his intent; he desired of him to continue working at the center and also to take up additional departmental responsibility at a nearby affiliated hospital and work at a pediatric hospital in Lakeville, about a one hour drive from Boston. Mustafa was not aware of his chief's plans for him, and it was only at a dinner meeting later in the residency, just before the completion of the residency, that he got wind of the chief's plan for him. By that time, Mustafa had already rehabbed the office space in the beautiful town of Brookline and signed contracts for part-time jobs at the army base and VA clinic. With great trepidation and much hesitation, he informed his chief of his plans for a private orthopedic practice and also of the fact that he had rented an office and signed contracts to work at an army hospital and a Veterans Administration clinic. The chief was greatly displeased and remained so for the next six months, but he forgave him and also complimented his decision at an office-warming party hosted at his Brookline office six months later, where he was the chief guest.

Chapter 21

Orthopedic Practice

Mustafa had spent all his free time each weekday and all free weekends in the last three months of the orthopedic residency preparing his Brookline office. He painted the walls with assistance from friends and dressed up the walls with red oak wainscoting and new red oak baseboards and crown moldings. He had washed the carpet several times using a rental carpet machine, removing grunge and grime of years of past use, bringing back to life the beat-up old carpet. He revived the carpet with sweat equity, as he was not able to budget in a new carpet in his limited budget. The bank that loaned him a startup loan was not ready to give him a loan initially, rightfully so as he had no proven creditworthiness, mostly because he had not used any debt services during the years of residency, but after submitting several supporting testimonials from practicing orthopedic surgeons, giving the bank information of the earning potential of an orthopedic surgeon, the bank approved a loan of eight thousand dollars. By the time he had completed the face-lift, lead lined the X-ray room, and furnished the office with used furniture from Goldstein's, he was ready to see his first patient beginning the first day of the year. New Year's Day was a holiday; however, he had agreed to take emergency calls during the holidays, so he managed to treat a large number of trauma cases that arrived at the two emergency rooms he covered during the New Year holidays. He was advised by an older colleague to make himself available at all times and assist other practices to ease their load, an advice that helped him immensely.

Word was out that a young resident who was a favorite of many practicing physicians had opened an orthopedic practice in Brookline, which was lucky for him, and also the ERs of both hospitals where he had privileges were housed by residents he had worked with in the past three years, so he received a large number of the trauma cases from the two hospital emergency rooms. Many senior orthopedic surgeons did not like working during winter nights and weekend days, so he gladly covered their practices and also covered orthopedic emergencies of their patients during those days. Being available, proficient, and likable were the key for his quick success in a solo practice in Boston, where many had failed to establish a solo practice. He worked at the Court Street outpatient clinic each Tuesday and at the army hospital every Friday, carrying out arthroscopic surgeries at the latter, as the older orthopedic army surgeons at the army hospital were not proficient in arthroscopic surgery, mostly because of the lack of learned psychomotor skill required for the more advanced arthroscopic techniques introduced to orthopedics in the recent years. His relationship with the army hospital was symbiotic, as he got to carry out six to seven arthroscopic surgeries each Friday, further honing his skills in arthroscopic surgery and also helping soldiers at the base receive the latest, high-end arthroscopic surgical care locally.

The Tuesday Court Street clinic was mostly a chronic care clinic, and many patients at the clinic were on narcotics for many years. At Court Street, Mustafa introduced alternative medications and modalities, such as physical therapy, yoga, and exercises, in an effort to reduce use of narcotics, as the latter was addictive and habit forming. Many of the veterans were also overweight and depressed, ate the wrong foods, and told winded stories of their war experiences. He was amazed and appalled with the high level of tobacco abuse amongst the veterans and surprised that the Veterans PX (post exchange), also sometimes referred to as the commissary, stocked cigarettes and cigars even at its medical facilities. He distinctly remembered a time during a major snow emergency when a chopper brought in cigarettes instead of much needed medical supplies to a busy hospital that had run short on medicines! He also noticed that a large number of veterans were receiving psychiatric care for suffering from vivid combat-related nightmares. This illness was ill understood at that time and routinely treated with tranquilizers and antipsychotic medications. He treated the veterans and also soldiers at the army hospital with great compassion and care, thereby becoming a welcome introduction to their health care. One of his patients even wrote a letter to the White House, praising the care he received from Mustafa, which resulted in a commendation from the commander in chief and also the DAV (Disabled American Veterans) Administration and a letter of praise from the White House.

Mustafa enjoyed his work and never fatigued or felt tired, even though he worked greater than sixty hours each week, and he worked on Saturdays and Sundays too. Some called him a workaholic, but he was not offended, as work was his passion; his work ethics had won him a title of an *iron resident* during his residency training. He knew his patients well and made it a practice to send them birthday cards and even remembered their children, who later became his patients. One such patient, an eighty-five-year-old female under his care for a knee joint disease for past several years, arrived at the office for a routine follow-up one day, and as he was chatting with her as was routine with him (he referred to it as warming up), he noticed tears in her eyes. Mustafa asked the reason for her sadness, and she said, "I just remembered that they brought me the flag today." She explained that her son was MIA (missing in action) in Vietnam and that they had brought her the American flag that day, some years ago. Mustafa could not understand an emotion of having a child missing in action, so he did not know how to console his patient, except saying sorry. His lack of understanding his patient's pain dwelled on him for a few weeks thereafter, and one night, he woke up from deep sleep with a troubling thought of an MIA, and he scribbled a poem titled "Missing in Action" on a scrap paper he found on his nightstand. The poem read as follows:

Missing in Action

Eyes searching the horizon
For long lost son gone without much reason
MIA, what does it really mean?
Ask the mother whose child she has not seen

Young in age at nineteen
Ready to serve his country with high esteem
No questions asked at the time
Now lost much before his prime

No folded flag or salute brings back the son
The mother questions of what her country has done
Did his life or death win peace or war?
Ask the mother whose heart it tore

At a latter follow-up appointment of his eighty-five-year-old, he apologized for not understanding her pain, handing her the poem as a note of condolence. She read the poem, and tears rolled from her eyes, and she asked Mustafa to read the poem to her, which he did. She got up from her chair, asking Mustafa if she could hug him, and Mustafa explained that medical ethics disallowed doctors from hugging their patients, but he was going to make this one an exception. She hugged him and sobbed on his shoulder, venting years of pain. The poem later appeared in a veterans' magazine and also on the first page of a book of poem titled *Poetic Musings* a few years later.

His orthopedic practice flourished, so he opened a second practice in an adjacent town of Cambridge, across the Charles River, about equidistant from the world-famous Harvard College and the Massachusetts Institute of Technology. He was financially secure but never found a pressing desire to marry. On rare occasions, he went out with friends but did not enjoy 'the party scene,' and did not enjoy imbibing alcoholic drinks, especially related to his painful memory of 'liver rounds' at a pub in Cambridge during his Harvard residency; however, he did not object his friends' consuming *som ras* (Kashmiri for "alcohol"), albeit he was amused how glib they got after a few drinks, telling him things they would not have shared except after an alcohol-induced loss of supratentorial control.

He remembered CM often as he grew older and cherished her memory, but many years had passed, and he was not in touch with her for at least ten years. He often wondered of her life with Prem Prakash. In their time together, he had joked that he would have a complete football team, as he wanted a large family, and he wondered if she had a large family just as he had wished.

Over time, his name became a household name with many patients and their families, and he started receiving patients from other states and even from abroad. He was once referred to the Indian ambassador to Austria, who consulted him for a back problem for which he was advised surgery in Europe. After reviewing his medical reports of his consultations abroad, he concurred with their recommendation and offered a consultation when he visited the United States. The ambassador made it a point to follow through with the recommendation, arriving in Boston within a month, with a request to have his surgery in Boston. Mustafa carried out an extensive clinical evaluation and viewed his MRI, following which he advised him of a nonsurgical plan of care, as he believed that he did not require a surgical intervention. Being a type-A personality, the ambassador was annoyed and a little disfranchised by Mustafa's recommendation as it conflicted with his European doctors, but his wife, who accompanied him, convinced him to at least give the nonsurgical treatment a fair try. He left for Vienna, and Mustafa did not hear from him for more than six months, and then out of the blue, he received a phone call from the ambassador, who was full of high praise. He had followed Mustafa's recommendation, and he was completely well and free of pain. He stated that he had also taken up hiking in the woods outside Vienna and enjoyed tracking the hills, something he could not even envision doing six months ago. He invited Mustafa as his personal guest to Austria. Mustafa eventually got an opportunity to meet the ambassador while attending a medical meeting in Vienna. The ambassador had recovered well and had taken up to the passion of trekking the woods of Austria and he also took Mustafa to his favorite forest just outside Vienna, where they walked for about an hour. He was in a much better physical shape than Mustafa, which made Mustafa realize that he had to care for himself, as he was getting heavier and out of shape. He decided to join a gym and also watch over his dietary habits on his return to Boston and address the obesity resulting from his affluence, improper eating habits, long hours of work, and lack of exercise. So the trip to Austria was with great reward—a patient cured and a doctor rehabilitated.

Upon his return to Boston, he joined a nearby sports club, which had a running track, all the desired machines, free weights, swimming pools, and a hot tub. Initially, going to the gym was a chore, but his gym buddies helped with keeping a regular routine. Just over a year in the gym, his waistline decreased from a fat thirty-eight inches to a trim thirty-two inches, and the chest size decreased six inches to size forty inches, close to how he was towards the end of his residency; even his belly firmed up, and he was able to see his recti muscles reappear (six-pack abdomen). The weight training not only improved his stamina but he also gained strength and power, as he was able to reduce joint dislocations without assistance or fatigue, and he also noticed that his lower legs did not swell after eight hours of standing in the operating room. The trip to Vienna was a win-win situation—a satisfied patient and a cured doctor.

With his renewed discipline of daily exercises, he also stopped gobbling large slices of cheesecakes or eating scrumptious chocolate-chip cookies steeped in butter brought in by the OR nurses or washing the junk he ate in the surgeon's lounge with a large bottle of Coke. The downside of the fitness routine was that his custom-made Armani suits did not fit him anymore, and he needed a new wardrobe, but that was an acceptable trade-off, as he was trim and fit and felt much better.

In the latter years of his practice, he realized that there was a loss of trust with the Board of Registration in Medicine, especially amongst the Boston area physicians. Physicians felt that the board was on a witch hunt, and the feeling was further deepened when a senior investigator on the disciplinary arm of the board, who was invited by the bar overseer to talk about the board, made some loose and unfortunate remarks. Unfortunately for the disciplinary attorney, his speech was transcribed and circulated to its membership. In his speech, he contended that the Board of Medicine was the *jury, judge,* and *executioner* all rolled in one and that a physician who confronted the board was asking for trouble. He went on to say that a physician who came on his knees before the board had a better chance of winning its grace than the one who was confrontational. To add to the insult, at about the same time, a very prominent physician was sanctioned by the board for prejudice against a homosexual patient, and his license to practice medicine was summarily suspended, mostly arising from the pressure exerted by a then influential lobbying of the Boston gay community. However, it later came to pass that the censured physician was also gay himself but in the closet at that time, worried of the repercussions to his practice arising from his sexual preference.

CHAPTER 22

Board of Registration in Medicine

Phobia of the Board of Registration in Medicine amongst the Massachusetts physicians was palpable in the recent past years; the lecture of the board attorney at the bar overseer convention raised the bar of bias to a higher level, not punning on the word *bar*, as the lecture was at a convention of attorneys. To the advantage of those unaware of the text of the address, the whole speech was transcribed and posted on many public sites. The arbitrary verdict against the prominent Boston physician for discriminating a gay patient added more fuel to the fire of distrust flaming in the medical community.

Mustafa, who by now was a trained investigator, decided to write a treatise, a white paper on the problems at the board, giving a physician's perspective to the newly elected governor. He named the treatise "A Fractured Board of Registration in Medicine." In his treatise, he summarized his review of available public records of cases that had come before the board, its subsequent judgment, and disciplinary sanctions of the board against the deposed physicians. In the treatise based completely on available factual data, he also presented his finding of delay and arbitrary denial of new license applications and delay in turnaround of renewal of licenses, which took an inordinately long time and most times greater than three months at an average. He presented data on the arbitrary handling of physician complaints, the weight given to frivolous whistle-blower complaints that generated volumes of investigative material and loss of physician practice time, the severe sanctions against physicians addicted to drugs or alcohol, and the desperate treatment of foreign medical graduates who were unfortunate to come before the board. The latter issue had little or no input from a foreign medical graduate who was on the board at that time, as he opted to recuse himself on each and every case that involved a foreign medical graduate who came before the board.

Mustafa presented the treatise to a newly elected governor, who thumbed through the pages with great interest, especially as he was repeatedly told of the problems at the board by his physician constituents, who had favorably supported his campaign. The governor scheduled an initial closed-door meeting with a handpicked staff, followed by a second meeting with a proposal for Mustafa's election to the board.

Mustafa observed the mix of the members on the board at that time, one a public member who was an attorney who had represented sleazy general building contractors, who had defrauded at least two physicians to the best of his knowledge; the other public member position was vacant, and he was aware of the foreign physician on the board, who was mostly towing the line for his own political aspiration and growth. He was also aware from his review of the board proceedings that the foreign medical graduate member on the board routinely recused himself on cases involving physicians trained outside of the United States. His review of the board and the available public records presented a strong disincentive of his being a part of it, as he knew of his inability to tow the line and the fact that he was too honest to be on the board; however, he conceded only under pressure and after a promise that the present governance would support his decisions and work closely with the consumer affairs and the board to bring about parity and accountability.

He joined the board with an agenda to bring back fairness and also to inspire a dialogue with the one body that it policed, 'the physicians'. He was aware that the federal government greatly subsidized the cost of medical education and therefore incurred great financial loss each time a physician lost a license to practice medicine. He also believed that abuse of drugs prevalent amongst certain groups of doctors and a higher incidence of alcoholism prevalent in young physicians were both dependency diseases, and the afflicted physicians, just like the general population, must be offered appropriate rehabilitation under medical supervision and allowed to return back to practice medicine under peer watch with proper checks and balances in place to prevent recurrences.

Mustafa had worked in busy emergency rooms and learned firsthand the importance of triaging patients, prioritizing care for severe and life-threatening trauma and medical emergencies. He wondered whether introducing a triage system, similar to the one adopted by major Boston emergency rooms, would work to streamline both licensing and complaints at the board. Obviously, he had cogent and innovative ideas that he believed would help solve some of the problems, but he was also aware that the board had an ingrained culture, and he harbored a trepidation that he would be treated as a pariah not only by the board members and its staff but also by the physician community, which eyed the board with a high level of mistrust. He was also fearful that physicians referring him patients may disfranchise him and stop referring him patients. He was aware of the time that may be required on the board to implement the changes, would also steal away time from his busy practice. The board offered a small stipend for the time spent on the board, which he had decided not to accept. He was aware that he would have to espouse confidence with physician associations and medical societies to encourage partnership and cooperation, which would involve public-speaking engagements to drive home his message to the public, as well as the physician community.

Nonetheless, he accepted the challenge of an appointment on the board, especially as he was aware of its turmoil and its obvious dysfunction. The challenge was quickly evident at his first full-board meeting, where there were two cases of boundary violation before the board—one of a very prominent neuropharmacologist, a head of the department of a very famous Boston medical school who had ongoing sexual encounters with a patient over five to six years, and another of a foreign-trained physician, an internist who had a single sexual encounter with a psychiatric patient, whom he evaluated on a consultation. In the latter case, the patient, upon her discharge from the hospital, continued to call the doctor, inviting him home, and eventually, he accepted the invitation, during which time he had consensual sex with the woman. Both cases were egregious, as they represented boundary violation in the purview of the board—one of a single episode of a sexual encounter and the other of multiple sexual encounters over a period of five or six years. The foreign medical graduate was slated for board review first, and as was routine, a boxful of materials arrived at Mustafa's home two days before the case. He had two days to review and assimilate all the materials, which were about two thousand pages of interrogatories, personal information, notes from the woman's psychiatrist, and a note from an anonymous whistle-blower, a health-care worker. He reviewed the materials, cross-referencing it and reviewing other similar materials of past decisions both in Massachusetts and other states, to help him understand the case before the board. Mustafa was not new to research, so he spent time at the Harvard's Countway Library, cross referencing the case.

When he approached the board on the day of the hearing, he was surprised that his presence at the hearing was questioned. The board asked if he was going to recuse himself, a fact that he found puzzling but was reminded that a second board member, also an FMG (foreign medical graduate), routinely recused himself from FMG cases that came before the board. He was not able to understand the logic of the precedence therefore questioned the logic, and a member said that he would harbor an innate prejudice, as the individual physician before the board was an Indian physician! That prompted Mustafa to ask the board if every white American physician recused himself when an American graduate or a white physician was before the board? One of the board member said that there was no obvious or inferred bias in the later case involving a white physician or an American graduate. Mustafa responded that the same case scenario was relevant in his case, as he had no prejudice, albeit he felt insulted that the board assumed that he would not be able to come to an unbiased conclusion just because the physician before the board was of Indian descent. He said in his defense that even with a jury selection, cultural make up, color or training was not assumed as a bias. The board voted unanimously that his argument was cogent and he be allowed to sit on the board hearing.

As the case proceeded, he was amazed that most of the board members had not viewed the documents sent to each member, with the exception of a consumer member, an attorney who was just elected on the board. As the hearing stumbled along, a decision was made that there was evidence of boundary violation; and accordingly, the physician's license was summarily suspended in keeping with the board regulations and past determinations. The hearing took the board just over six hours, mostly because a majority of the board members had not taken the time to view the documents sent to them and had to depend on the board disciplinary attorney for explanations and clarification. It was obvious that all the board members with the exception of the two, Mustafa and the newly appointed consumer member, had not taken the case seriously enough to spend time viewing and cross-referencing the materials sent by the board, two days ago. The second consumer member also an attorney who had represented sleazy general contractors and who was on the board for past two years was very verbose and comfortable but lacking in cogent evidentiary material. At the end of the meeting, the newly appointed female consumer member, an attorney, complimented Mustafa for his understanding of the case and for his argument for not to being recused.

The second case came before the board four weeks later, and as requested by Mustafa and voted by the members, the boxful of evidentiary and investigative materials arrived one week before the date of the hearing. The physician before the board, as indicated, was a very prominent psychiatrist at a famous Boston medical school. He was sexually involved with his patient over a six-year period and whom he had taken on holidays and to professional meetings outside Boston. Mustafa's review of the case and cross-referencing did not leave any doubt of boundary violation, which had taken place over a long period of six years, which in his mind was more egregious than the previous case of the FMG Indian doctor before the board four weeks ago.

The second board meeting was more streamlined, as most but not all members had read the materials that had arrived at their doorsteps. Obviously, the longer review time had made a difference if not for the fact that Mustafa's in-depth understanding of the prior case of boundary violation had prompted most to read the materials. What bothered him was the repeated mention during the hearing that the physician before the board was a prominent physician who was regarded very highly in the Boston community. One member even suggested that the board show leniency in this particular case not because the sexual misconduct over six years was not egregious but because he was such a prominent member of the medical community. Something else became evident as the case proceeded; it seemed that there had been a discussion of the case amongst some members outside the board and prior to the board deliberation. On a five-member board, three members voted that the physician's license not be summarily suspended for his multiple acts of boundary violation but the deposed physician be allowed to continue practicing his profession under peer review. Mustafa and the female attorney, the consumer member, voted for summary suspension as was appropriate and in keeping with the board policy and regulations. The majority vote carried; however, he was surprised that one member suggested that the two nay votes reconsider reversing their decision so as to arrive at a unanimous vote, a decision that would look more favorable in the public eye. Mustafa wondered if he was on a board of medicine, where fairness and compliance of the law was paramount, or on a politically influenced consumer body. The two nay votes stayed, so a unanimous decision was not entered. As expected, the matter was in the press the next day, some reporting the disparity in the board decision. At a later date, one of the board members, a prominent inner circle member of the Republican Party and a party appointee, had the audacity to remark that Mustafa should have considered changing his vote, as the physician in question was a prominent member of the party. Mustafa responded, "Indeed, I reconsidered and did follow my conscience and respect for fairness outside my party or political affiliation."

Mustafa was appointed chair of the licensing committee mostly because other members did not prefer spending extra time on the board and also because he had shown interest, an understanding and knowledge of the board regulations and policy. On his first day on the committee, he was inundated with a few hundred files of renewal of licenses and a few applications for new licenses. Both renewal and new license applications were treated the same, each file was cross-checked, and each application was checked for credentialing, academic records, medical school transcripts, etc. Mustafa thought that the criteria used were appropriate for new licensees but the scrutiny redundant for renewals, as their credentialing and transcripts had already been checked during their initial application. He found out that all physician-data was stored on the server at the board and also regularly backed up to protect the data from a rare case of hardware failure. The data was also encrypted to protect it from a rare possibility of a hacker accessing or disrupting the system.

After reviewing a small sample of renewals, he proposed the adoption of a triage system for renewals, which grouped renewals into two groups: one of physicians without existing or pending complaints and another of physicians with complaints filed against them. And as he reviewed the latter group, he found out that majority of the cases had frivolous complaints. For example, a doctor charged the patient for a medical report (board regulations allowed the physician to charge copying and retrieval fee), or the physician did not spend appropriate time, or the physician did not respond to a telephone call in a timely manner. With the knowledge gathered from his random sampling of the license renewals, he was able to triage the renewals of physician license with complaints further into those with egregious complaints and those with frivolous complaints. He brought the proposal to the full board after discussing the changes with the licensing arm of the board, its attorneys and also the administrative attorneys, and the chair. After a very short discussion, the board voted an approval on an adoption of the proposed triage system, and a policy decision was appropriately introduced. The licensing attorney was charged with its implementation, but as the triage progressed, it was evident that the board had hired more clerks to view the large number of past renewals, and now there was a surplus of clerks that had to be either transferred to other departments or services of nonunion clerks terminated. The system came into play very quickly, thereby streamlining the relicensing process and improving the turnaround time. The first compliments came from the local medical associations and also from individual licensees who received their renewals within two weeks of reapplication. The newspapers got wind of the change and complimented the governor for bringing about the changes within a few months of his taking office. A change that he proudly presented to a body of doctors as 'keeping his promise to the doctors of Massachusetts', promising more changes in the days to come

The board term was a three-year stint, but some members lingered on to do extra services after their term was over. In those three years, Mustafa learned much at the board but did not see any compelling reason for his continued stay; some referring physicians had stopped sending him patients after his appointment on the board, and his practice had also suffered because of time lost away from the practice. Of course, the board gave a stipend of about seventy-five dollars, which Mustafa refused to accept, as he believed that his service on the board had to be voluntary and without any financial incentive, as he was not an agent of the establishment but a physician volunteer who wanted a semblance of fairness in the proceedings of the board.

During his time on the board, there was an incident when he witnessed a dog and pony show when a prominent Filipino psychiatrist was before the board for alleged boundary violation with a client, a medical student at a prominent Boston medical school. The student was suicidal and had already made multiple unsuccessful attempts to terminate his life prior to coming under the care of the psychiatrist. He had also allegedly skewered multiple lab animals and placed them on Bunsen burners, producing a stench of burnt flesh, which was witnessed by an incoming early morning lab staff, during the time he was under her care. Review of the lab security cameras identified the culprit as the student who had attempted suicides. The student committed suicide eventually when under her care, but before his death, he stole his psychiatrist's personal diary, in which she had documented her personal feelings of a conversion reaction she was suffering from, and for which she was receiving psychiatric help, and upon recommendation of her psychiatrist, she was documenting her feelings in her diary. The stolen diary was found in the personal possessions of the student after his suicide and the contents of the diary released to the media! Mustafa also learned from other psychiatrists working at the top Boston hospitals that a conversion reaction was not unusual with psychiatrists, and he was informed that she was dealing with her conversion appropriately.

There was much hue and cry about the case, and the case material had become first-page- news in all Boston and national newspapers for weeks on end. Newspapers sold well on sensationalism, and this was an opportunity they did not miss. The psychiatrist's home was sieged by newspaper and TV reporters, who camped outside her home. The verdict in the press for the psychiatrist was guilty without any chance of proving her innocence. The news sensationalized the unfortunate and tragic episode as a suicide resulting from a love affair between a treating Filipino psychiatrist and a Latino medical student at a most prestigious seat of medical studies in Boston! In the frenzy of the event, the board, in its ultimate decision, decided to hold its hearing at a Boston's historic public auditorium instead of what was usual and customary, in the privacy and sanctity of the hearing room at the office of the board. The verbose consumer board member an attorney cashed in the free publicity, as his name was in the papers almost daily. Mustafa was worried of a potential miscarriage of justice, and after reading the two boxes of materials over and over again and referencing and cross-referencing them, he was more aware of the case, and troubled by the board's conduct. But everyone else on the board was enjoying the limelight that the case had brought. The board chair at that time sidestepped as was his usual practice when confronted with high-profile cases, allowing the second in command, none other than the attorney who had betrayed the trust of some physicians when representing sleazy general contractors, to run the dog and pony show.

Not surprisingly, the psychiatrist succumbed to the pressures generated by daily media barrage, loss of privacy, and threats from the board and other consumer groups and surrendered her medical license, a travesty in Mustafa's mind, as she had shown good judgment in consulting a fellow psychiatrist when she developed a conversion and followed his recommendations. She had not stopped counseling the patient, as she and others in her profession believed that a transfer of care at the time would have triggered a suicidal reaction in the medical student, who had already made unsuccessful attempts in the past. So that brought an end to an illustrious career of a great psychiatrist. What an irony, Mustafa thought and wondered if it was because the psychiatrist was a Filipino? Whatever, the case, justice was not served he believed.

The board appointment was not based on academic excellence but on a random selection by the governor as a return favor and, in most times, to the party loyalists. When Mustafa was chairing the licensing committee, he received a call from the governor's staff to facilitate licensing of a non-American-university-trained physician, who was a wife of a strong campaign contributor and an owner of a huge financial empire built on gambling businesses based mostly in Las Vegas. Mustafa reviewed her application as a priority as instructed but found out that she did not fulfill the licensing requirements of the board, and she had not passed any of the American qualifying examinations, such as the USMLE or ECFMG, therefore not even eligible for a Massachusetts license. A short time thereafter, he received multiple calls from the Beacon Hill office whom he informed of the board requirements. To help with her application he volunteered to send the applicant a copy of the board requirements for a Massachusetts medical license and names of the preparatory schools for foreign doctors who desired to complete the USMLE. His action left him in disfavor on Beacon Hill, but he was at peace with himself, as he did not have any personal aspirations other than to do what was morally right. His aspiration was to be *Maryada Purushottam* (a person with an unshakeable morality) therefore the political pressure from Beacon Hill was a non-issue.

The three year service on the board came to an end, and in due course, he forgot all that he did with his time on the board, and the board forgot him too. He received no thank-you for the changes he brought to the board. On one far corner of his office hung a tall certificate of appointment to the board, the only material memory of his service to the board. The system of triage was adopted and continued, but he wondered if later FMG board members recused themselves from proceedings involving fellow FMG physicians?

CHAPTER 23

Return Home

Mustafa worked extremely hard in Boston, where he continued his research and buried himself in his orthopedic practice. He derived an unusual joy from his work; his love and commitment was evident from the letters of praise that adorned the walls of his offices, now three. He had won many awards from various academic institutions and medical associations and also awards for his global humanitarian work and contributions. In a way, he held an enviable position amongst academics and private practitioners alike, but he still felt unfulfilled.

He was not married not because he did not desire to marry but because he had not found the right person, no one matched CM or even come close. There were some fleeting moments when he dated gorgeous professional women, but none of the short affairs culminated in marriage. He still thought of CM with great fondness and often wondered of her whereabouts and her life; she was truly his first and only love. He had information mostly from friends that she had married an IFS officer, who was a very well-placed diplomat in some foreign land. She had written to him when he was in Africa, and over time, they took divergent paths and just drifted away not by choice but by circumstance and were now out of touch. He was looking for CM in every woman he dated—not at all fair to the women he dated, but that was the way it was. He made a very robust income, so he managed to accumulate substantial wealth in the two decades of a high-end, well-paying orthopedic practice. He was a loner who loved food, but he did not consume alcoholic drinks, therefore a bad company for his drinking physician friends for whom he was a designated driver most times because of his abstinence from alcohol.

His heart was still in Kashmir, and he dreamt of home more frequently and of the *shikaras* on Dal and Nagin Lakes; he had been to Banff and Jasper but could not stop thinking of the Kashmiri Mountains; Pangong, Hari Zoji, and his favorite Amarnath Purvath, all of which he had been on with his school friend Krishna eons ago. The appleblossoms, the *chalum* and *akhrot* trees, and the snowcapped Himalayas populated his dreams constantly. As the popular saying went, "Home is where the heart is," and his heart was truly far away from Boston in the valley of Kashmir. Boston, his adopted land, had given him all, but the call of his *matrabhumi* (motherland) was strong and irresistible, even now.

After one very severe Boston winter, he decided to return home to Kashmir. He had been away from Srinagar for more than thirty years. He flew in to New Delhi and thence took the highway, retracing the path he had taken when he escaped from Kashmir. The roads were much wider and easier to travel on, and the tunnel had been widened and took less time to cross, but the fresh crisp mountain air with the hint of eucalyptus and Himalayan pine had remained frozen in time. He closed his eyes for a little while and woke up surprised, as in his mind, he was still the twentysomething travelling his country. When his cab reached Srinagar, it was nightfall, so he checked in, in a hotel and slept the best night ever in at least past thirty years. He felt the energy of his homeland imbibe deep into him as he slept. The sounds of the *koyal* songs awakened him early; he walked to the bathroom and froze in front of the full-length bathroom mirror- he had forgotten that he had grayed much over time, but his piercing green eyes still looked the same. He took the hair off his face and held them back as in a ponytail and remarked, "Mustafa, you look like a hippie. Time to get a haircut." So after eating his usual four boiled egg whites, he walked outside the hotel and returned to the hotel to change some of his American money into Indian rupees, as he had run out of rupees during his trip. Back out on the street, he hailed a bicycle rickshaw and gave the rickshaw driver an address; his first stop was Krishna's house, only to find out that both of his parents had passed away, and Krishna was still in the United Kingdom where he had gone for postgraduate education and never returned to Kashmir. The shop was run by another Brahman, who supplied him all the information of the pandit family.

His next stop was his medical school, and he did not recognize it. The city had encroached to the walls of the medical campus, and there was a lot of filth laying around outside the walls and also within the campus. Even the lakes had more water chestnuts than when he left. The houseboats were unkempt and dirty. The people walked the streets like zombies, without smiles on their faces, so very unusual for the valley where the people were once unusually warm and friendly. The whole valley had transformed from a heaven on earth to this twentieth-century cement jungle, where people walked shoulder to shoulder without even noticing each other. The roads were congested, and the sewer ran out from broken pipes. His heart sank seeing the sorry state of his home.

He found his way to the barbershop he frequented when in Srinagar, where he met whom he thought was his barber and surprised how young he looked, only to find out that it was his son, who had taken over the family business. As was usual at a barbershop, he got all the gossip of the town, from the price of onions to the frequent visits of the army personnel and police. He also heard the barber refer to his old house as the *bhutiya ghar* (haunted house), as whoever ventured to live there vacated the house days after, as they all felt a presence in the house.

He decided to walk to the house and found it locked and in disrepair. He walked behind the house to find out that nature had reclaimed the back walls, where vegetation had grown over the fence and over the window railings all the way to the roof. He sat outside the house and said a silent prayer; thence, he walked to the graveyard to find an old fakir (beggar) who knew the location of all the graves. He first located his mother's grave, where he said his *Ziarat*, and next his sister's, which was nearby, and last his father's grave on the other side of the cemetery. He prayed at all the graves and promised to return with flowers and some garden tools to plant flowers around them. He actually felt great relief as he left the graveyard, as not being present for their burial had bothered him most of his adult life, and today he said prayers and asked their forgiveness and blessings as was usual in the Indian culture. He sat by the graves, reciting some poems from *Mind's Eye* and from Saadi's *Gulistan* and *Bustan* that he had memorized.

He hailed a cab and returned to the medical school, which too was in need of repair. He went to the library and visited his old lab, where he worked as a student. The students were still dressed in their pearly whites and moved around busily as overworked medical students did all over the world. He thought if he would displace these students to Harvard Medical, they would completely assimilate, as they looked no different in their state of well-intentioned hurry. All his professors were long gone; thirty years was a long period, and much was erased from the memory bank.

He returned to his hotel room very tired but felt great that he was back and visited his family and prayed at their graves. He slept well once again but dreamt that he was in his father's house; in his dream it was very well kept and grew a very fragrant garden in the back. In the front of the house, he saw a long line of people, some on crutches and some with a cane. In his dream, it seemed as if the folks were waiting their turn to see a doctor.

The next day, he passed by a garden shop, where he bought flowering shrubs and digging tools. When he returned to the graveyard, the fakir was still there, and as he talked with him, he found out that he lived in the graveyard. The fakir helped him plant the flowers and helped him water the plants. When Mustafa gave him some rupees, he put his hands together, refusing the gift, which reminded Mustafa of his own Kashmiri heritage of selfless giving. He promised that he would bring him food on his next visit as was customary in Kashmir.

He found his way to the city clerk's office to gather information on his father's house. He found out that it had been sold and resold many times, but the tenants just did not seem to last, and eventually, the owner had given up a hope of getting rid of the property. He managed to find the owner, who was too pleased to sell it to Mustafa for a few paisa on the rupee.

That night, he once again slept well and saw the same dream as in the previous night. He wondered why he bought the house in such an impulse but felt much at peace that he did. The whole journey back to Srinagar was a pilgrimage and tremendously fulfilling in a metaphysical way; he felt peace deep within him. Mustafa felt peace and quiet in his home town, a feeling he had forgotten in the rat race of his Boston living; he had forgotten his identity during his stay on foreign soil. After a few more days, he paid his hotel bill and retraced his path to New Delhi and back to Boston.

CHAPTER 24

Born-Again Indian

Once back in Boston, each night, he revisited the recurring dream of his old house and a line of sick people outside, waiting for their turn. A few months later, he decided to sell his house in Newton, a suburb of Massachusetts, give away some of his old belongings, and pack his bags to return to Kashmir permanently.

He was now in his fifties and had found his identity not in Boston but back in Kashmir, where his heart and soul frequently returned to the place he saw in his dreams.

Returning home was not without its share of problems. Sending shipments of medical equipment for a proposed clinic, transferring money, and setting up accounts in India took much effort, and completion of Indian formalities was not without frustration. During his previous visit, he had spent almost a full day at an Indian bank just cashing his traveler's checks, which required production of a passport and cross-checking of an ID, endless formalities, all traces of the past British occupancy of India. And now he was planning a transfer of a few million dollars, an act that would be inundated with typical Indian red tape and also lot of blue ink. Repatriation to India was much, much more difficult than emigrating; hands needed to be greased, an act not palatable to Mustafa, who wore a badge of highest morality, so he had his political contacts help smoothen the process.

But once he was on the plane in Newark, he felt a return of serenity and peace. His custom Armani seersucker[14] suit was perfectly creased and his Boston bow tie hand tied to perfection. He noticed the looks he got from both sexes when he was at the airport, and when he went to the restroom in the business lounge, one grey-haired man, who introduced himself as Solomon, commented on his immaculate look, salt-and-paper hair, well-trimmed full moustache, well-manicured fingernails, and piercing green eyes. He called him a *GQ* man after the famous men's fashion magazine out of Boston. He went on to add that he too loved dressing up, and as they reconnected in the plane, Mustafa found out that he was a multimillionaire, who also owned a professional ball team in Boston. They hit it off, and after the plane took off, he moved to the empty chair next to Mustafa. He told him that he was going to India to an ashram to rejuvenate himself after living a life on the extreme edge for more than thirty years. He said he had a faint, remote memory of Mustafa when he briefly consulted him for his sick wife, who was dying of cancer. Mustafa once again realized that all meetings in life were with a purpose, and a Hebrew saying of '*HaShem (God), Middah k'neged middah*' came to mind. The saying was depicted as a weighing balance (scale) and essentially meant that God HaShem rewarded one measure for measure and in simplistic U.S. terms meant 'what goes around comes around.' Indeed, there were no coincidental meetings; all meetings, he believed, were predestined.

In the eighteen hours of flight, the two gelled together and promised to stay in touch. Solomon promised that he would visit Mustafa in Kashmir someday, and Mustafa responded, "Insha Allah" (with the will of God). Solomon reminded Mustafa of the Somali gentleman, Mohamed, on his first travel out of India to Kenya. The two were an absolutely identical personality and thinking, except that Solomon was an ardent Jew and Mohamed a Muslim but both sons of Abraham and prayed in the name of Abraham and believed in one god. Mustafa mused, *Indeed both are sons of Abraham.*

His mind wavered. He remembered that the most sacred place in Islam, the *Kaaba*, was built by Ibrahim (Abraham) to worship the one god, Jehova. As he was thinking of Abraham's temple, his memory drew him to childhood stories told by his dad. He had said that *Kaaba* was the point to which direction all Muslims pray; the point was known as *qibla*. Even Hagar's search for water was ritualized and emulated by Muslims

14 Seersucker is a cotton material popularized by the colonial Brits in India. The actual definition of the cotton fabric is *sheer*, meaning milk or cream, and *shakar*, meaning crystalline sugar, as it is smooth as cream and textured like sugar.

as they walked and ran between the two hills *Safa* and *Marwah*. Some historians, he later found out, stated that the circumambulation around *Kaaba* was dedicated to *Hubal*, a Nabataean deity, and *Kaaba* had 360 idols, which probably represented each day of the Lunar year. The seven circumambulations were performed by naked men and partly clothed women, and the past circumambulation was believed to be a fertility ritual; however, today the ritual was carried out by Muslim men wearing two pieces of spun cotton, one covering the upper body and the other the lower body, and by women with their hair covered as a ritual for accessing the gates of heaven. And he wondered that all this started with Abraham building his temple for one god.

He wondered how the two people with the same origin, Ibrahim, were now at each other's throats mostly originating from the Balfour Declaration—which was essentially a favor to Lord Rothschild, an English Jewish baron—and reduced in a single-page letter written in November 1917, promising repatriation of the Jewish people to Palestine, which forced displacement of the Palestinians from their homeland, but its enforcement did not come to pass until after the Second World War and a latter commandeering of the territories known as the West Bank.

The flight landed in New Delhi at around 9:00 p.m.; Solomon slept most of the night after downing a few highballs and an aperitif after dinner. When he awakened, it was about an hour before touchdown. The visa forms had been distributed, and Mustafa completed his soon after and kept his travel friend's form in the pouch in front of his seat. Solomon snored a lot, mostly breathing from his mouth and making gargling noises prevalent with people with a large midriff. Mustafa thought that his decision to spend time in an ashram may most likely change his lifestyle and infuse some youth in him, which he had lost with his Western lifestyle, and the great the American past time of over eating. After visiting the restroom and brushing his teeth, Solomon showed some semblance of the man who had boarded the plane with him in Newark.

They exchanged contact information, and Mustafa offered to give him a ride to his hotel, as he had arranged for a vehicle to pick him up at the airport. After dropping off Solomon at his hotel, Mustafa went to Shangri-La, his usual hangout whilst in New Delhi. He had a meeting the next day with the health minister, who was a Kashmiri, and a meeting with the secretary of home affairs to discuss his plans to open a free clinic at his birthplace in Kashmir.

Mustafa was as always very organized and meticulous in all that he did. He had already prepared a brochure, outlining his plan for the clinic in Srinagar, and attached architectural plans of the proposed clinic and also information on the rehabilitation work already underway. The plan was in three phases, phase one being a basic outpatient clinic and in phase three a final progression to a fully accredited medical school. The meetings went off well, and the health minister was thrilled with the prospect of a second accredited medical school in his home state of Kashmir. Mustafa did not want to change his U.S. citizenship mostly for political reasons but got a residency card, allowing him same and equal privileges as an Indian citizen.

Once the ministry meetings were done, it was evening, and there was no time left to go to the bank, as banks in India closed shop much earlier than in the United States, and the machinery moved at a snail's pace, so he decided to dedicate the entire next day at the Hindustan Bank. He went in just as the bank opened its doors, and fortunately, he had arranged his meeting in advance through his connections at the ministry. The bank manager was very courteous and at the end of the meeting offered to take him to Khyber restaurant in a building adjacent to the bank that served a Kashmiri cuisine. Mustafa had requested a wire bank transfer of a million dollars as an initial transfer, some of which was placed in high-yield CDs, and he was surprised that the CDs in India promised a much higher return than in the United States, and the CD also offered him an ability to receive the principal and interest in dollars if he so desired, as he had retained his U.S. citizenship.

The day after the bank appointments, he met with an architect to discuss his short- and long-term plans. The architect had a sister firm in Srinagar, so the meeting was very productive. When he returned to the hotel, there was a message from Solomon, with a wish to meet him over lunch or dinner. Mustafa was planning to travel to Kashmir the next day but agreed to meet Solomon. He offered to meet him at India International Center, a place where most foreign Indian intellectuals boarded during their stay in New Delhi. He had stayed there when he launched his first book and when he was conducting readings in India, so he knew the place well and also subscribed to its platinum membership.

He chose the place as it was quiet, and the food was excellent and not challenging to the stomach. He had his driver pick Solomon at his hotel and pick him at Shangri-La on the way to India International Center. At dinner, he found out that the legendary tabla player Allah Rakha was performing at the center. A phone call later, he procured two front-row VIP seats for the performance. The artist as always outperformed himself and received a standing ovation at the end of his performance. Solomon was thumping now not because of the highballs downed but because of the great tabla performance. He was so impressed that Mustafa had a hard time getting him back to his hotel. It was past midnight when he dropped him to his door, and Mustafa was completely exhausted. He had travel planned for the morning. Most of his luggage went directly to Srinagar, and he was travelling with a single roll-away bag, which made packing and travelling easy.

Mustafa and his driver started back to Kashmir from New Delhi much before daybreak so as to make their way into the mountains and across the tunnel before nightfall. They stopped only to use the restroom and for food and drove at a remarkable speed. The Chevy truck, a replica of the Blazer, was well made for the mountain roads and the ride very comfortable. Mustafa sat in the front seat so as to keep a running conversation with the driver, as he was worried that the tedious journey would cause loss of attention. They reached Srinagar just before nightfall, and he checked into his hotel and gave some rupees to the driver for the night, as most Indian hotels had a more subsidized food and lodging not too far away from the hotel for the drivers.

Mustafa woke up very refreshed just as the *Koyal* started its cooing. When he came to the lounge, the driver was already there, waiting for him. He was meeting with a construction crew at his old house, which by now looked much better as all the excessive vegetation was removed, with the garden dug up and replanted to his specification. He had the preliminary plans he had carried with him, and he was surprised that the foreman had already in his possession a copy of the plans. He intended to keep and preserve the structure of the original house much for sentimental reasons, as it represented his heritage, and all the additions would be done on adjacent land. Much of the house was already rehabilitated and upgraded for comfort and practicality; the patio where his parents sat after the evening prayers was redone to its old specification, just the way it used to be thirty or so years ago. Mustafa was indeed surprised with the care and love by which the rehabilitation was carried out and at a fraction of the cost compared to the Unites States. The house was now habitable.

They had also prepared the room where his sister was shot as a reception-cum-waiting room and the room where his dad was shot into an examination and treatment room. The kitchen was upgraded to introduce all the modern amenities, and his and his sister's bedrooms were both rehabbed as modern bedrooms. He had decided to occupy his old room, and his sister's room would suffice as a guest bedroom. The house was move-in ready, but Mustafa was not ready yet, as there was too much pain that needed days of healing before he could move in.

He started seeing patients in a few days but continued living in his hotel room, kind of living from a suitcase like a tourist. As days progressed, he rested for siesta in the house and worked into late hours of the night, as the trickle of patients was incessant. He had kept an open wood box in the waiting room for voluntary donations, as he did not charge a fee to his patients. As days passed, he felt more comfortable in the house; and so one weekend, he decided to make a final move to it.

The night he moved in, he felt extremely comfortable; he felt the warmth and love of his old home. The dreams that troubled him in the days when he was in the United States vacated, and he slept in peace and much comfort. One Friday night, as he slept just after the evening prayers, he heard and saw his dad as if in real life. He touched his shoulder and thanked him for his return home and for realizing his dream of serving Kashmir. He awakened from this very realistic, dreamlike meeting with his dad, ate his supper, and went into deep and peaceful sleep. He knew deep within him that he was home, and his decision to return to Kashmir was a right decision.

He was still an *Armani-man* dressed in sharp custom suits and French cuffed shirts, a complete aberration of the country and place he lived in. As he continued working in the clinic, his coat jacket sat on his chair and the cuffs rolled up to the elbow, which was more practical, as he was washing his hands constantly and caring for very sick patients. As time went by, the jacket remained constantly on the chair, and the French cuffed shirts were replaced by short-sleeved shirts and his Armani wool pants for white cotton pants. A transition was happening. However, he was not a frequent visitor to his barber, and his hair was getting longer, so for practical reasons, he tied his hair back in a ponytail. Even with a ponytail, his sharp features, deep green eyes, and now silver-grey hair and well-proportioned body made him look like a movie star, but he aspired to live the life of his personal hero, Albert Schweitzer.

Construction work continued as planned, and the clinic was taking shape. It was designed like any high-end outpatient clinic in Boston. All the equipment made its way from Boston either as a donation of surplus hospital equipment or purchased by him prior to his departure. Patient care was outcome based at the clinic, which offered personalized and compassionate care to all. For the public, the name of the house soon changed from *bhutiya ghar* (haunted house) to Dr. Sheikh's clinic, and people thronged outside, awaiting their turn, sometimes until late evening.

Many arrived at the wee hours of the morning, traveling down the rabbit paths down the neighboring mountains and hills; some walked for hours to come to the clinic. Each left feeling the warmth and kindness of personalized care they received at the clinic. Some mothers from the community had approached him with an offer of assistance, which was welcome, as he was inundated with work. As time went by, nurses from the nearby hospital volunteered their time at the clinic. The word was spreading much too quickly, as most patients related, "Dr. Sahib has *jadoo* in his hands." (He has magic in his hands.) Some even exaggerated that his mere touch was enough to cure illnesses and that one did not even have to take any medicine. He was becoming a local legend; people even stopped on the roadside to wish him, and when he walked into a grocery store or any of the local shops, crowds parted to allow him to walk ahead as if he walked on water. The storekeepers refused to charge him for things he bought, which embarrassed him tremendously, so he stopped going to the shops and instead sent emissaries to buy for him, and after the first few times, the shopkeepers identified them as his emissaries and stopped charging. The shopkeepers were pretty smart and kept a mental note of his buying habits, so they recognized the destination where the goods were going to. Some even went to the extent of delivering the groceries each month to his doorsteps. Families and friends of patients started arriving with cooked delicacies, dried and fresh fruits from their orchards, and vegetables, most of the time more than what Mustafa could ever consume, and when he refused to accept, they were hurt, and they falsely believed that the doctor did not appreciate their simple gifts, which was truly not the case. The refusal created even a bigger problem, as now the patients arrived with even more food. He talked to a wise local man, who advised to dedicate an unlocked room where his well-wishers could leave their gifts on shelves and also recommended that he place an old refrigerator in the room to store perishables. The wise man hoped that, over time, the well-wishers would realize that they were bringing in too much food and fruit, and they may stop or, even better, pick up off the shelves what they needed so that a banana farmer would leave bananas and pick up apples and so on and so forth. He thought that the solution was simple, practical, and doable, and he had just the room for it. In the first week, nobody picked any of the gifts, but as the excess food started spoiling, they realized that they were giving too much, and the *doctorsaheb* was unable to eat all that they brought, so some started picking up excess stuff mainly to avoid spoilage, but also, a barter system started; thereby, a potato farmer left potatoes and picked up okra or other vegetables that overpopulated the shelves.

By now Mustafa had completely assimilated and readopted his original Kashmiri culture; his French cuffed shirts and his smartly tailored suits were now a fixture in his closet, a reminder of his past. His attire was now more practical—a white Kashmiri kurta with removable buttons, a white or cream trousers, and a cloth belt. He still continued to wear shoes mostly for convenience but removed them before he entered the bedroom, mostly as he said his prayers in the room where his dad was shot by the mujahideen whilst on his prayer mat. To him, life had taken a better shape, as he was now in tune and harmony with his own elements.

Each morning at dusk, he awakened to recite prayers and went for a long walk thereafter on the shores of the lake and at times across the bridge. During his long walks, he carried a cane, which he had found in his dad's house, not out of necessity but because it made him feel connected to his dad.

Each day was very fulfilling for him; he was given more in return than he was able to give back. He had believed that, in a few years, he would have run out of the cash he had accumulated in his years in Boston, but he did not anticipate the giving power of the people he treated and the gratitude of the community at large. The wood donation box was always full, and at times, people left their gold jewelry in the box. There was so much left in the box that he did not need to subsidize the clinic with personal money; it had taken off and now on autopilot.

CHAPTER 25

Sadhu Solomon

The clinic expanded sideways with additional rooms, where nurses and social workers instructed patients on health and hygiene. The well-baby clinic was always full, and the vaccinations were available for free, mostly supplied by an Indian public health grant. Mustafa had also started doing basic outpatient orthopedic procedures and he trained a crew of young medical students to assist and also carry out simple procedures, such as suturing wounds, incision, and drainage of abscesses. He had a basic laboratory, which measured serum and blood chemistry using spectrometric analysis by machines gifted to his clinic by well-wishers abroad and in India. He also had an X-ray machine, which was a God sent, as he was able to reduce and treat fractures at the clinic. In Boston, he had used intravenous medications for conscious sedation, which he adopted at his clinic in Srinagar. His clinic was given an electronic photometric machine, which measured the blood pressure, pulse, and blood oxygen when he administered the intravenous sedation. He had trained a group of high school students, nurses, and aides in basic CPR, so the clinic's operational safety followed the highest standards and at most times was better than most other local outpatient medical facilities in Kashmir.

One Friday, just as he completed his evening (Magrib) prayers, his helper and friend Rammu walked in to announce that there was a sadhu waiting outside, who refused to come in. "He had a few followers with him. The rumor was that he had walked all the way from Haridwar for your darshan, and he will not eat, drink, or rest until he has seen you."

Mustafa wondered, *a sadhu from Hardwar, and he had walked eight hundred kilometers to see him. Who could that be?* He quickly changed his prayer clothes, kissed the *Yassin* that he was reading, and rolled up his prayer mat, placing it on his bed. He walked outside to find not less than thirty *bikhshus* (self-acknowledged beggars) all in saffron robes, most of them in their twenties. As he walked to them, the group parted, revealing their guru, a white man fit and trim, wearing a saffron wrap around robe of a *Bikshu* and carrying a *lota* and begging bowel. He hesitated, as the person had a distant resemblance of Solomon, his fellow passenger on the flight from Newark. However, he looked much younger, and fit and trim and had a tremendous radiance on his face.

Indeed, it was Solomon, and he had managed to turn the clock backwards; he had regained youth, vigor, and vitality. The two embraced each other for a very long time, and Mustafa let his surprise out, "What happened to you, Solomon?" he said, "You have turned the clock at least twenty years backwards." His friend replied that he had found the right and only reason for human existence at the ashram and later proceeded to spend a year in Gangotri, meditating in an absolute quiet seclusion. When he walked off the mountain, he was rejuvenated, and he had adsorbed so much knowledge of human existence during his meditative months, something he would not have gained during an eternity of his materialistic existence in Boston.

Solomon, his Jewish friend, said that he was a born-again Indian— he was a *Bikshu* without any need, malice, anger, or want; he was living a perfectly balanced life, living in nature and with nature, without any internal or external conflicts. He said he was one with the cosmos now. Mustafa noticed a distinct halo around his head, which radiated in the dimly lit hallway as they entered the house. He wondered if the halo was real or just his imagination.

When they reached the living room, Solomon refused to sit on the padded chair but squatted cross-legged on the floor without even a slight hesitation. Mustafa tried to do the same but had to grab the chair to get to the floor, and he felt the power of Solomon's hand, which somehow took away the pain he felt in his knees as he squatted. Solomon asked Mustafa to close his eyes, and he kept his right palm on his forehead and the left on his chest, just at the level of his heart. Mustafa felt a searing heat emanate from his palms and almost lost consciousness, and when he came through, he was sitting just like Solomon squarely in a perfect lotus position, something that he was not able to do even though he stretched each day for an hour or so. Solomon smiled as if knowing what he was thinking. He said, "I have come to you to repay your kindness and guidance. If it were not for you, I would have taken the next flight out of Delhi, but I proceeded to the ashram, and now here I am, a changed man." He said that he was very powerful in Boston with all his money and powerful only because of his money, but here, he was powerful without even a penny to his name because of his inner strength. He said that he ate what people gave him, and in return, he brought peace to the path he walked and to the people he touched. God had given him salvation, he volunteered.

"Moses," Mustafa remarked, and Solomon smiled the most blissful smile, which was full of love and understanding.

He said, "I am just a plain old *Bikshu* without an ego, I have no possession and no destination, and I just walk the path he guides me to. Forget me, what happened to you, Mr. *GQ*? You are transformed too. In all the towns and villages I crossed to reach your house, everyone told me that you are the incarnate of the prophet. You care for people, rich or poor, blind or seeing, without a want in return. My friend, you are one of a kind, and it is my pleasure to meet you again, and I can tell you that there is more pleasure in meeting you than even what Stanley may have felt when he met Livingston in Africa."

Mustafa asked him if he would like to eat something, and his visitor folded his hands, saying, "I do not eat after sunset." Mustafa excused himself to see to it that the other *bikhshus* were all taken care of, only to find out that they had all retired in the courtyard. He came to escort Solomon to the second bedroom, and he thanked him. When he returned to the room, he found Solomon sleeping on the floor with a roll of his folded robe supporting his neck, and he looked very peaceful in his state of absolute sedation.

When Mustafa awakened for his *Fajar* (morning) prayers, Solomon was already out of the room and sitting outside in deep meditation, facing east, where the sun was to rise at daybreak. He completed his prayers and joined Solomon in a perfect lotus position. The two sat for a long time, but as they were sitting down, there was a conversation going on between the two without a word spoken. In trance, Solomon told Mustafa that his family was at peace and that they were pleased that he had returned to Srinagar. He told him that his sister appreciated that he thought of her each time he ate *Zarda*, her favorite desert, and that she was happy and free of any care, and she liked the flowers he had planted at her grave, especially the dark pink ones. He told him of his mother and father, transmitting terabytes of information in quick succession without a spoken word. Mustafa was truly amazed that a person he had met randomly on flight was now transmitting thoughts and communicating in rapid succession information that he had not even shared with any other living soul. When Solomon came out of his meditative trance, Mustafa looked much rested and divinely peaceful as if a great weight was off his shoulders; he bid Mustafa good-bye but promised to return someday soon.

When Mustafa asked him where he was going to, his answer was simple, "Wherever the road takes me." When Mustafa requested to allow him to walk with him a short distance, he said, "Your destiny is here and mine at an infinite place." He hugged Mustafa, and he said, "Assalamu' alaikum Warahamatullahi Wabarakatuh" (Best wishes to you. May God bring you his choicest blessings?) He spoke in perfect Arabic, leaving Mustafa wonderstruck with his complete transformation. His friend had truly transcended to a higher being.

After Solomon left, Rammu approached him to inform him that Solomon was rewarded by *Shiv Avatar* during his meditation in Gangotri, where he did not eat or drink for a month and remained in a complete trance during the time. He said that his followers believed he had been blessed by *Shiv Avatar* and that he was able to communicate without speaking and was able to cure the sick with just a touch of his hands. What he had experienced over the past eighteen hours was difficult to explain on the basis of science. But he knew for sure that he communicated with him in trance, giving him very personal information of his family, who had died a very violent death a long time ago.

When he entered his bedroom, he found an envelope, which contained a check of one hundred thousand dollars payable to the Sheikh Foundation and a letter. The letter was short and written in long hand. It said, "I have come to you to help you with your outreach program. I believe you should invest the money in a mobile clinic that will allow your clinic personnel to travel to distant villages. Go there, and disseminate simple and much needed information on disease prevention. Mothers are feeding their children infant formula when mother's breast milk is the best nutrition for the infant." And then he realized that Solomon's visit was not a coincidence; he had read his innermost thoughts from miles away and arrived in Kashmir just to offer him a helping hand.

Chapter 26

Young British Apprentice

A few days had passed following Solomon's visit to his clinic when he received a fat manila envelope containing information on a Shalini Sharma, MD, a recent summa cum laude medical graduate of the prestigious London University, who wanted to work in his clinic for a year. Her credentials were excellent, but Mustafa was not very sure if Srinagar was a proper place for a single female and he was also concerned as he was not married, and her presence, he believed, may give the public something to talk about, so he wrote her a polite thank-you note and an apology for not having an opening to suit her qualifications.

About a month after his letter to Shalini Sharma, Rammu came to his examination room to let him know that a young *Maam* (a foreign woman) was waiting for him in the waiting room. After taking care of his patient, he walked to the waiting room, where he found a young female wearing a Punjabi *kurta salwar*, reading his degrees and commendations mounted on the walls of the waiting room. Her back was turned to him; she was quite tall, about five feet, ten inches, and carried herself well. On an adjacent seat rested a midsized suitcase with plane tags hanging from its handle. He stepped in and said, "May I help you?" and she turned around.

Mustafa was speechless; standing in front of him was a younger and taller spitting image of CM. He just continued staring at her as if in trance. She came forward, saying, "I am Shalini Sharma, and yes, I did receive your denial letter, but I decided to visit you and personally convince you to give me an opportunity to work in your clinic for at least a year, and if I fail your expectations, I will leave. Sir, I will only need a small stipend and a simple lodging if possible. I am independent and very reliable." Her voice was that of CM. He was shaken by the tremendous resemblance—her poise and her affirmative attitude, a signature of CM he knew from many years ago. Mustafa was obviously shaken, he was tongue-tied, and did not know how to respond to this very forthright carbon copy of CM, so he selected a quick exit. He said in a single breath, "I am busy at this time, but let us explore possibilities at lunch. Rammu will take you to the guest room so that you may freshen up, and we will have lunch at noon—sharp. Please let Rammu know what you would like for lunch."

He was not able to focus on his patients thereafter, and he kept looking at the wall clock to see if it was already time. At exactly noon, he walked across the clinic to his house, and as he entered the dining room, Shalini was waiting. He could not believe how Shalini looked like CM. Shalini was an easy conversation partner, and she loved to talk. She volunteered her history; her mum was a doctor, and she lost her father in Dubai. Her father was an Indian Foreign Service (IFS) officer, working at the consulate in Dubai, where he died when she was a little girl. He did not pursue the topic but asked her about her mother. She had trained at Lady Hardinge in New Delhi but moved to London after her dad's death, where she completed a doctorate in biostatistics. She worked in a hospital-based job in London, where she was still working a few days a week. Shalini went on that she had read of the clinic and read some of his publications in the *Lancet, Journal of Tropical Medicine*, and *AMA Journal*. Her desire to work in Kashmir was more instinctive and compelling, as her mother had talked about Kashmir often and with great passion. Mustafa could not reject the young physician, especially after hearing her story and, of course, her strong resemblance to CM, and her story removed any doubt of her relationship to CM.

Mustafa told her that she may live in the adjacent room, which had an attached bathroom, allowing the required privacy. Mustafa asked Rammu to move his meager belongings out of the house to a room adjacent to the clinic, which he believed would be sufficient for him. The morning after, when he walked to the clinic, he was surprised to see that Shalini had already arrived and had not only oriented and introduced herself to the staff but also gone over the patient charts and rearranged the equipment to expedite processing of patients. Dr. Sharma, as she was known in the clinic, was a people person and loved cooking too. During the afternoon break, she went home and baked a cake and made *zarda*. When Mustafa arrived for dinner, she complained that she was not happy that he had moved to a room in the clinic and that she would move to the clinic bedroom instead. Mustafa told her that the house offered greater security for a single woman; therefore, it was imperative that she lived in the house. After dinner, she brought out the cake she had baked and also the *zarda*. He was surprised that a Punjabi girl brought up in the United Kingdom knew how to make *zarda*, a Kashmiri specialty. But she explained that *zarda* was her mother's favorite dessert, and as it was her mother's birthday, she had also baked a cake. Mustafa had not seen CM for more than three decades and forgotten her birthday completely. He wondered what other coincidences providence had in store for him.

Shalini was a great addition to the clinic; she picked up the Kashmiri dialect and spoke Hindi fairly well but with a British accent at the onset. Patients loved the new lady doctor, and her ability to diagnose and treat tropical diseases was excellent. She also helped in the fracture clinic. She was getting to be an expert in making casts out of strips of cotton bandages impregnated with plaster of Paris and also with X-ray diagnosis of fractures.

The mobile clinic arrived just as Dr. Sharma was working in full swing at the clinic. The clinic was growing by leaps and bounds, and the mobile extension of the clinic allowed doctors and health-care workers to go to remote villages all over the state. Some patients also started coming from adjacent states and, he believed, from across the border, as the border with Pakistan was quite porous. He was surprised to see some Xinjiang Chinese Muslim patients who walked the old silk route.

Dr. Sharma took charge of the mobile clinic and travelled to villages, training mothers in basic hygiene, especially related to infant care. Infant mortality was high in Kashmir, as many children suffered from marasmus—a protein malnutrition—and also kwashiorkor, which gave the babies red hair and an emaciated look. The infant formula industry had brainwashed mothers with a barrage of well-baby advertisement of their product; however, a can of baby powder milk cost so much that mothers watered down the formula for the can to last at least a month instead of a week as the can was intended to be used. This paradox was difficult to overcome, so Dr. Sharma attacked it from a different angle—prevention of disease that resulted from the use of the formula. She talked about the disease-preventing quality of mother's milk; there was no need for baby-bottles or washing them, as mother's milk was dispensed from a natural container, the mother's breast. It eliminated a need to warm as in formula milk, as it was optimally warm at body temperature. It did not need to be mixed with water, which removed the possibility of contamination with protozoa, and saved so much money each month too. She additionally supplied the information that mothers who breast-fed children had a lesser incidence of back-to-back pregnancy during the time they were breast-feeding. The latter information of back-to-back pregnancy drove home the message, as most mothers did not want to contend with another pregnancy until the child was old enough to care for himself.

Dr. Sharma also collected vaccination data from mothers and entered it on an Excel spreadsheet on the clinic computers and also backed up all the data to an external drive and her personal computer for safety. She compiled the data for a presentation to UNICEF and WHO, as accurate data was scarce, and the available national data was mostly falsified. She made slides of river and well water to identify contaminants and protozoal infestations, which she routinely projected during her health information talks to the villagers. She boiled the water to show families how it killed the protozoan and also talked of the signs and symptoms of early detection of protozoal infections. She trained local mothers to relay her talk to other mothers and made them a part of the preventive campaign, so the mothers disseminated the message of healthy living to other villagers. Dr. Sharma was able to achieve in a short time what the local government had failed to achieve over a long haul of many years and at a fraction of the cost. All in all, she was a great asset to the clinic and in a short while she was indispensable.

One day, about eight months in the clinic, she asked Mustafa if it would be fine if her mother travelled to Kashmir for a visit. The request took Mustafa completely by surprise, and he responded, "That ought to be completely fine, as she could live in the house with you and as long as she wishes." Shalini got up and spontaneously hugged him, saying, "Mustafa, Dr. Uncle, Abbu you are the best. She will love you, I assure you, as she is just like you, very compassionate and caring and very organized. She is called the data wiz at her hospital. You may not even let her go back to London." Mustafa knew all of CM's attributes only too well, but how was he going to be able to face CM after so many years and how would she react, were unanswered questions. He thought about it and just resigned to allow destiny take its course.

CHAPTER 27

CM

Spring in Kashmir

Spring in the valley of Kashmir was always remarkable, with wild flowers sprouting everywhere. But this year, the spring was even more exuberant. An excess of winter's snow and early spring rain helped rejuvenate the valley with great vigor. The natural scent of the wild flowers and spring blossoms was truly heady this spring. Children with rosy cheeks played in the parks and the streets.

The grass was emerald green, and the geese had returned to the Dal and Nigeen Lakes. The shikaras adorned colorful canopies and the shells repainted for the season in a rainbow of colors. Shikaras laden with freshly cut flowers and fruit travelled on both lakes and all the interconnecting waterways. The shops catalogued new merchandise; the carpet weavers had worked over the whole of winter, weaving newly spun silk and wool carpets, and new cloth and shawls were sewn.

The clinic was running at a more than full capacity; the mobile clinic was now making daily day trips to villages. Dr. Sharma had started wearing Kashmiri garb, and even the color on her cheeks matched the locals. She had picked up Kashtawari, Poguli, and some Rambani - Kashmiri local dialects. In the early days, when she had just joined the clinic, she called Mustafa as Dr. Mustafa with an English accent to the first four letters and later as Dr. Sheikh, followed by Dr. Mustafa Uncle, and now she called him Abbu, just like everyone else in the clinic. Interestingly, a father was lovingly referred to as Abbu, short for *Abbu Jaan*. They referred to Mustafa as Abbu, as he was a father figure at the clinic, and even his patients and some of the citizenry of the town called him the Abbu. Someone once said that he was *Jag Abbu,* a father of their world. Shalini's calling him Abbu had great and deep meaning, as he had always dreamed of having a daughter like her—caring, poised, and respectful and a perfect daughter in every which way a father could ever wish. He considered himself very lucky.

Dr. Sharma made frequent trips to the town in the following weeks, buying *daries,* quilts, and carpets, as well as Kashmiri stone crockery in preparation for her mother's arrival. She had learned to cook almost all Kashmiri delicacies to perfection from Abdul Razaak, the *boty* (cook). AR, as she called him as a short form of his name, loved to teach Dr. Sharma cooking. She had shortened many names; even Mustafa Sheikh was now Abbu. There were times when Mustafa was inundated with work and felt tired and defeated, and she would sit with him and cheer him up, with stories of her childhood and at times of her mother, who was a mother and a father rolled into one. The relationship between the two was symbiotic, as Mustafa did not have a daughter, and she was not able to enjoy the love of a father, as her father had passed away when she was just a little child; therefore, their relationship was evolving into a father-daughter relationship. She could make Mustafa smile even after a tough and exhausting day, and he loved to listen to her adventures when she travelled to the villages. Mustafa had assigned Sikander, a six-foot-two-inch-tall

Pathan, as an escort to accompany her to the villages during clinic visits and even when she went out shopping so that no harm came to her.

The house was now about ready to receive their guest. Shalini had bought a bus ticket, but Mustafa convinced her to fly to Delhi and fly back with her mother. Mustafa bought the tickets for both, and she hugged him, saying, "Abbu, you are too good to me." Mustafa left Shalini at the airport very early that morning and waited until the plane had taken off before he left; he felt sad that she would be away for the day.

Once he returned to the clinic, his work took over, and he did not even realize that it was time to go to the airport to pick up the mother and daughter until Rammu came by to the clinic to remind him of it. Rammu started off for the airport on his bicycle whilst Mustafa went in the clinic car. They crossed paths just outside the airport, and by the time the car was parked, Rammu was already standing outside the arrival gate.

Mum and daughter came out together hand in hand, and as Shalini saw Mustafa, she dragged her mother towards him; Shalini hugged him and said, "This is my wonderful Abbu." CM froze in her track as she recognized the piercing green eyes, but he had grown older, with a salt-and-pepper head of hair, a push-broom white moustache, and a little fat in his midriff. She came towards him and shook his hand, saying, "Shalu has been writing to me about you, referring to you as Abbu in every letter. I am so glad she found you." In a few words, CM told much, but that was CM; she could convey a lot of meaning by just the glitter in her eyes and a quick smile. She had aged but still very graceful; her hair was jet-black but showed a few grey roots, which escaped the coloring dye. She had smile wrinkles on either side of her lips, which wore well on her face. The twinkle in her eyes told stories of past mischief.

Rammu with Sikander, who also had arrived at the airport, helped pick up and bring the bags to the car, and as the two were taking the bags, Shalini turned to her mum, saying, "Abbu has this big guy accompany me everywhere I go." Looking towards Sikander, who nodded in submission.

The bags were loaded in the dickey of the car and tied down, and Mustafa sat in front with the driver, and the mother and daughter sat comfortably in the bench backseat. CM searched for the seat belt, and Shalu said, "Mum, you are not in London. There are no seat belts in the backseat here in India and definitely not in Srinagar. And, Mum, you should see how they ride the auto-rickshaw here. It is outrageous, absolutely no protection." She informed her mother that the motorcycle was the most popular family conveyance, where sometimes four family members travelled on one motorcycle.

They jostled as the car made to the main road, and the engine misfired, and CM ducked down, and Shalini said, "Mum that was a backfiring of our car. You have been away from India too long. Do not worry, you are safe here." The banter between the two was nonstop, but it was refreshing to see how close the two were.

The car slowed as they entered the clinic; Mustafa had described his home a million times when they were friends in Delhi, but CM never realized that it would be so pretty. In the last rays of the sun, she could see the colorful bougainvillea flanking the clinic, and the smell of *Raat ki rani* filled the air. CM took a deep breath as if to fill her lungs with the pleasant fragrance of the evening jasmine. She stepped out of the car and noticed that there was a floor mat of fresh flowers, and as she walked to the house, petals of roses fell from a canopy overhead. Shalini knew that she had not made all these arrangements, so it had to be Abbu. *How very thoughtful,* she mused. Mustafa stood outside and then disappeared into the shadows and back to his room behind the clinic. Shalu showed her mother her room and was surprised to see rose petals on the bed. The quilt she had bought was neatly placed over a soft cotton bedsheet. Every detail was perfect, and she knew that Rammu was not capable of such a perfect reception; it had to be Abbu. After freshening up, they gathered in the dining room, but Mustafa was not at his usual place at the head of the table. Shalu asked Rammu why Abbu did not join them, and he said that Abbu was tired, as he had to handle a lot of patients alone when she was away, so he excused himself to retire early.

The dinner was exemplary Kashmiri cuisine and served in the stone crockery, which Shalini had bought with much love. Everything was just exquisite. Shalu joked with her mother that her welcome was that of a new bride entering her *sasural* (husband's house), just like in the Indian movies on DTV she watched in London. But Shalini felt sad that Abbu did not join them for dinner; after all, she had every dinner for the past so many months with Abbu, and this was the first dinner without him on the table, so it felt strange.

After her mother was tucked in, Shalu snuck outside to the bedroom behind the clinic. The light was still on, so she peered in through the window; Abbu was still reading as was his habit. She knocked on the door and entered the room. She hugged him, saying, "Abbu, this was the first time I had dinner alone."

Mustafa corrected her, "Not so, you were with CM," and corrected himself quickly after the Freudian slip, "I mean your mum. I thought it fit to give you two private time." She sat for a little while chatting, hugged him, and said, "Kuddha Hafiz." (God be with you) "Sleep well. I will make up tomorrow for the lost day."

Mustafa joined them at the main house for a quick breakfast and excused himself to go to the clinic, as patients had already thronged outside. Dr. Sharma joined him, and in a little while, CM joined them. She started taking patient history and triaging patients so that the more serious ones got immediate care, and the less urgent ones she counseled. The day passed very quickly, and Mustafa noticed his patients were triaged more efficiently than on the previous day. When he left the clinic, CM was still going over the intake forms and talking to the staff. She spent the remaining evening revising the intake form and other forms. She requested the reception staff to meet her at seven the next morning to discuss changes that may help with efficiency. At dinner, she discussed the suggested revision to the intake form and methods to improve efficiency at the clinic. Mustafa smiled and mused, knowing CM's modus operandi, efficient as before.

After dinner, Mustafa sat on the *jhula*, a large swing that is usually in the *angan*, a central vestibule or courtyard of most Indian homes, but this one was in the garden next to the jasmine bushes. As CM started walking towards the swing, Shalu held her arm, saying, "Abbu enjoys his private time." CM nodded and said with motherly assurance, "That is fine. I want to talk to him about tomorrow, and this is the best opportunity." She went to the swing and sat next to him.

"Musu, it has been a very long time. How are you?" she asked.

Mustafa said, "I have not been called that since the last time we were together in Bombay, when I was about to leave for Africa. God knows how good it sounds." They talked, telling each other's life's story. She told him of her husband and how he died, and he told her about his life after he left Bombay, his stay in Africa, his acceptance to Harvard and the orthopedic residency, his practice in Boston, and his return to Kashmir.

She asked, "But you never married?"

"No, I did not find the perfect woman. Everyone paled in comparison to my CM," he said.

"How sweet" she said, spontaneously moving sideways, resting her head on his shoulder, "Yes, and I have always missed you. If I had known that you were here, I would have come over without a second thought."

They talked for a long time, and she moved away as she saw the house door open and Shalu walking towards them. Shalini said, "Abbu, I told you, you would love my mum. She is a wonderful person, isn't she? She has already started making changes in our clinic." Mustafa felt good that Shalini felt that she was an integral part of the clinic. The next day, Shalini was scheduled to go with the mobile clinic, and CM had arranged to meet with the reception staff to implement changes, and she had already structured a questionnaire to assist collection of patients' demographic and disease data.

Shalini left with the mobile clinic, with Sikander not far behind. Shalini's being away gave the two private time to catch up on lost time. Between patients, they teased each other just as they had done in New Delhi. Much time had lapsed, but their love for each other had stood the test of time. Even now when she accidently bumped against him, she felt the electricity that had doused in the past thirty-plus years. Too many years had passed, and he believed that it was impossible to think of a life together. She teased, "Shalu is calling you Abbu. Was it your idea?"

He said, "No, you may have noticed that everyone calls me Abbu at the clinic, and now even when I go shopping, the shopkeepers call me Abbu, so she started calling me Abbu too."

Together, they must have seen and treated more than a hundred patients. The triage implemented that day seemed to bring in efficiency in the process, and the patients were pleased. By the time Shalini returned, she was just in time for dinner. Her mother had told Rammu to have the boty make *dhal and bhat,* Shalini's most favorite food. Shalini excused herself when she saw what was on the table and returned with a *limbu* (lime) from the garden. "Mum," she said, "Abbu has the best *limbus and mirch* (chili peppers) in the garden." She put a large helping of *bhat* on her plate and poured *dhal* over it; she then squeezed half the *limbu* on it, mixed the *bhat* and *dhal,* and spooned her way to an absolute bliss. CM looked at Mustafa and smiled. "I told you she loves *dhal and bhat.*" CM did exactly as Shalu, squeezing the remaining half of the *limbu*. Mustafa asked Rammu to pick a few more *limbu* and *mirch* from the garden. He reached for the *kofta* curry but decided to try the specialty of the night, *dhal and bhat* topped with *limbu* juice.

After dinner, there was a choice of *kheer* and *zarda*. Instinctively, Shalu reached for the *zarda* and mumbled a silent prayer for those who had passed on as was the routine in the house. CM loved *kheer* but had *zarda* instead. If anybody had walked in, they would have thought that this was a model Kashmiri family, as Mustafa was wearing his Kashmiri garb, and both mother and daughter had *kurta salwar* and a *pashmina* shawl, as the evening chill had set in.

After dinner, Rammu lit the fireplace, and the three sat in front of the fire, enjoying the glow and smell of walnut wood burning. CM looked at Shalu, and she said, "Shalu, Mustafa and I were very good friends when in college in Delhi. We lost touch when he left for Kenya and later for the United States."

Shalu said, "Mum, you never told me of Abbu."

CM said, "There was never an occasion to talk about my college life."

So Shalu let the cat out of the bag; she said, "Mum, I found your old diary when I returned home after graduating from medical school, so I started a Google search on Mustafa Sheikh, which led me to his whereabouts in Kashmir. I kept my Google search alive, and after my internship, I decided to apply for a job he had advertised in the *British Medical Journal*. I needed and yearned for a field experience, so I applied for the job and arrived at his doorstep, even though he did not respond to my application and several letters of inquiry. I needed to know the person my mum loved and respected, and after coming to Kashmir, I had a firsthand opportunity of knowing Abbu better." Both CM and Mustafa were taken aback by the story of this Cupid. She went on to say, "Mum, both of you need to make up for the lost time now that you are together. Stay here in Kashmir as long as you wish, and if you two still have a place for each other, you may want to get married and spend whatever time is left, together." Mustafa looked at CM, but both did not say a word. That night, when Mustafa sat on the swing, CM did not join him, as she had been outsmarted by her daughter. She went to bed but could not quite fall asleep. Mustafa sat on the swing, expecting CM to join him, but she did not.

Next morning at the clinic, the work went on without a mention of the discussion of the previous night. The discussion did not come up for several days thereafter, and then one afternoon, Mustafa asked CM if she liked being in Kashmir, and she replied, "Very much. I enjoy the people, and I am glad to be able to help."

"But is that all that you feel, CM? Honestly, I have never stopped loving you, and that is my reason for not marrying," he said. She looked at him, saying, "I am sorry. I did not show the same commitment, but you must know that I never stopped loving you, and I even told my husband of you before we got married so that he knew of us, and he was very understanding, stating over time I would love him as much, and I did, as he was the most wonderful human being and he was so very compassionate and giving. Most do not get an opportunity to have the love of one man in a lifetime, and I am fortunate to enjoy the love of two."

Mustafa looked at her, his green eyes more inquiring than ever. "So would you consider living the rest of your life in this valley?"

She looked at him teasingly, saying what most women would have said, "It depends." Mustafa wondered what it meant.

Next day, Shalu suggested that he take her mum to Char Chinar, a little island on the lake that had four chinar trees on it. The island had sealed many couples in a romantic future. Shalu made all the arrangements, even the Shikara to take them there, and a picnic basket, wrapped in a food quilt to keep the food warm. The Cupid sent off the two to Char Chinar. Once they reached it, the *Shikara-Wala* told them that he would return that evening. The two spent the remaining time together. Mustafa, who was an eloquent debater, was tongue-tied, but as the day wore on, the two became their old selves again. Mustafa had brought his mother's ring with an intention of proposing to CM, but the words did not come through, even though he went over it mentally several times. After lunch, CM eased the situation. She told Mustafa, "You asked if I would like to stay over in Kashmir." The answer is, "I would love to." At that moment, Mustafa got on his knee and asked her if she would marry him, and she said, "Of course," in her no-nonsense way, so stereotypical of CM. He found the ring and put it on her finger, a perfect fit. So the legendary magic of the Char Chinar had sealed the fate of yet another couple.

When the Shikara took them home, they were more sublime and became one with the beauty of Kashmir. After dinner, they sat for a long time, talking to each other. A few nights later, Shalu told the two that she was planning to join the famous Guy's Hospital in London to complete a family practice house job, and she would like the two to be married before she left. The Cupid struck again. The two discussed the prospect and decided to marry under the justice of peace. After filing the required papers and putting in a public notice, the two decided on a private wedding, but that was not to be, as the public announcement was enough for the clinic staff and most of their patients and citizenry of the town to be part of the wedding. The justice of peace announced that he had the pleasure and privilege of marrying the top bride and bridegroom of Kashmir. He praised the work of the free clinic and pronounced them husband and wife. The town took out a *Julus* (a parade), carrying them on a *Palki* (palanquin) over their shoulders to a public hall, where they had arranged a *Dhawat* (a public dinner) for the whole of Srinagar. Later that evening, the town had a fireworks show and Kashmiri *ghazals* (Sufi poetry sung with music of sitar and tablas) for the son and daughter of Kashmir. Tired and surprised, they returned home as husband and wife; their love from days at college had survived changing of times, changing of venues and separate travels across many continents.

The house too was at peace, as the son had brought home his bride. He dreamt of his parents, and next morning, they both went to their parent's graves to receive their blessings and to tell them of their love. The work in the clinic continued without days off for a honeymoon. The two worked as a team. When Shalu left, CM took over the mobile clinic work. She too assimilated well, and the folks started referring to her as Bhabhiji or Bhabhijan (sister-in-law). She learned the dialects just like Shalu.

One day, as Mustafa was seeing patients, a very old man came to the clinic. He was tired and gaunt; he had a distinct limp from a shattered leg bone, which had left one leg shorter. He fell on his knees in front of Mustafa and laid his face down, holding Mustafa's feet, asking for his forgiveness. Mustafa held his shoulders, helping him up on his feet. When he looked into his eyes, he knew that the man was haunted by his ghastly deed of many years ago, on the day of *Rakhi*, when he and others had massacred his family. He sat him down on a chair and asked one of the clinic staff to get him a glass of cold water. Time had changed, he had changed, and Kashmir had changed. He looked in his eyes and held his hand, saying, "I forgive you for your crime, go to your maker in peace. And if he asks you of your crime, tell him that I have found my God of forgiveness through you, and he too will forgive you."

That day, Mustafa rose to a greatness many aspire to reach but may never reach. He was now complete. He was back home in Kashmir, he was married to his first love, and he was eternally thankful for the opportunity to serve his country and his people.

His tireless and selfless work earned him India's highest award, the *Bharat Ratna*, for his contribution to the health and well-being in Kashmir, but he respectfully declined to accept the award, mostly because he genuinely felt no need for yet another award, and there were so many others more qualified and deserving than he was.

He had found himself, his love, and a daughter, who, he believed, was the greatest award ever, as now he was at peace and one more wall mounting; even the *Bharat Ratna* meant very little to him.

The story ends, but life goes on.

 End

About the Author

Onaly Abdulkarim Kapasi was born in Mombasa, Kenya, and brought up in Zanzibar and Tanga, Tanganyika. He went to medical school in Pune and Bombay and returned to Kenya, where he worked as a house officer at the Coast General Hospital in Mombasa and later at the Kenyatta National Hospital in Nairobi.

He came to Boston, Massachusetts, on a Harvard fellowship to Boston Children's Hospital Medical Center. He subsequently trained at the Harvard University surgery program and Tufts University orthopedic program.

He practiced orthopedic surgery in Boston, where he opened his first office at the prestigious and historic 1180 Beacon Street, Brookline, address and later expanded orthopedic practices to Cambridge, Dedham, and Haverhill.

His first publication in 2014, *Mind's Eye*, a book of personal poems, is well received; proceeds of the book are entirely donated to medical charity.

He has helped finance and operate a free clinic in the Himalayan town of Mandi for the past twenty-one years and he has also carried out medical missionary work in Africa, also supplying Tanzania and Sudan with much needed orthopedic hardware and equipment. He carries out free joint replacement surgeries in India for patients in need of his services.